THE TROUBLE WITH
TRIPOLI

Tim Paulin

The author gratefully acknowledges permission to quote from the song "Don't Fence Me In" words and music by Cole Porter. Copyright © 1944 (Renewed) WB Music Corp.

ISBN: 1484152646
ISBN 13: 9781484152645
Library of Congress Control Number: 2013907883
CreateSpace Independent Publishing Platform
North Charleston, South Carolina

DEAR ANN,

YOU'RE GOING TO CALL ME FOR ENCROACHMENT, POACHING, TRESPASS-ING, VAGRANCY — BUT I CAN'T HELP IT — I HAD TO WRITE THIS!

IT'S COALS TO NEWCASTLE, I KNOW, BUT IF YOU'RE IN THE MOOD FOR SOME-THING DIFFERENT IN THE NEXT FEW WEEKS ... PLEASE BE MY GUEST!

HAPPY HOLIDAYS,

Tim

DEPARTMENT OF CLASSICS • GRANVILLE, OHIO 43023
740-587-6251 • www.denison.edu

FOR ANN,

WHO KNOWS ABOUT

NEW DIRECTIONS &

NEW BEGINNINGS.

με φιλία και αγάπη,

Tim

PART ONE

το χωριό

the village

1.

He recognized him as soon as he saw him.

It had been years. Even though Daniel was passing along the square exactly opposite the spot where he was drinking a coffee and getting over his jet-lag, Knightly recognized Daniel at once. The hair was now cropped close—in his student days Daniel usually had a mop of unruly curls. Knightly also remembered that stride, though the figure of Daniel was quickly obscured by the gaggle of people in and around the *plateia*. He knew him instantly. But it also occurred to Knightly that he might just be stoned from yesterday's ordeal of a long, sleepless flight and the drive down to Tripoli and that this was perhaps just some kind of hallucination or waking-vision.

But why a vision of Daniel just *now*?

Knightly shook himself. He threw some money on the table and took off in pursuit. Daniel had already turned off the square, and was now out of sight, on the north side of the stately Agios Vasilios. Where was he going? If he's headed for the street of George I, Knightly thought, maybe he could catch him on the other side of the church, if he hurried.

Easier said than done. Old ladies with young children, old ladies without children, young girls in pairs, with shopping bags, or without bags, arm in arm, an old man stopping dead on the sidewalk, looking at a store window, into a *kafeneíon*, or just at the people passing him by. Knightly tried to dodge this casual scrum of humanity without banging into anyone, but he couldn't help it, and he got the expected looks—surprise, annoyance, or outright hatred, especially when the victim was older. He had the uncomfortable feeling he was making a spectacle of himself.

He passed the church and saw Daniel was already on the street of George the First, at least a block ahead. Daniel's head bobbed above the heads of the others, though not by much. He had always had a peculiar ability, Knightly recalled, to blend into a crowd, walking across campus, somehow managing not to tower over other students, though he was well over six feet and solid as a young oak. Standing next to him, you realized he was a big kid, but put him in a crowd and he seemed to disappear. A mysterious talent. A good thing, no doubt, given the line of work Daniel finally decided to go into.

"I'm not going to catch him." Knightly cursed under his breath. He was sweating now. He wanted to break into a run, maybe he could catch up to Daniel with one decent sprint. But there was no opening. Knightly could only keep pushing and weaving through the mob in front of him, as Daniel's lead increased. In desperation, he called out, "Daniel!" But it was no use.

Knightly was little more than a block from Kolokotronis Square when he stopped himself. There was a bus waiting on the square and Knightly saw Daniel climb on board. The moment Daniel got on the bus, it seemed, the doors made a squeaking sound and then let out a belch of hot air as they shut tightly. Knightly heard the bus driver fire up the big diesel and watched as the bus lurched around the circle of the Plateia Kolokotronis and then down Venizelou. As the bus lumbered past, Knightly looked up, but too late to make out what destination was showing on the glow-lit sign over the driver's broad window. Then he caught a glimpse, through one of the dusty green-tinted passenger-windows, of a familiar profile. It was Daniel's, who was staring straight ahead.

Knightly was stunned. He knew that the local buses stopped in Kolokotronis. But did the Athens bus stop there? And since when does a Greek bus ever leave on time, he thought? Daniel had no sooner climbed aboard than the bus left, almost at once. It was bizarre. Either Daniel had an uncanny sense of timing or had gotten lucky or else he had managed to slip the driver a twenty. And what the hell was Daniel doing in Greece anyway, I mean, why now, after all this time? And for Christ's sake why of all places here, in *Tripoli*?

The bus accelerated as it left the square.

Knightly watched it go. What he couldn't see was that other eyes were watching him as he looked at the bus making its way out of the city.

2.

THIS IS CRAZY, KNIGHTLY THOUGHT, AS HE DROVE THE car along the steep and winding road into the mountains.

After he had missed Daniel, he went back to his hotel and fell on the bed, less exhausted than simply perplexed. His head was no longer foggy, but now it hurt and, when he closed his eyes, the room spun slowly. While he was sitting at the café, drinking coffee and staring into space, he had begun to feel the exhaustion leave him, but after Daniel appeared like that, out of the blue, what had been a mildly, almost tastily surreal morning suddenly turned into a jarringly atonal piece of work.

He lay on the bed for two minutes before he realized he was too restless to sleep or even to stay in the room. Yet he wasn't ready to leave, either. If he was honest with himself. He had come to Greece because that is what he did almost every summer. But this time he had also come because of Eleutheria. He had decided he wanted to see her again. Yet he wasn't ready. That made no sense. He had planned to spend a day in Tripoli to relax and unwind, and then go see Elli. It seemed like ideal timing. But the sudden appearance of Daniel had thrown him off balance.

The truth was, ever since the divorce, he had felt off balance, especially where women were concerned. He didn't know why he wasn't eager just to dive in. He had his freedom, after all. And though at times it seemed to him, in his newly liberated state, that ninety-nine per cent of humanity were married to one another, when he bothered to look closely he saw that there were women out there, even his own age, who were unattached and unencumbered and so, in theory, approachable.

But he felt no keen wish to approach. Casual encounters, fine. The thought of anything other than light-hearted conversation paralyzed him. The sparkle of a first or second date was exciting. Then he'd think about the vast distance he'd need to travel to enjoy any of the intimacy and depth of a true relationship. It made him feel depressed. The problem was that after the divorce he did not feel liberated. He felt exhausted. It's normal, he said to himself, to take some time. Except that the time had already started to weigh heavily on him, after only a year, as if it had taken up a seat in his apartment, like an uninvited guest, and when the spring semester ended he thought, *I am going to lose my marbles soon, maybe my entire collection, if I don't get out of Dodge.* And if he did not reconsider his increasing acceptance of being alone—or aloof.

So he had called Elli a week before he left for Greece. Now it felt like the wrong decision. Why hadn't he waited till he got here? He could have settled in, gotten his head straight about what he wanted to say to her and how he wanted things to go. It felt rushed. It was a crazy idea to start with, he thought. *Or are you just making way too much of this, Will?* The truth was that his relationship with Elli—or at least the image he had of that relationship—struck a balance between the freshness of a new love and the depth of age and experience. He leaned his head out the window to let the hot wind pummel his face, just enough so that the streaming air did not force his eyes completely shut.

Jesus Christ! he muttered. He saw in the side-view that a car was coming up fast on his tail. He pulled his head back in and checked the dash. Converting from kilometers, he figured he was going about seventy. But the car passed him as if he were standing still. Knightly laughed to himself. He had forgotten the exquisite technique the Greek driver applied to a fundamental problem of driving on mountain roads. The road had become steeper and the first set of the inevitable switch-back turns was now straight ahead. How did the driver that just blew by him plan to negotiate the first hair-pin turn? The back lights of the Mercedes popped bright red, as the driver slammed on his brakes, and crawled through the series of turns, up and up, back and forth, until the car cleared their snaking course. The Mercedes accelerated as soon as it hit the straightaway, tearing up the road once again, like a ballistic missile homing on an unseen target, far away. *There's your answer, Will,* he thought. Drive like hell and slam on the brakes whenever necessary.

He got out of the car at the parking lot of the site of Apollo's temple at Vasses, leaned back against the hot car, and took a bite of the *tyropita* he had bought in the city. He was hungry and the cheese and flaky crust were delicious. He finished it in three bites and took a long drink from the bottle of water he bought at a kiosk before he started driving. By some miracle the water was still cool.

The rest of the ride was uneventful, fortunately. He had been passed another five or six times, though the route was as usual thinly travelled. He had made Chrysovítsi in good time, even driving at his paleolithic pace of sixty to seventy miles an hour. The real stroke of luck came after he had turned on the road to Andritsena and Vasses. Just before reaching Ellinikó, he had seen trouble ahead. A herdsman with a vast flock of sheep had his animals about fifty feet from the road. Knightly knew from bitter experience that, once the animals began to cross, there was nothing to be done but contemplate the landscape in precious detail until man and beast had made the crossing according to the same timeless fashion they had practiced since shortly after the creation of life on earth.

But Knightly beat the man and his fleecy hordes to the spot where their paths would have crossed. As he passed the flock, he slowed to a speed that seemed respectful but not quite unmanly. He happened to catch the shepherd's gaze. Neither old nor young, the man stared at him and the look on his face was not a grin nor yet a completely neutral expression. Knightly got the feeling that the man knew something, but the relevance of what the herder might know simply escaped him. Knightly was satisfied, at least, that he could ponder the mystery of this exchange of glances from a distance and while driving on toward his goal.

The parking lot was deserted, which would have struck him as strange had it not reached that point in the afternoon when the sun was strongest and beat down on the land without mercy. The booth at the entrance to the site was also empty. Knightly looked around for the *phylax*, the caretaker, who sold tickets to visitors and generally looked after the site. Maybe he's inside his cottage, which would be sensible enough in this heat, Knightly thought. He decided to go in and let the caretaker catch up with him later, or vice-versa. The ground rose slightly at the entrance and after a slight dip there it was, the temple of Apollo, which the Phigaleians had dedicated to the god in his guise as *Epikourios*, the Helper, or Healer, since the temple was built in thanks for the Peloponnesians escaping a plague that had ravaged Athens early in the great war between that city and Sparta in the last quarter of the fifth-century.

The temple was situated within its landscape in a way that was stunning, nestled amidst the deep ravines that gave the place its name, *Vasses*. The temple itself was also striking, with a number of interesting features, but none of these were apparent anymore to the visitor at first sight, because since the nineteen-eighties the temple had been covered with an enormous canopy of a space-age material. The canopy did not reach all the way to the ground but was tethered to the earth with taut cables. The Big Tent, protecting a remarkable cultural artifact from the elements. Knightly tried not to be fussy about it, but admittedly he was glad when he had walked down to the temple and gotten inside the canopy to view the structure again without its now-permanent addition.

It was an odd feeling to be in the tent with the temple of the healing god, almost as if it were two old friends huddled together on a camping trip. One of the friends, in that case, being fairly massive. Knightly walked around his "old friend" slowly, enjoying himself as he began to feel lost in wonder once again at the quiet beauty of the building—a beauty he might even have called "grim" owing to the darkened shades of the limestone of the temple's columns and blocks, that had been graying even before the intercourse with wind and weather, in this remote location high in the mountains of Arcadia.

On the other side of the temple, Knightly found an audio display. He doubted it worked, but he was studying it when he was startled by a sound behind him, at the entrance to the tent.

He turned around and saw five men who had just entered the canopy-area. They were dressed almost identically: three of them were wearing blue track-suits, with white stripes down the leg of the pants. Dark and swarthy, but not necessarily Greeks, the men looked like a detachment of Olympic athletes from somewhere in the old Eastern bloc. Not so much like tourists, and certainly not a team of archaeologists, unless I have missed the latest thing, Knightly thought. Two of the men looked at the information-board that stood at the entry-way of the tent and exchanged some brief comments, while another looked vaguely in the direction of the ruined temple and the other two stared blankly at the insides of the enormous canopy.

Knightly wondered who in the world these jokers could be. Had they really made the pilgrimage to see the remains of the temple? Or....

He laughed to himself. *You really are losing your mind…why would they be up here, following you? What would they be planning, to knock you on the head and throw your body in a ravine?* He determined to get hold of himself. The sudden appearance of the Bulgarian track stars had struck him more with curiosity than terror. On the other hand, there were five of them, and no one else seemed to be around. If they had come to do him in, it wasn't clear what he could do to stop it. It would be a fitting end to a day that had refused to resemble anything like normal, if he were to die at the hands of a small Balkan clan dressed in tacky exercise clothes. Trying to appear as if he wasn't looking them over, he thought about which one he would have to take down first, to have any chance. Not a great prospect, but maybe there was a hope that the others would be shocked enough, if he sucker-punched the leader, that he could run to the car and maybe get the hell out of there.

No sooner had he formed the doom's-day plan than the *phylax* walked into the site. Not a giant of a man—he looked to be about five feet and change—but a savior nonetheless. His appearance seemed to put the band of five into a sudden consternation. With a shuffling of feet and nervous laughter, they began to sidle toward the door of the tent and slip away. Knightly was relieved, but now he was more confused than ever. Had these guys in fact come to see the temple of Apollo at Vasses, but didn't necessarily want to pay for the privilege? Or had the caretaker intervened at just the right moment, helping to avoid a scene of carnage on the site of the god's sacred precinct?

After exchanging a few pleasantries with the old caretaker, Knightly paid him and left the canopy, looking once more at the austere and lovely ruins. He went back to his car. The track-suits were nowhere to be seen.

The sojourn to Apollo's temple had been a marvellous distraction. As he drove away, however, he realized that the uneasiness he'd briefly shed returned. Knightly began to chew it over again. It wasn't just his apprehension at seeing Elli, he realized, though that worried him. The possibility of the whole thing going wrong with her posed a disappointment that he was beginning to admit would crush him. But it was also Daniel. The boy had been the best student he ever had and they had become good friends. They kept in touch, even after Daniel joined the army and began to travel. It was only when Daniel had become involved in more specialized training that it grew difficult to keep up the contact. They hadn't communicated for five or six years at this point. It made Knightly feel ridiculous, even guilty in some way, that he had let it happen. But that wasn't exactly fair. It had just happened. Now suddenly Daniel shows up utterly at random. Just before his beloved former teacher is nearly assassinated by a hit team composed of shabbily-dressed Bulgars.

Knightly was passing by the spot where he had seen the shepherd with his flocks. The man was gone. He had taken his animals to their resting-spot for the afternoon. It couldn't be far off; as he passed, Knightly heard the raspy clanking of bells that the shepherd had tied to the necks of one or two animals, maybe a couple of rams. If he stopped, what would he have asked the shepherd, if he had still been on the side of the road? The old man had the look of knowing something. Of course, Knightly would have learned whatever he would have learned only depending on what question he asked. The exasperation of oracles. He would have asked first about Elli, then about Daniel. *Also, who were those five guys at your god's temple, by the way?*

"My god? Who—?"

"Come on, Apollo's, I meant."

"As a matter of fact, I worship Hermes, his younger brother."

"Oh, sorry, I get it. The shadowy one."

"Right. The rich men who come here, especially the pilgrims, they worship Apollo. They make him up to look like them, you know? But I worship Hermes. Less fancy. He can even be a pile of rocks. Anyway, the important point is, he increases my flocks, if you get my drift. And those rich men, they buy sheep and goats from me, then they give the meat and hides to the local priests. So, you see, I guess we all worship Hermes around here. Something for you to think about, my boy."

Shit!

He hadn't seen it coming. His mind was so taken up with everything that had been happening since he got to Tripoli that he'd stopped checking his mirrors. A car with a sleek black outline shaped like a torpedo was racing up on him at a freakish speed and was about to ram him from behind. He flicked a glance at the rear-view and braced for the impact. But at the last moment the black car suddenly swerved into the other lane to avoid the crash. Luckily that side of the road was empty.

Knightly was furious. *Go for it, moron!* he sputtered, screaming out the window. *Genius, absolute freaking genius!* Then he saw the driver of the black car, though only for a second, and it silenced him. It was a young woman, and he saw she was as excessively beautiful, naturally, as she was impeccably coiffed and made-up. And dressed to the nines. She paid no attention to Knightly, whose car she had just blown off the road. She certainly didn't hear him cursing. The windows of her BMW were rolled up snugly, and Knightly could suddenly sense the icy elegant leather-interior of the Beamer. The mounting tensions of the day and the sudden terror of the moment let loose all at once. Knightly was stupified, but then it hit him just how hilarious the situation was. He stopped cursing and began to laugh. Tears came to his eyes and he could hardly see the road.

The lovely girl in her luxury car was merely following an acquired impulse (the idea she'd been "taught" seemed dubious)—she drove like a fury blazing out of another dimension while preserving the most exquisite air of indifference toward all other life-forms. *Ah, you Hellenes, lovers of freedom!*

Knightly began to sing,

"Oh, give me land, lots of land under starry skies above
Don't fence me in!"

The girl was pulling away as they came to another stretch of switch-back roads. The girl hadn't bothered to pull back in. She stayed in the wrong lane so she wouldn't be forced to brake quite so hard as she took the turns. There was a problem, however: in the other lane, just down the hill, there was a giant Mack truck that was tackling the turns aggressively and with startling speed, despite the fact that it was climbing, and suddenly it looked as though the Mack was going to plow head-on into the girl as they met in the bend of one of the hair-pins. Knightly stopped singing and looked on in horror. But at the last second the girl swung the BMW back to the right and into the proper lane and drove on. As far as Knightly could tell, she hadn't missed a beat of whatever song was playing on her car's magnificent sound system. No problem. Knightly made a note to himself never to worry about such trivialities ever again. That's how it's done, and he had simply forgotten, on the long and winding, steep and fenceless roads that lead one into and out of the magical mountains of Arcadia.

"Send me off forever but I ask you please,
Don't fence me in!"

3.

This must be the place, he thought.

Stavros turned the car off, settled back, and looked at the building, which was lacking in any distinguishing features whatsoever. He had followed the directions. Take the road out of town to Kalamata. Exit on Philippou. He had seen his landmark, the tire store, a weary-looking building of medium size, which looked like it was half-busy some of the time. He had driven past three warehouses spread out along the deserted block, then turned into a gravel lot just after the third warehouse.

This must be the one Alexis meant.

He had minded the directions, and he had also been careful when he left the city that he was not being tailed. He had noticed for about a week or so that he was being followed. As soon as he suspected, he had been more alert, and he was sure he had caught them at their game a couple of times. They were cops; he could tell by their clothes. Trying to look like regular guys, he snorted. It was easy enough to pick up on the tails. Even so, it had bothered him. Why was the pressure going up all of a sudden? It was also strange that Alexis had told him to go to this place. Why not make the handoff like usual? He liked doing the exchanges at his own place. Or at the *Paradisos*, in the neighborhood, where he knew the owner was cool, and where he knew even the cops on that beat were being made comfortable. Which made it even more strange that he was being followed. Must be some failure of organization, he thought.

He got out of the car, dropped his cigarette on the gravel and crushed it under his shoe. He looked around at the desolate area. Nothing for a kilometer or so. The closest thing around was a big squat apartment building, situated across a parched weedy field. It was far away. He had to squint to make it out clearly. He was five minutes early, okay, might as well go in.

The door was open. The building was bare inside and not spacious. As he stepped inside, his shoes scrunched on the gritty floor and the place echoed uneasily. Against the walls were old crates. He wondered what this place had been used for. He looked at the crates, but they were scuffed from handling so that the lettering on the sides was hopelessly worn. Who knows what they kept here, he thought. There was plenty of small manufacture in Tripoli and always had been and of course the area was famous for its farming. He knew many old-timers who remembered when certain streets of the city were lined with saddleries and hardware-stores and the city itself served as the general store for the whole region.

There were the crates piled up around the inside of the building, but not a stick of furniture. Absolutely nothing. Only a fly that buzzed right in front of Stavros, so that he threw up his hand out of instinct, to brush it away from his eyes. *Stinking fly*, he cursed. What the hell are you doing in here? Enjoying the view? Quite a kingdom you have here, or is it some kind of holiday resort? Can't say the food is fantastic, he imagined, looking around at the emptiness.

There was a sound at the door. It opened, and a man walked in whom Stavros had not seen before. Alexis had said it would be somebody he hadn't seen before. Bringing in new people, he said. We're going to make a couple of places for them to stay, you know, safe places. They can work from there. There's plenty of work to do. And it's good to have new people once in a while. Keeps the cops in the dark.

The stranger who just came in was standing in the dark. It got on Stavros's nerves that he couldn't see the face of this guy. But Stavros didn't feel like moving toward him. And the stranger didn't move from where he was standing.

"So this is the place?"

It sounded stupid, but Stavros felt the need to say something. "It was easy to find, but I like doing business at home, you know…?"

"Yeh, I know," the other man said.

Finally, he said something, Stavros thought to himself. It was a relief to hear him speak. But it was obvious even from a few words that the stranger wasn't Greek.

"You got the stuff? I have the money right here, so give me the package and I'll give you this." He pointed to a small duffel he was carrying. Get this business over and get the fuck out of here, Stavros thought. Then he shivered.

"Sure, let's do it," the stranger said as he came toward Stavros. Stavros stared at the guy. He couldn't see any package. Where was he hiding it? What the fuck.

The stranger took the gun from inside his belt. It took longer to get out of there because it had a suppressor on the end of the barrel, and that made the gun longer than usual. At last the gun cleared the stranger's belt as he raised it, calmly.

Stavros saw the gun pointing straight at his face. Jesus, it looked close, but then it looked far away, as it coughed. A piece of stone must have come off the wall on the other side of the building, a chip or something, because he felt something sharp hit him in the forehead. Stung like a bitch.

The fly was there. It flew past him, over the barrel of the gun. But it had slowed down. Stavros thought he could see a wing moving. Only once, downward. Just one stroke of that tiny flipper. The fly dipped its thin wing like a gauzy-panelled oar into its beloved, every-bit-as-good-as-infinite sea of air. That was how long it stung, the rock that flew at him from the wall. Or from the gun. It hurt in a spot on his forehead. It hurt so fucking much, but just that long, until a darkness deep as a gorge swallowed him, taking him down into its chilly depth, almost like a comfort, like he was a small boy again and the gorge was telling him to sink down, to hide away in it. *No one will ever find you here.*

The fly sat on the wall. It crawled six inches, to two o' clock, then sat still again. It didn't seem to move after that.

4.

Knightly wanted to see Elli's picture again. She had attached it on one of the e-mails she sent in the small barrage they exchanged after he contacted her again. He had printed it out. In order not to fold it, he placed it in an envelope and put it in the side of his bag.

The picture showed she was as beautiful as he remembered her. She was not a young girl anymore but somehow the years had not had much success leaving their mark on her, he thought, like a lake hidden in the woods that the breezes barely trouble, thanks to the high tops of the trees surrounding it.

But there was something in her eyes. The photo had been taken outdoors. She was sitting, relaxed, yet concentrated, her thick hair falling over her shoulders. She was slim and she clasped her hands around her knees. The hint of a smile began to appear on her face but it wasn't clear whether she had fully committed to the idea of smiling or not. Perhaps it was just impatience with the person taking the picture. *Could we please get this over with?* But her eyes. That look was pensive, if not downright sad, an unsettling contrast to the tenderness and whimsy that Knightly saw radiating from the portrait.

Knightly couldn't explain that look and though it bothered him he loved staring at the picture of Elli. She had been a young girl and distressingly pretty when they met and now she was still a beautiful woman. A beautiful woman with a certain sadness in her expression. It was as if her eyes betrayed a wish that the camera or the person holding the camera would just go away—or that something else would.

Knightly found Kremni and the center of town easily enough. He circled the *plateia* once and then parked the car and got out. He looked around and saw the usual furniture: a taverna and *zacharoplasteio*, or sweet-shop, at one end of the square, a bank and various shops around it, and then just off the square a building with the town's offices.

Knightly took off down the street Elli indicated in the directions she'd sent him and he quickly got lost. He hadn't walked more than three blocks or so before running into a church. Elli hadn't mentioned any church. He decided to go back to the *plateia*, consult the directions one more time, and try again.

The town wasn't that big. And of course there were no street signs. No one in this village, or in most others in Greece, lived at such-and-such an address on Main or Maple Street. Knightly concentrated on the landmarks Elli provided. The long street that bends around the large white-washed house with the over-grown yard—it was owned by a former mayor of the town who had quarrelled bitterly with the town's council and had decided to let the weeds in their profusion demonstrate his annoyance to the entire village, not to mention his insouciance.

Walk past a bakery; turn right at the pharmacy, then follow the street until it comes to an open area where the market is held every Friday. There's a little kiosk there: turn left. Go straight until you come to a three-storied house with construction going on in the first story that hasn't been finished yet. The street divides here: go right. When you come to the sign that points to a shrine of Agios

Theodoros, go right again. Follow along the wall and the third house is mine, on the left. You'll see a lemon tree right behind the gate.

As he opened the gate, he saw the lemon tree was indeed growing luxuriantly between the gate and the house and spreading out so generously that it shaded a verandah next to the front door, where Knightly saw Elli was sitting. The sudden epiphany startled him. Elli got up.

"You found me, Will!"

"I did, Elli. Hello!"

"Kalispera." *Good evening.* I hope it wasn't too difficult to find this place."

"No, not too bad, a little confusing…."

"You should have called me! You have my cell, I would have come to the *plateia* to get you."

"What would have been the fun in that?" he said, grinning. "All my cherished illusions of being the Pathfinder gone, just like that!"

She smiled. "Wait a minute, I'll open the door for you," she said, going into the house.

She opened the door and ran out to greet him, kissing him on both cheeks. She was tall and slender, and her hair was gathered on top in a way that made her look taller still.

"You look beautiful, Elli, absolutely beautiful!"

She smiled, embarrassed. "Oh, no, come on" she said, "*you* look great. It's just too bad you've lost your mind, apparently!"

Knightly laughed. "Are you kidding me? You look just like you did back then…."

"Only even a little better, with the mellowing of the years…" she added, mocking him. "Come inside, you sweet man, and let me get you something cold to drink. I'm afraid you've gotten sun-stroke and soon you'll be seeing Pan frolicking with nymphs in my garden."

"Okay, okay," he said, "if you insist on puncturing my rapturous visions—a glass of water would be great."

"How about *vissino*? My neighbor's trees had so many cherries, she didn't know what to do with them all. She made some and brought it over this morning."

Elli led Knightly to a couch in the living room. When she came out of the kitchen, she handed him a glass and sat down next him. She looked at him. She was beaming.

"I just can't believe it! Thank you so much for coming all this way. I've been so excited all week. I could hardly wait to see you."

"I felt the same way, Elli," Knightly said. It was true. Any hesitation he had felt, he now understood, was really just excitement that had been building up and turning to apprehension over what might happen—or not happen—when he finally saw Elli again.

"So how was your trip?" she asked.

"Not bad. I didn't sleep on the plane, of course, so I was a little zonked yesterday, which I decided to spare you. But now I feel fine."

He decided to spare her, too, a long story with all the strange things that had happened to him yesterday, from the moment he arrived in Tripoli.

"What would you like to do tonight?" she asked. "I thought we might go to the taverna."

"I would love that," Knightly replied. "In fact, would you want to go now? I enjoyed walking over here, and I wouldn't mind stretching my legs a little more."

"It would be nice to walk," she agreed, "we could take our time. Are you hungry at all?"

"Famished, now that I think of it. But let's take our time."

They left the house, walking slowly to the square, the same way Knightly had come.

"So you moved back to Kremni after Tripoli?"

"Yes." She didn't say more.

"Why Kremni? You're not from here, if I remember right."

"No. I'm from an even smaller place." She laughed. "My sister's husband is from here. They live here, so it seemed like a good idea. It's nice, being close to them."

Knightly recalled she had mentioned some of this in an e-mail.

"I work in a bookstore. It's close to the *plateia*."

"I walked by it, I think."

"Yes, you must have."

"What happened with Tripoli?" he asked. "Too congested, noisy? It's peaceful here…"

"But there's not much happening, you're thinking?"

He was about to answer when he was stopped by a high-pitched screech, ostensibly made by a human voice, though it was hard to be sure, a sound that seemed intended to deliver either a greeting or else a dire warning. An old lady, dressed in black, was sitting outside the door of a two-story house, where an over-hang shaded an area of slated courtyard large enough for a couple of chairs and a small table. She was sitting and watching the street in front of her house. Elli turned and skipped over to her, kissing her in greeting. It was difficult to tell the old lady's age. She was dressed in black. Another woman was sitting with her who was also dressed in dark clothing.

Elli began to speak with the old lady. Knightly could hardly make out the old lady's Greek. *Indifferent dentition making for indistinct diction*, Knightly mused. Elli understood her perfectly. Knightly caught a few phrases: *Nice evening…a little hot…friend from America…to the tavernaki*.

Knightly glanced at the other woman. The look on her face took him aback. She was looking at Elli in a strange way. Solicitous, Knightly thought.

Then he heard his name. He was being introduced. As Elli rejoined him in the street, Knightly smiled at the old woman.

Chairomai, he said. "Pleased to meet you."

Kalispera, the old lady answered. "Good evening." Να είστε καλά. "Be well."

"Who was that?" he asked Elli, as they walked away.

"That's *the old lady*," Elli smiled. "She sees everything, or at least everyone who passes by her house. And she sets up shop there and retails her news like a rich merchant from early in the morning until the end of the day!"

"But she won't say a word about the two of us to anyone?"

"Oh, certainly not!" Elli laughed.

It wasn't clear that the old lady would even have a scoop on the news, since there were many people out, and everyone who passed them on the street looked away after a casual greeting, making it clear that they could barely contain the urge to flip open their cell-phones and tell their news to somebody.

"Am I being conceited or in the space of ten minutes are we becoming an item?"

"I don't think you'd be far off to say so." She laughed again.

As they came to the square, Knightly saw the lanterns of the taverna, that were lit and hung amidst grape vines spreading over a wooden trellis. They sat down and ordered simply: a salad, bread, *tzatziki*, fried potatoes, and *kotosouvli*—slices of pork grilled with peppers and tomatoes, all of which was chopped into small pieces—and a rosé, *spitiko*, house-wine, that came to the table chilled in a glass pitcher.

They talked a while about the place itself, which was, like most, a simple affair, but with its trailing vines and ivy creating a bower-like effect, and with its lanterns throwing a soft light underneath the trellis that was open to the night-sky, above their heads, as they sat next to one of the plane trees in the courtyard, a pillar supporting the local heaven—taking in all of that, they allowed themselves simply to sit and enjoy the atmosphere of the place and the heady scent of the pines that stood all around the corner of the square the taverna occupied.

Knightly decided to ask Elli again what had happened with Tripoli.

"So why did you leave the city, after all, Elli? Why didn't you stay in Tripoli? You had a plan—work at the restaurant until you were ready to take your University-exams, then study to become a teacher. English, right?"

"It became obvious it wasn't going to happen."

"What do you mean?" he interrupted. "You were good. I mean your English was really good. I remember, I could not believe that you had never been to England or the States. You had—I mean, you have—a natural talent for languages."

"You're very sweet, Will, thank you. It was a lot of things. First of all, my family couldn't afford the lessons I needed to prepare for the exams."

"You mean the *phrontistirio*—was that really necessary?"

"The exams to get into University are very difficult here. You know that, how competitive they are."

"It just seems like such a shame."

"And then my father became ill. My sister was already married, with a baby, and she had moved to Nikos's village."

"So you went back to your own village?"

"*Nai*," she said. "yes, Aetorachi."

"Aetorachi," Will repeated. "That's right, I remember the name now." He paused. "Was it hard on your mother, when your dad got sick?"

"Yes, it was. And when my father passed away, I ended up taking care of my mother."

"But why didn't your mother move in with your sister? Chrysanthi wasn't working. You could even say it was her turn at that point. You could have gone back to your studies."

Elli smiled. "You sound just like Chrysa. She said the same things. She offered and she tried hard to convince me. But it didn't seem fair. She had a small child at the time, and I knew they wanted another. She got pregnant again. Even so, she kept on insisting. But it just didn't seem right. It would also have meant moving my mother from her own village to a strange one. You know what that means. In the end, I felt like it was the least I could do to take care of *mama*."

"*Peismatara*," Knightly laughed, as he looked into Elli's eyes. *Stubborn*!

Somehow, during the conversation, without realizing it, he had ordered another jug of wine. Was it the crisp chill of the wine melting the heat of the summer night or the delicate, slightly vulnerable beauty of this woman sitting across the small table that was melting his heart?

It was a hot night and the air had, in fact, become somewhat heavy and oppressive. The wine was thirst-quenching and tasted so good with the food that Knightly half-noticed he was drinking too quickly. He felt a pleasant buzz coming on.

He thought back to when he and Elli met. It was the first time he had ever come to Greece. He had just defended his dissertation and he had been lucky enough to land his first job and so he had made it a sort of present to himself to go to Greece, at last, before starting teaching in the fall. He had travelled everywhere in the country during the first couple months of the summer, north, south, east and west, islands and mainland. He was almost at the end of the trip, making a circuit of the Peloponnese, when he landed in Tripoli. Elli was a waitress there, working in a restaurant on Deligiani. He showed up at the place with a couple of other American students he had met in the hotel where he was staying. While she was serving them, he had started up a conversation with her, and eventually asked if she would join them for a drink when she finished work.

Knightly smiled at the thought. It had been unlike him. Anything but impulsive, he also disliked it when he felt that he was imposing on anyone.

But that night, he recalled, had been like this one. A sultry, slightly stifling evening, whose very heat, when mixed with the cool wine created a heady elixir with an extraordinary magical power. And Elli had just been so damned sweet. It had seemed that there was maybe half a chance she wouldn't say no.

They made an excellent *parea*, the whole group of them, and passed the next few nights together in high spirits, until it came time for the others to leave, one by one. It was close to the time that Knightly had planned to go, too, but he decided to forget about the rest of his time-table and stayed in Tripoli. He would eat at the place where Elli worked every night and then walk the streets of Tripoli until she was free. Then they would go out—a bar, a park bench—laughing and talking into the small hours. It was the most innocent relationship he had ever had with a woman, but also the most intense. He had no explanation for the chemistry between them. As the end of August arrived, the time came when he would have to leave. He had even contemplated staying in Greece, working at the taverna or a bar himself, or trying his hand at writing, anything so that he could stay with Elli there. Despite his noble attempt at acting on impulse, it was Elli herself who insisted that he go back and start his career. He had worked so hard, she said, it would be a crime to throw the opportunity away. *We will keep in touch; you can come back to Greece.*

It was at that point that the relationship turned physical. An intense, almost desperate passion suddenly burgeoned and poured out of them, the very night that it became plain that the feelings they had discovered for each other would now have to wait indefinitely and that they were going to have to say goodbye in less than a week.

"What are you thinking?" Elli asked him, her voice coming to him from far away.

Knightly smiled at her across the table. "You don't want to know!"

They both laughed. "No, really, I was just thinking about when we met," he continued, "You know, how we met…." His voice trailed off.

Elli looked at Knightly. He noticed her eyes were moist.

"I'm so sorry about what happened," she burst out.

He reached over and squeezed her hands gently.

"It wasn't your fault, Elli! It was a mistake, a bizarre mistake, that's all. It wasn't anyone's fault."

It seemed she was beginning to cry. She covered her eyes with a napkin, trying to move out of the light.

"It was my fault, really," Knightly said. "When I got back, I was so busy—I should have written to you right away. By the time I wrote…"

Elli looked again as if she might cry. "I'm so embarrassed," she said.

"Elli, I should be embarrassed. I kept meaning to write. When I finally did, you had already moved, I guess."

The truth is that he had been shattered when she did not answer his letters. The new job and all that was involved with it had caught him off-balance. A deer in the headlights. And he had dallied in Greece. It had taken him almost a month to sit down and write to Elli. Within a week or two, though, he had sent her three long letters. She never answered any of them.

They sat in silence.

"I couldn't believe it when I read in your e-mail that you never got my letters. I assumed you'd decided to give up on me and moved on. It's unbelievable what happened, like something out of a bloody Hardy novel!"

"I am so glad you sent that first e-mail!" she said.

"I am so glad you answered it. I was afraid you'd blow it off. When I found Chrysanthi on the web, and asked if she had an address for you, she said yes and told me to try. She said you would answer."

"Chrysa is an angel."

"I guess we just had to wait for the electronic age to make contact."

He took her hands again. He looked into her eyes and she gazed back at him. Finally, Elli squeezed his hands.

"Will, can I be perfectly honest with you—you look exhausted!"

They burst out laughing.

"And slightly wasted, you mean."

"You have to drive back to Tripoli. I feel terrible."

"It's no problem," he quickly added. "I'll snap out of it while we walk home."

Knightly paid and they left the taverna. He wobbled for the first few steps but by the time they were half-way to Elli's house, Knightly felt steady on his feet.

"Was it meant to be this way?" he asked her.

"You met someone, didn't you, Will?"

He swallowed. Thank god it's dark, he thought. He felt himself blushing and he felt his own eyes growing moist.

"Yes, I met someone. That first year. Twenty-four years later, two great kids, both grown up, out of the house now."

"The marriage ended?"

"Yes, last year."

Elli seemed to be thinking this over.

"What happened, Will?"

Knightly sighed. "At this moment in time, my dear Elli, I am not drunk or sober enough to talk about it. If I ever will be."

"I'm sorry," she whispered.

"Don't be sorry, Elli. I don't mean to be elusive. It's just hard to talk about. And it's been such a lovely night."

They stopped abruptly. They had reached the house, and the lights were on inside. There was also sound coming from the house, people talking but in an artificial, mechanical rhythm that made it obvious after a moment that the sound of voices was coming from Elli's television.

"What's going on?" Knightly said. "We left the house dark, didn't we?"

Elli calmly took his hand. She opened the front door.

"Chrysa?" she called. As they entered the house, Elli's sister appeared from the living room.

"Will!" Chrysanthi ran and embraced Knightly eagerly. "τι κάνεις;" *How are you?*

"Καλά. Και εσύ;" *Fine. How about you?*

"It's so good to see you, Will. It's been a long time."

"Something like twenty years or more, Chrysa, I hate to say it."

"Ouf!" Chrysa exclaimed.

They laughed and went into the living room together. The conversation started with their evening at the taverna but quickly moved on to the old days, when Knightly had met Elli in Tripoli and Elli had introduced her new American friend to her older sister, Chrysanthi. Knightly had liked Chyrsanthi immensely. What was not to like? Elli's sister was vivacious, out-going, and as gentle and kind as Elli herself. And equally beautiful. Tall, slender, with chestnut hair that at the time she used to wear long, falling over her shoulders or down her back in a thick braid, but now wore short in a pert bob that Knightly dimly recognized as the current fashion.

After they had talked for an hour or more about the old days, Elli sipping on a glass of ice water, Chrysa and Knightly drinking beers, Elli looked at Knightly and said that he looked tired. He nodded, "Yes."

"Do you want to come by tomorrow morning, Will? We could go to the sea, before it gets too hot. It isn't far from here."

"That would be great, Elli, you're on. How about if I get here around eight-thirty—could we get to the sea by nine or so?"

"That would be fine," she said.

"Or we could go for a swim right now?"

Elli smirked at him. As she pushed Knightly toward the door, he caught a glimpse of something on the television. Apparently it was the late news report. There was a breaking story. Knightly stopped, taking Elli's hand gently.

"Could we turn this up?" he said. Elli turned the sound up.

...the body was found in an abandoned warehouse by boys from a nearby apartment building. The victim, who has been identified as Stavros Korakogenis, was known by police to be involved in the sale of narcotics in the city of Tripoli. The police have stated that they will release further details as they become available.

"That kid must be in shock," Knightly muttered. In fact it had been one of the boys, as Knightly gathered from the report, who had found the body. He had been playing a game of *petropolemos* with his friends—basically, an all-out dodgeball contest, only played with rocks. No more stupid than a lot of things the kids I grew up with used to do, Knightly mused. When the boy decided he'd taken enough of the action on his backside, he had ducked into what he assumed was an empty building. And it was empty, Knightly thought, more or less. Except for a corpse.

"Does that kind of thing happen around here often nowadays?" he asked.

"Not really," Chrysanthi said, slowly.

Knightly shook himself. "Okay, well, I'm going to get back to the hotel and get some rest. I will see you bright and early tomorrow, Elli."

"I can't wait, Will."

He kissed both sisters as he left, and then he looked at Elli.

"This has been fantastic, Elli, really. Seeing you again—"

"Me, too."

"Good night."

He hadn't lied. It had been a truly wonderful night. He couldn't remember when he had felt so happy. Yet as he walked back to where he left his car on the *plateia*, he found it hard not to think about what he had seen on the TV.

"A murder in Tripoli? Of a known drug-dealer? *An assassination, for God's sake?*"

While he was driving back to the city, as much as he tried to focus his thoughts on the now vivid image of Elli—her raven black hair, radiant dark eyes, and sweetly smiling face—he kept returning in his mind to the list of bizarre events comprising the mere day and a half he had been in Greece, that had just been added to by one more very strange, and very violent, item.

5.

WHEN KNIGHTLY STUMBLED INTO THE HOTEL, THE NIGHT CLERK avoided looking him in the eye. It struck Knightly as odd behavior. But he was too exhausted to care about the strange little man at the front desk. *Victory,* he thought, as the door of the elevator opened. As soon as the door closed, he leaned up against the wall of the elevator. The air was stale but at the same time it felt sweetly relaxing to draw in a deep breath. He exhaled slowly and began to imagine how it would feel to fall into bed: the soft pillow cradling his head, the mattress accepting his weight, his limbs sprawling as he slipped into oblivion. He felt as if he were falling asleep on his feet.

The elevator opened on his floor and as he staggered out he was abruptly shaken out of the dream. The door of his room was open and light was flooding the carpet. Knightly was suddenly, brutally awake. He looked in cautiously. There was a man sitting in the chair in front of the flimsy desk that stood against the wall. The chair was turned around and the man was sitting in it, facing away from the desk. The man looked up at Knightly as if he had been waiting for him and gestured to him to come in. Knightly entered and saw his suitcase lying on the bed, the contents—all of his things—lying in an imperfect heap next to the empty suitcase.

"Who are you and what the hell is going on?" Knightly said in a stony voice.

The stranger stood up and reached out his hand. "Professor Knightly, I am with the police. Your room was broken into, I'm afraid." He gestured toward the armchair in the corner of the room and Knightly sat down. "Please allow me to introduce myself. My name is Aris Kazantzakis. I am a Chief Inspector of Police in Athens." He leaned toward Knightly to show him his badge and credentials. "I happen to be in Tripoli because of an ongoing investigation and what has happened here may be of interest, so I waited for you after my colleagues were finished with the room. The long and the short of it is that someone broke into your room and emptied your suitcase. They do not seem to have done much else."

Knightly was stunned. "So that's why the fellow at the desk looked so sheepish. But how did they get in?"

Kazantzakis paused a moment, looking at Knightly.

"I am very sorry that this happened, Professor Knightly, and may I offer you my apologies for such a rude welcome to this city. The hotel's security leaves something to be desired. We found a door in the back of the building that was unlocked. And one sheepish clerk, as you put it. But if you don't mind, I would like to ask you a few questions. I am mindful of the hour," he added, "not to mention that you may be upset, given what has happened. It will save you a trip to the department tomorrow if we may speak now, if you don't mind."

Knightly nodded. "Of course, Inspector, ask whatever you want. I'm exhausted, but at the moment I don't exactly feel like going to bed, either."

"Is this all you had in the room?" Kazantzakis asked, looking at the suitcase and the pile of Knightly's things on the bed.

"This is everything," Knightly said, "except for a briefcase."

Kazantzakis turned and took a briefcase from the desk behind him, handing it to Knightly, who gave a quick look inside it and tossed it on the bed.

"That's it. Nothing exciting, a couple of books and some papers. It's all there."

"Is there anything missing from your bag?"

Knightly got up and looked at the things on the bed.

"I didn't bring anything valuable to Greece, Inspector. No computer or camera. I had my wallet and passport with me, and my phone. The thieves must have been broken-hearted...."

"It might have been a robbery, Professor, though I think that's not likely."

Kazantzakis paused again, looking closely at Knightly's face. "You seem to have picked this hotel, if I may put it so, more for the sake of its possible historic charm or out of a sense of nostalgia. It's not a natural target for thieves."

Knightly laughed, in spite of himself. "It's true, Inspector, I'm not such a fan of boutique hotels."

"And whoever broke in seems to have taken nothing. It looks instead as though they were looking for something and, when they didn't find it, they simply left."

Knightly shrugged, sighing. "I am at a loss, Inspector. I have no idea what's going on here." He suddenly looked up at Kazantzakis. "You said 'they'? How do you know it wasn't just one person who broke in?"

The inspector smiled slightly. "I said 'they' because we are fairly sure we've found the prints of at least three individuals, besides your own and the housekeeper's. They appear to have been somewhat amateurish, Mr. Knightly, if that offers you any comfort." Then he leaned over and asked in a tone that was level, but firm. "Do you have any idea why someone would want to have a look at your things?"

Knightly stared blankly at Kazantzakis. Not one intruder, but three or more. Willing to break into his room, somewhat bungling and incautious. He suddenly thought of the Bulgarians, or whoever they were, at the temple of Apollo the day before. Slightly comical, but also somewhat menacing. Then he thought of the strange and disturbing piece he had heard on the television as he was leaving Elli's place. And then he thought of Daniel.

"I can't imagine who would have the slightest interest in me, Inspector!" he blurted out, half-sincerely.

"You haven't been in Greece long?"

"Only about two days now."

"But you come often?"

"I'm a professor of Classics, Inspector, ancient Greek, ancient history, et cetera…so, yes, I come to Greece often."

"Did you make this trip with any special purpose in mind?"

"Not really. Well, I mean, yes and no. I am visiting a particular friend who lives in the area."

"Would you mind telling me who that is?"

"Her name is Eleutheria Parthénis. She lives in Kremni."

"Forgive me, but have you known her long?"

"You mentioned nostalgia, Inspector. Eleutheria and I met many years ago. The fact is that tonight is the first time I've seen her in over twenty years or more."

The Inspector raised an eyebrow. "I'm almost finished, Professor. Please think about this next question very carefully before you answer. Have you seen anything in the past two days that stands out as unusual? Anything strange that's happened, before tonight, I mean?"

"Nothing, Inspector. Absolutely nothing." Knightly answered flatly. He wished the Inspector would suddenly disappear. *Thank god I'm so exhausted*, Knightly thought to himself, *or it would be tough to pretend that I don't think this has been the strangest two days I have ever spent in Greece, or anywhere else for that matter.* It was the sighting of Daniel that was bothering Knightly in particular, but that bit of information was the very last thing he wanted to mention to the Chief Inspector without carefully considering the entire matter, preferably after some sleep and a cup or two of strong coffee.

Kazantzakis looked at Knightly with the same calm expression. "Very well." He got up from the chair. As he went to the door, he took out a card and handed it to Knightly. "There's really nothing more for me to do here, except to thank you for your patience and your willingness to answer my questions."

"Will you need me again, Inspector?"

"No, Professor. Unless you think of something else that is slipping your mind at the moment. And please, let me repeat, if you notice anything out of the ordinary, contact me right away. Please don't hesitate."

Kazantzakis looked at Knightly. "Will you be alright, Professor?"

"I don't think I want to stay here tonight, Inspector."

"Of course. Your friend, perhaps?"

"Yes, I think that's where I'll go."

"Do you need a ride? I would be happy to arrange it." Kazantzakis looked at him sincerely.

"No, thank you, though, that's very kind. I have a car. It's only a short drive and for some reason I don't feel sleepy, at least not right now, anyway."

Knightly looked at Kazantzakis as the chief inspector stood in the doorway. Slightly taller than average, he seemed solid, perhaps wiry, though the suit he was wearing fit loosely and disguised his build. He had a tangle of curly black hair which he had apparently made an effort to comb at some point in the day. And he wore a thick black mustache.

"Inspector, you said you work out of Athens?"

"Yes."

"But you are in Tripoli…"

"…working on an ongoing investigation. Yes, Mr. Knightly. It's not unusual."

"One last question, Inspector," Knightly said, eyeing him curiously, "are you from Athens, then?"

"No, as a matter of fact."

"You wouldn't be from Crete?"

"Yes, as a matter of fact, I am from Crete."

"And your name is Kazantzakis…"

"…just like the writer's," the inspector winced, "yes, Professor. And now may I urge you to get to your friend's house as quickly and as safely as you can and get some sleep!"

As he left, Kazantzakis turned to look at Knightly one last time. "Please, Professor Knightly, keep in mind what I said. Nothing was taken from here tonight, apparently, but I am still concerned. If you think of anything else I should know, please contact me. There's nothing more I can do for the moment, other than to ask you to be very careful about what is going on around you:

When danger seems to pass you by, and you take an easy breath,
You choose to ignore the danger, and may fail to see the rest."

"A *mantinadha*…!" Knightly exclaimed.

Kazantzakis smiled at him. "A specialty of my island, as I am pleased to see that you know, Professor. Good night." And the chief inspector left.

Knightly sat for a moment. The room was quiet. He felt drained and exhausted. *You choose to ignore the danger, and may fail to see the rest.* He forced himself to get up. Then he gathered his things and left the room himself, closing the door behind him.

6.

ELLI WAS STARTLED WHEN SHE OPENED THE DOOR AND saw Knightly standing there, looking disheveled and worn out.

"Will, I don't understand. What are you doing here?"

"Elli, my room was broken into—"

"What?!" Elli shrieked, her eyes widening.

"I don't know what's going on. When I got back to the hotel and went to my room, the door was open and there was a policeman sitting inside!"

"What in the world is going on, Will? Come in, please."

She took his arm and led him straight into the kitchen, where he sat down at her table.

"Do you want something to drink?"

"Yes, please."

"Tsipouro?"

"Perfect."

She poured a glass and put it in front of him. Knightly drained it and asked for another. Elli filled the glass. Knightly lifted it and stared at the clear liquor, as a dull fire began to spread down his throat and into his chest. He glanced at the one-liter bottle that Elli had poured from. It was plastic. Knightly chuckled.

"You've got the good stuff, eh, Elli! Let me guess—another neighbor?"

"A friend of the son of a neighbor, actually."

"Good god, such bounty! Do you people need to buy anything at the store anymore? Ah, Nature smiles forever on the Greeks! May Fortune smile on them as well."

Knightly downed the contents of the glass. Elli put a chair close to Knightly's and sat down beside him. She put her hands on his arm.

"Do the police know who broke into your room? Was anything stolen?"

"Nothing was taken. My stuff is all there, not that I had much to steal."

He was about to add that the inspector with whom he had talked did not suspect robbery, in fact, but was considering other motives for the break-in. Better not to tell Elli that, he thought. Why cause her to worry even more? He began to think of what else he couldn't tell her. Or didn't want to. The same scruple that had kept him from leveling with this Kazantzakis also held him back from confiding in Elli. It was his uncertainty, for one thing. But it was also a fear. He was worried about Daniel. There is little reason to believe in coincidence, he thought. We say "accident" or "coincidence" just to give a name to an event whose connection to other events or circumstances we haven't fully traced. He had spotted Daniel, lost him in a crowd—or was lost by him—had been stalked by goons, had his room broken into, and had been interviewed by the police. Knightly was believing more and more that the pieces fit together. He was just too tired to figure out how.

"Maybe whoever broke into your room thought that there would be something valuable to steal?"

"And then found out that they were hitting up an academic?" Knightly joked. "The police really don't know what to think, Elli, and since nothing was stolen I don't think they are going to put much energy into pursuing the case. If there even is a 'case,'" he said, trying to reassure her. "The inspector I spoke with was very decent. Kazantzakis was his name. He's from Crete—"

Elli smiled at this.

"I know, I thought the same thing. He works in Athens, but for some reason he's here in Tripoli, working on another case." He realized he had probably said too much.

"Another case? Why was he there in your room?"

"Maybe he's investigating a burglary ring or something. I really don't know. But I do know that I'm exhausted, and I am a stranger in a strange land, my dear sweet girl."

He looked at Elli, who answered him by tugging on his arm and lifting him out of the chair. She led him to a spare bedroom and pulled back the covers.

"The jet-lag was nothing, Will. I'm so sorry you had to go back to the room and find that. It's crazy! Will you be able to sleep, after all?"

"I think so," he said. "Thank you, Elli. What would I have done if I couldn't have come back here? Slept in the car somewhere, only to be rousted by gypsies?"

She smiled and drew close to him. Kissing him on the cheek, she pressed herself up against him. The feeling of her body suddenly pressed so tightly against his own was electric and gave Knightly a pleasant jolt. Despite his weariness, he began to feel an instant, delicious longing. Elli gently brushed his cheek with her hand.

"Good night," she said, and left the room.

"Good night, Elli."

Knightly managed to strip off a layer of clothing before he fell on the bed. He knew he should be worried about what had happened, but the numbness weighing on him was too great, and he had a vague sensation that he was muttering something even as he felt himself drifting into sleep.

Before he woke up, he had a strange dream.

He dreamed he was skating over a large pond—pond or small lake, really. It was winter and the pond was frozen over, its surface swept smooth as glass by the wind. Knightly was skating at high speed over what seemed the vast, unending expanse of the pond, which was framed by cattails and white birch. The sky was a pristine blue with nothing but thin wisps of cloud and the air was cold and crisp around him as he sailed along. It dawned on him that the place was familiar—it was a pond that was located in his own hometown in New England and he had indeed skated there when he was a kid. There had been a bucket factory at one end of the pond, but that had closed down long before his time.

At some time in the dream, Knightly heard the ice begin to make booming noises, the great sheets covering the pond contracting and making the *boom!* just as Thoreau described it in *Walden* and just as Knightly had often heard it himself when he used to skate on the great pond. It was a terrifying sound. You knew it was safe from talking to the locals and testing the ice yourself in various spots, but all the same it was disconcerting, to say the least, to hear the ice buckle and crack and go *boom*. Many just kept to the smaller ponds behind their houses or, if they had no pride, a rink in the nearby city. There was this trade-off—a total certainty and lack of risk paid for at the price of giving up or never even knowing the utter exhilaration of skating full-tilt with no boundaries ahead or behind or anywhere else in sight.

It was at about that point in the dream when he looked up and saw Daniel skating ahead of him. Daniel was travelling over the ice just as fast as Knightly was. He tried to catch up to Daniel by skating faster, but it was no use. No matter how hard he tried, he couldn't come up to him or cut down on the distance between them. And Daniel seemed to take no notice of him, even as Knightly struggled to catch up.

Then Knightly saw something odd, out of the corner of his eye. A shadowy figure, someone from the family of his ex-wife, had come out on the ice, and was holding an axe, which the phantom hoisted up and then brought down hard, chopping at the ice vigorously, blow after blow. Knightly cried out, *No!* but the odd spectre kept up with the chopping, without making any sound, until there were big chunks of ice floating loose all around the edge of the pond.

Knightly looked up, searching for Daniel on the horizon, and finally making out the figure of his former student some distance ahead of him, only to see him suddenly fall through a great crack in the ice that had opened up among the large chunks that were now floating everywhere.

Then the scene was changed. Knightly was on a slope, the air was still cold like winter but the sun was overhead and hot as it often is late in the season, and the combined heat of the sun and the cold had made the snow on the slope of the hill crusty and slick, so that Knightly found himself struggling to get up it. He had too many clothes on, he felt himself over-heating, he could not get any traction or find his footing at all, and his lungs began to burst as he tried to scream for help. He woke up in a cold sweat and the sheet that had covered him was soaked.

Jesus Christ, what a dream! he thought, and he looked around at the room, trying to remember where exactly he was, until it came back to him how he had left the hotel the night before and come here to Elli's house and found a momentary respite from all the weirdness that was going on. It felt good to put his feet on the floor. He looked at them, took a deep breath as he stretched his arms over his head. He didn't hear the sound of anyone in the house. What time was it? It seemed the sun was up. Maybe Elli was out of the house already. Knightly got up and dressed and went through the door of the bedroom. He was about to call out to see if Elli was in the kitchen or another room when he stopped in his tracks. In the living room, sitting on the couch and staring at the television, which in any case was not turned on, there was a young man of about twenty years or so. He took no notice of Knightly and just continued staring straight ahead, either in the direction of the television or at nothing in particular. Knightly realized that he looked remarkably like Elli. At that very moment, Elli walked in the front door, holding a bag of groceries and a smaller bag from the bakery. She looked at Knightly and she looked at the youth who was sitting on the couch and staring. It was clear to Knightly from Elli's reaction, if he hadn't already realized it before, that the boy was Elli's son.

7.

Kazantzakis arrived early at the office that the department had provided for him. He opened the door, looked at his desk and saw a surprise waiting for him: a small tray with a cup of coffee, a glass of water, and a plate of *loukoumades*, lightly doused with honey and a sprinkling of cinnamon. He sat down and tried one, cutting it in half with a small fork that was next to the plate. It was crisp and warm. *How could this be?* The police department was in a building on the edge of town, too far from the central squares where cafés and sweet shops are packed in great numbers for anyone to have walked from there to here without the doughnuts going cold. As he contemplated how the miracle might have taken place, he sensed that someone was standing in his doorway. It was Athena, a young detective who had been assigned to assist him while he was in Tripoli. It hadn't taken Kazantzakis any time to realize that she was an excellent police officer. She had graduated from the academy with high marks, only to be submerged in the work of various departments conspicuously lacking in glamor—traffic, passports—until finally she could not be held back any longer. After assignment to a routine patrol, she was promoted to detective ahead of the usual schedule.

"Athena, do you have anything to do with this?" Kazantzakis asked as he waved his hand over the plate that was already nearly empty.

Athena said nothing, but only changed the subject, laughing.

"Good morning, sir. You had to work late last night, I hear. How are you?"

"Yes, it's true. I'll tell you all about the conversation I had with our visitor in a minute, when Mitsos gets here. I'm feeling fine, thanks. How are you?"

"I'm fine," she said, though as she spoke she turned to stifle a yawn. She came into the office and sat down.

"Feeling fine, are we?" Kazantzakis laughed.

"Well, I did have a late night, too."

"But you weren't on duty last night, were you?"

"Not any official duty, Chief Inspector, no. It's the name-day of my uncle tomorrow and I was cooking all night."

"I see. And how did you acquire this honor? Weren't there others waiting in line for the right to prepare the feast?" he teased her.

"My mother is cooking, too, don't worry. Apparently we have to feed the entire village that she and my uncle come from!"

"You're a good daughter, Athena. What are you making?"

"The usual suspects, sir," she said, "and tomorrow I'll be roasting the meat. We're having wild boar."

"Don't tell me you went into the mountains and hunted it down yourself!"

"No, no, we're getting it from a market, don't worry!"

They were laughing and talking when Mitsos walked into the office. He was an older man, a veteran of more than thirty-five years and an experienced detective. He had a medium build, brown wavy hair, but cut short, dark brown eyes that protuded, like those of a fish, a prominent, bulbous nose, and a long face and square jaw-line that made his head look like a lantern. He had a reputation for being solid and reliable, though he could appear plodding at times. He had also failed to acquire any fame within the department for his sense of humor.

"Good morning, Chief Inspector," he said, as he sat down in the other chair in front of Kazantzakis's desk.

"Good morning, Mitsos. How are you?"

"Fine, sir."

"Very good. Why don't we get down to business, then? Let's have our briefing and then we can all get back to work."

"I'm afraid the news is not good, Inspector," Mitsos said glumly. "Whoever killed our boy didn't leave us a thing. Our people have gone over the warehouse, the parking lot, the whole property, for that matter, but they couldn't come up with anything."

"He left a bullet, didn't he?"

"Yes, sir, he left a bullet. We ran it, but it's not telling us much. A nine-millimeter. But we couldn't trace the gun."

"A pro," Kazantzakis said.

"Yes. It's as if he floated into the warehouse on wings, popped our boy, and then flew away."

Kazantzakis grimaced. The death of Korakogenis was a real blow.

"So be it, then. Do we have anyone else that we're working on?"

"This Stavros was it," Athena said. "We hadn't turned him yet, but one of our guys was about to make contact. We had enough on him to apply some pressure. It looked promising."

"It looked promising because it's all we had," Mitsos chimed in.

"It's been difficult to get at anybody above the street," Athena continued. "We're finding plenty of people dealing, but we just can't climb the chain. Korakogenis was the first person who was up the line of distribution at all. It was promising, though even he was probably a small fish."

"It's the same problem we've been having in Athens. The network is well organized. The links in the chain seem to be discrete and the communication from one level to the next is carefully controlled. Their discipline is superb, I regret to say."

Kazantzakis paused. Then he began again.

"We know that the stuff that's showing up in Athens is coming from Patra. A good amount of it takes a detour and gets dumped right here. The man we're hunting in Athens has a healthy franchise in Tripoli and in the rest of Arcadia, too."

"Skorpios," Athena said.

"His nom-de-guerre. And that's about all we have. He's shrewd. Whatever he's making, he's hiding it well. There's hearsay about certain businesses he's 'interested' in. He's a serious investor. But we have nothing concrete and we have not come close to identifying him, let alone locating him. He's not only built up an effectively opaque network. He's also terrorized most of the people who have dealings with him. Up and down the chain, he's feared. Very effective, I'm afraid."

"Skorpios," Mitsos muttered.

"What about the break-in at the hotel?" Athena asked. "It was an American who had the room?"

"Yes. Wilson Knightly, American, a professor, university-level, ancient Greek, of all things. I had a chat with him, but there's not much to report. I don't think he's involved in any way with the merchandise that's involved here. He doesn't have a clue about it, I'm sure. But I saw that the forensic tests turned up something."

Kazantzakis opened a folder on his desk.

"Right," Athena said, "we got a match on some of the prints from the hotel room. There were at least three men who broke in, and Interpol had two of them. They're Romanian, and small-time. We received photographs, too, and one of the cops who was tailing them the day we found them following the American recognized them from the photos."

"They are definitely the B-Team," Mitsos said. "They only got on our radar because they're careless. Scoring some dope as soon as they hit town. Not very bright!"

"But why were they following this Professor Knightly?" Athena asked.

"I don't know. It's odd, I admit, but I can't see a connection and, frankly, I don't want it to distract us. I'm not worried about Mr. Knightly. He won't be hard to find, if we need to talk to him again for any reason. As for our Balkan brethren, they must be extra hands for the network and probably highly disposable. But find them and bring them in anyway, Athena," Kazantzakis said. "Let's see if you can get something useful out of them. I am afraid they will not be very well-informed, unfortunately. Which brings us back to the point. We need to get back to work and cultivate some contacts who can throw light on the middle levels of the network. Then we can move on up the line. That's why I came to Tripoli, my dear colleagues, because they are moving a lot of stuff in this area. The network is flourishing around here, and there has got to be somebody who is pulling strings, at least locally, and who has a perspective on the organization. We need to get to that level, even if that means starting from the bottom again."

"We have a list, sir. We don't have to go back to square one. We'll keep working on them."

"Thank you, Athena. Tell your people to keep at it. And anybody they're working on and they think will be useful to us—tell them to watch the backs of those people!"

"Yes, sir."

"That's all. Thank you both."

Kazantzakis noticed the two were quiet. He straightened himself and looked at his two colleagues.

"We're flying blind at the moment, there's no arguing that. And the man we're after is a first-class bastard. He's ruthless and he's successful, thus far. But I've been in our present position before, as I am sure you have been, too." He looked directly at Mitsos, but then nodded to Athena as well. "We just keep doing what we do. We will find what we need, given time, and we will nail Mr. Skorpios. It is only that, a matter of time. And diligence. Tell your people to keep working.

The hound will chase the cunning fox who cheats in ev'ry way.
But the hound keeps on; well he knows that the dog will have his day."

Mitsos had begun to roll his eyes, when he glanced at Athena, who was making no effort to hide the grin on her face.

"Good day, sir." Mitsos got up and left the office.

"Good day, sir," Athena said, as she got up, too.

"Good day, Athena. And, by the way, *chronia polla* to your uncle!"

"Thank you, sir. But not to the old boar!"

"Exactly."

Kazantzakis watched her leave.

"Good kid," he mused. "Good cop."

May luck and fortune bless her and the blessed fates be kind.
Whatever our fates and fortune and the future have in mind.

He picked up his cup and took a sip of the coffee, which was cold.

8.

When you get to the bottom of the cup, you can tell the future from the grounds of the coffee. At least, certain women of the villages say they can. Knightly stared at the surface of the coffee in his cup, which was full. "Here's a sign—clear liquid, undisturbed, with froth around the sides, signifying that what is directly in front of one's face will make sense, to a point, but that obscurity is close by, surrounding what little you will ever know, waiting to swallow all certainty within a turmoil of foam. What omen could be more sure than that?"

He looked up from the café table and around the square and thought about Elli.

They had sat down together for breakfast in her kitchen—himself, and Elli, and Elli's son, Giannakis. Only a pale light filters into the kitchen in the mornings. Through the window that stands over the sink you can see the mountains that lay to the west of the village. Elli set a place for Giannakis and put out food for him, even though he did not touch a thing.

Knightly was moved by how Elli cared for her son. She did not dote or fuss but simply included him in the proceedings.

When they were finished with breakfast, he and Elli had walked Giannakis over to the house of Chrysanthi, who had in fact called her sister as soon as she realized Giannakis had left her place. Chrysa had met them at the door. "You have a good time, you two!" she said. "Giannakis can stay here. We'll be fine." So they walked back to the house, collected a blanket and some food, and got in the car and drove to the sea.

They didn't swim. They just sat and talked. Mostly, Elli talked. She explained how it had happened to Giannakis. How everything had been fine when he was a young boy. Growing up, he had been a normal kid. It was only when he entered the *Lykeio*—high school—that the trouble started. And it wasn't even trouble with *him*, but rather with some of the boys in his group. There was plenty of pot around. Giannakis tried it, once or twice, with his friends. It didn't take a detective to figure out what he was doing. Elli knew immediately. The smell stayed in his clothes, never mind the odd behavior, the stumbling, when he would return home after being with his friends when they were passing joints behind the soccer field. Elli was firm with Giannakis and told him that those other boys could do what they liked but that he and his friends must not take part in it. Any time the boys with the drugs showed up, he was to leave. *I should have forbidden him to hang out with any of them. But I trusted his friends—or rather I trusted their parents.*

Elli said that Giannakis had done what she told him to do, despite the fact that he took a lot of abuse, not only from the boys who would light up and egg on the rest, but from his supposed friends as well.

She recalled the one night that, in her mind, proved to be fatal. She had convinced herself that she and Giannakis had worked it out and that they would get through these few remaining teen-age years unscathed. He was out with friends and they were at a club. It was very late, they were having a good time. Anyone who was smoking or anything of the sort was doing it outside, not making a big deal of it. And somebody passed him something. She said she still didn't know to this day if Giannakis knew what he was doing or not. His friends swore he was given the substance—whatever it was—by someone else, no one knew by whom. "Giannakis didn't know what he was taking," they said, "it was in his drink," they swore it. *That night and the next two days were the worst days of my life. I thought he was going to die.* He would be raving one minute, incoherent, wild, and then just as suddenly he would become silent, comatose, she said. He was sweating profusely and then he would shake as if chilled to the bone. He was never the same after that night.

He became moody and withdrawn. He would no longer talk with her about what was going on. She told him he was forbidden to go out with any of those boys but he began to ignore her. She knew that he must be using, but it had come to a point where nobody would talk with her — neither the boys nor their parents. She became furious. She even resorted to locking Giannakis in the house at night. Chrysa tried to help as well. But nothing worked. It wasn't long before he began to slip into his present state. At last, she said, she had to take him out of school. *Catatonia*, they called it. None of the other boys suffered anything like this. She took him to doctors who tried various treatments. Some of the drugs made his symptoms worse. Nothing helped. He would just sit, staring, for hours, or walk around town, without any apparent purpose. *He may have had a susceptibility to these symptoms on account of an underlying condition, they had said, perhaps the onset was hastened by his substance-abuse.* Chrysa helped her to take care of him, though they fought viciously once about whether Giannakis would be better off if he were staying in an institution. Elli had absolutely refused to consider such a thing, even when the doctor treating Giannakis agreed with Chrysa. She could not bear the thought of her son in an institution, she said, especially any of the kind she could afford. *We do the best we can do for him now. I only wish I hadn't let it happen—*

At that point Elli's voice had given out. He hesitated to ask her but he had to. *Where was Giannakis's father in all of this, Elli? He should have been there. It sounds like it was all on you. Where the hell was he?*

She could not answer the question. He could see that she was in an agony and that her eyes were burning but no tears would come. It was impossible for him to watch her like this. He was afraid she would explode. She was trembling, her face was red and it looked to him as though her eyes ached but she could not cry. He realized then that she had most likely already shed every last tear that one could. He held her and told her not to answer, not to talk. He was sorry. "Let's just sit here," he had said.

Leaning on him, she told Knightly she was sorry, she just could not talk about it anymore. Giannakis's father was not a good man. She didn't mean to speak badly about anyone. But he just didn't care, she cried. He was never in the picture. *What happened, happened. There's nothing to be done about it now.*

And then they just sat there, looking out at the sea, and at the sunlight that played carelessly on its surface. Or closing their eyes they listened to the sound of the waves as they washed up on the sand. It was strange, but this was the first moment that he had felt at peace, he realized, since he had arrived in Greece, despite the terrible things that Elli had just been compelled to tell him.

It had been difficult at that point to tell Elli that he had decided to go back to Athens for a few days. Not that she gave him a hard time. Quite the opposite, she was understanding about it, when he told her. But he felt terrible. He felt as if he was abandoning her, or as if he were running away, as soon as he had found out that her situation in fact was a complicated one and that her life was made difficult by the need to take care of her handicapped son.

He also found it was impossible to be totally honest with Elli about why he was going back to Athens.

Knightly looked up from his table. He looked up at the church, Agios Vasilios. Its two towers that faced the square were imposing, but they were not monstrous or outsized. They were human in scale, and somehow comforting. He was sitting in the same spot where he had been sitting when he saw Daniel. Something was bothering him. As he replayed the scene in his mind, catching sight of Daniel, jumping up from the table, the fruitless pursuit, Knightly was sure that Daniel had seen him. *Daniel had seen him and ignored him.* That was the most troubling thing of all. There could only be one explanation for that. Daniel was doing something that could not be interrupted. Daniel was doing something that he did not want to involve his old professor in. As if that would have endangered Knightly, or Daniel himself.

The logic was simple and prompted a conclusion that worried Knightly deeply. Daniel is either in some kind of trouble, he thought, or he is engaged in making some kind of trouble, and Knightly's own sudden appearance here in Tripoli must have represented a serious inconvenience, to put it mildly, which Daniel had remedied by escaping the scene. *But to where?*

How could he tell Elli about all this? How could he tell Elli who Daniel was—at least, as much as Knightly knew about it? Daniel had passed up a host of opportunities after graduation—law school, graduate school—and joined the army instead. And he flourished. Knightly recalled the e-mails. Daniel's joking complaints about the training and the rest of it could not disguise his satisfaction with what he was doing or the fact that the young man had apparently found a calling. Daniel's career accelerated, in a particular direction. He told Knightly he was applying to the Army's Ranger school. He not only got in, he excelled. It was around that time that Knightly began to hear less and less from Daniel. Knightly was under no illusions as to the level of his own naiveté, but he understood what this probably meant. Daniel was travelling further and further, if that was the right way to put it, into the world of special operations. He had entered and was passing through the curricula of the various special forces of the United States Army. Where had it led him? *Black Ops?* Had Daniel submitted to the training and succeeded in entering the legions of the *shadow warrior?*

Knightly had grown convinced, in fact, that what he had seen a couple days before at the edge of the square and in Tripoli's busy streets was just that—a passing shadow.

So he was protecting—whom? If it was true that Daniel was in Greece and carrying on activity in his particular line of work, the last thing Knightly wanted to do was to tell a Greek policeman about seeing Daniel! But why not tell Elli? Was it to protect Elli herself—or Daniel? The admission that he didn't trust Elli enough left him feeling queasy. But he quickly told himself that, if he lacked any trust in Elli, she had acted in a similar way. She had been reluctant, after all, to tell him about Giannakis. Yet he knew that wasn't fair. She had good reason to hold back. She had explained to him, as a matter of fact, that she didn't tell him right away about Giannakis simply because she had wanted some space. *She had wanted to see him again, for the first time, at least, without any*—and she had begun to grow red again. She said that, once again, her sister had urged her, had insisted. Chrysa took Giannakis for the night so that Elli and Knightly could meet on equal terms. At least for one night. She was planning to tell him the next day, only Giannakis came home ahead of schedule. Finally, they had managed a laugh over that.

Knightly decided he was ready to leave. To Athens. Where else would Daniel go? Well, about a thousand places. And that's just counting the islands, Knightly thought. The buses leaving from Kolokotronis don't go to Athens. But maybe getting on the bus was just a dodge? Knightly had made up his mind to look for his former student in the capital. Half the population of the country is there, he thought, for Pete's sake. And, if it's an insult to the rest of the country to say that everything happens in Athens, there is at least a grain or two of truth in saying so. He had decided that he would give himself three days—or four, tops—to find Daniel in Athens. If he didn't find him, he could tell himself that he had tried. And he figured that he had maybe a fifty-fifty chance of being right that Daniel was in Athens or had gone there, at least. What his chances were of contacting Daniel or finding him in the city, he didn't want to contemplate. "Three days, Elli—four, at most—I can't explain why, but I have to go to Athens to take care of something. I promise I'll explain what's going on when I get back, however it turns out." Elli had smiled and said she would make him keep his word.

Knightly glanced at the newspaper he had bought. There had been demonstrations in Athens. Protests against austerity measures being enacted by the current government and cuts in benefits and programs and legislation proposed or passed affecting protected statuses among various professions in the public sector etc.

And clashes between anarchists and the police. Marble-slabs broken up, weaponized, thrown, tear-gas, fire-bombs, sticks, and stones. Knightly shook his head and sighed. Amid the carnage, a building was torched on Stadiou. "You're pushing it now, boys. Looks like you left the familiar and accepted bounds of your tedious little theater. Useless cretins," he muttered. He folded the paper and put it under his arm as he got up from the table.

What Knightly didn't read—what was not there to be read because it had not been reported and indeed was likely never to be reported in print or on the air was an incident that went on later in the day after the demonstrations had petered out and clashes between the violent groups and police had subsided.

A figure wearing a black hood had followed a group of five of the anarchists, themselves called κουκουλοφόροι—the ones who wear hoods—to an apartment in the neighborhood of Metaxourgeio. After giving them a moment to settle in, but only a moment, the hooded stranger knocked on the door of the apartment. One of the group looked through the peep-hole. He opened the door a crack. The chain-guard caught and though he strained he couldn't see anyone in the hallway.

Then the door exploded, jumping off its hinges. The hooded figure strode into the room and as the young man who had opened the door tried to stop him the intruder punched him in the jaw, a sound like a rotten pumpkin being thrown against a brick wall. One of the anarchists, sitting close to the door, lunged at the man in the black hood, but the attacker was too quick. He hopped on his left foot as his right leg scissored upward. It looked strangely like a dance-move, like an odd slice of ballet, as if he were flicking his foot, but in fact his boot struck the man hard in the solar plexus. A second *flick* and this time the toe of the boot caught the anarchist just under the jaw. Another rotten pumpkin. The victim crumpled and fell to the floor like a heavy sack dropped from a window. The attacker did not pause but instantly spun and unleashed a lightning-quick backward roundhouse kick at a third member of the group, who had sat in stunned silence on the other side of the room. The back of the attacker's heel—the steel-reinforced heel of his black boot—caught the man in the side of the head. The blow smashed into his right temple with a sharp *crack* and he slumped to the floor, silent as before.

The black hood approached the last two anarchists. He was holding a combat knife whose handle incorporated brass-knuckles. The blade had been sawed off to about three inches and then sharpened to a new point. Easier to hide. The black hood landed three blows in swift succession with the brass-knuckles to the face of one of the anarchists. He pushed the man up against the wall, holding him by the throat, and with a single concise and continuous movement of the stubby blade he cut a figure in the man's belly like a butterfly paper-clip, as the blood blossomed where the knife had made long gashes in the thin fabric of the t-shirt.

The dark hood now confronted the last anarchist, the only one left, except for the fact that he was not quite alone. Even as the attack began, he had been sitting on the couch with his girl-friend. He had already rolled a fat joint and launched into the latest of his adventures, with some relish, perhaps, before the man in black arrived.

The black hood stood over the girl—her boyfriend was at this point gibbering in the corner of the sofa. "What do you see in these fucking pieces of shit!?" he screamed at her, in a mix of Greek and English. "What the fuck are you thinking? Half of their bullshit is all for you, you stupid cunt!" He moved closer, pointing the blade at her throat. "You move, and I'll cut your miserable fucking head off." His voice was steely. *"Do you understand!"* She moved her head slowly, *Yes*, weeping and shaking.

The black hood grabbed the last anarchist by the back of the boy's own hood and put him in a wooden chair in the center of the room. He pulled the young man's hands behind him and bound his thumbs with a thin wire.

"It's time to do some decorating. You're going to remember this day, you little pussy. It's not right that people don't know who you are—you are one motherfucking big-shot, yessir," and he broke the boy's nose with one punch, "one great motherfucking big-shot. And everybody should know what a superior kind of asshole you are." His voice rose hysterically. "Fucking savior of history! Fucking liberator! Fucking popular resistance fighter fucking people's fucking hero—"

At this point, the figure in the black hood himself was shaking, trembling. He stood over the young anarchist, whose mouth was covered in blood running from his nose. The black hood leaned over the anarchist and spat at him, "Let's decorate our little pussy of a hero," and he cut an A into one of his cheeks. The terrified man moaned and writhed but hardly resisted. "That's beautiful," said the black hood and cut another A, this time into the other cheek, and then one last A, cut deep into the forehead of the anarchist. "Everybody's gonna know you now, motherfucker."

He stood back and looked at the young man for a moment. Then he struck him. A heavy punch in the side, his ribs cracking and giving way. Then another punch, lower down. Then another, and another, smashing the ribs on the other side of the young man's body. The dark figure lifted the anarchist out of the chair and dumped him on the floor. One last savage kick to the groin. The youth coughed and wretched as he lay on the tile, half out of his senses, half filled with sickening pain.

The black hood dragged the girl off the couch to where the anarchist was lying. He pulled her arms tightly around the boy's body and tied her hands with plastic cuffs, leaving the two of them lying there together on the floor.

Then the black hood left the apartment, after he had cut the throats of the others.

Knightly never read the story of what happened in that apartment, because word was sent back to headquarters by the first officers on the scene, who received word back just as quickly that they were to secure the apartment, which was soon visited by a special team who sanitized the site and removed all evidence of what had happened. Given the awful mess, this was no small task. Whether or not all the evidence present at the scene was in fact destroyed would remain unclear. If anyone with an acute political sense or indeed any sense of a future opportunity was by chance in the loop when the officers first called in the massacre, then that certain person or persons might have issued instructions to see to it that some of the evidence made its way into safe keeping. Most of it, presumably, was destroyed. One of the anarchists who had been murdered was the grandson of a prominent member of a leading left-wing opposition party. And the young man whose face had been so brutally marked by the figure in the black hood happened to be from a wealthy family and himself the nephew of a minister serving in the current government.

PART TWO

το δίκτυο

the net

1.

KNIGHTLY WAS IN THE CAR AGAIN. HE HAD DECIDED to drive along the coast to the old highway and then to the section of the National Road that had been built not so long ago between Tripoli and Athens. The coast-road was as stunning as ever. Across the gulf lay the Argolid, its hills crisply outlined by the morning sun that was already flinging its rays wantonly over the deep-blue waters of the bay. It was difficult to drive only because Knightly's eyes kept straying, even though it blinded him to look at the dazzling sea.

Knightly enjoyed this part of the trip. The old national road went inland following a winding path past towns like Koutsopódi, *Lame-foot*, and Fíchti, and then it slowed even more as one passed through fields and by farm-stands that sold honey and melons, until at last one reached the new highway. The landscape was attractive even here, with the vineyards of Nemea stretching out on either side. Once one arrived at the hills in the northeast of the Peloponnese, however, culminating in the imposing bulk of Acrocorinth, the terrain grew more and more austere as the land itself withered into bare rock and scrub.

Then the wasteland. Megara. Eleusis. Across the water one could see Salamis, the island with a name as famous as almost any ancient name. Now industrial facilities and dry-docks and refinery capacity lined the shoreline opposite the fabled island and rusted tankers sat abandoned in the waters between shore and island. From this point the trip from the Peloponnese to Athens was as deflating to Knightly as the coast road was delightful. It reminded him of that equally bleak stretch of the Jersey Turnpike that greets travellers to New York City with a vision of the Inferno. But the wasteland leading to Athens had a reason, after all. Half of the country's population had decided to reside in the capital city and the supply of goods and resources needed to sustain them came at a cost.

Once one entered the western reaches of the city, the desolation took on a different character. Instead of barren, open terrain against which the industrial works stood out in stark relief, one drove through a landscape that was increasingly settled and urban but barren and brutal in its own fashion. The wide avenue was flanked by mile after mile of concrete sidewalks and the buildings along this great western artery alternated between ugly, non-descript apartment blocks and stores of various types—plumbing, appliances, lighting, furniture, paint, hardware, cars, motorcycles, scooters, sporting goods, clothes, shoes, computers, cellphones, toys. These purveyors of life's necessities were interspersed with eateries, most offering some variety or other of food-on-the-go. The numbing gauntlet was salted with the occasional strip joint or sex club. While the rest of Athens, especially those neighborhoods in and around the historic center, seemed intent on aping the character of the villages from which so many of the city's inhabitants had fled, the area leading into the city had lost any semblance of the essence of a Greek village—with its life-supporting comforts and charm— or never had it to begin with.

Gratefully, the Attiki Odos that was built at the time of the Olympics of 2004 allowed one to go around the city to the north instead. Some of the prosperous and exclusive suburbs lay still further to the north of this beltway—Kefissia being the ultimate example—while other humbler neighborhoods like Iraklia or Nea Philadelfia lay to the south. Knightly took the Attiki Odo all the way to the new airport, another crucial improvement completed before the Olympics. He dropped off his rental car and took the metro into the city. He had no need for a car in Athens, given the nature of his plan to contact Daniel, if Daniel was indeed in the city at all.

After an easy walk from the metro station, he checked into the Pelopidas—one of his favorite hotels in the center of town. He dumped his bag in the room. No worries this time, he said to himself, the security's a little better here. He left the hotel and headed for his destination. He thought of walking directly, along Veïkou, but then decided to go by a more indirect route to get some exercise after the long drive. He even walked for a while on Syngrou, though only briefly, since the noise and congestion of the busy avenue quickly drove him back to the quieter streets of Makryiánni.

At last he reached his goal, a street that had been turned into a pedestrian zone and that was home to one of the best beer haunts in Athens. The restaurant served premium beers on tap—mostly German—and so originally it was called *Vom Faß*, with the old spelling preserved. Then the economic crisis intensified, in effect pitting Germany and Greece against one another, as though each represented nothing more than the two opposite poles of economic fortune, and thus things German began to be held in bad odor among Greeks. The business suffered. So the owner renamed his pub *Varelisia*, a good enough native equivalent of the German phrase. Business picked up again and the owner was happy that now his customers could go on enjoying their fine German brews without feeling they were having their noses rubbed in it. In any case, Knightly was relieved that salvation had arrived in time so that the best place in all of Athens to procure and enjoy a heady Weiße had not been allowed to disappear.

His plan to find Daniel was simple: let Daniel find him. Knightly had realized somewhere along the morning's drive, if not before, that there was little chance that he could locate Daniel in Athens. He possessed neither the tools nor the experience in hunting for people nor even the time. Daniel was, presumably, an expert at this game. If Daniel did not want Knightly to know where he was, there was no point in Knightly even trying. On the flip side, if Daniel was willing to meet with Knightly, then what Knightly needed to do, it seemed to him, was to make himself available. Obvious and conspicuous. Hence he conceived the brilliant plan of drinking beer in public, something that made sense on its own terms, in any case, and of waiting for Daniel to pass him a message that would indicate to Knightly where Daniel thought they should meet, and when, and how.

It might seem like a frivolous tactic. But Knightly remembered that Daniel loved beer. Especially the really good stuff. In fact, Knightly had a hunch. He was sure that Daniel had noticed him in Tripoli and that he had indeed taken evasive action, ostensibly in order to avoid an encounter. That had to be a tactical move on Daniel's part, Knightly thought—*or I am going to be damned offended*. If Daniel had a good reason to shun contact with Knightly at that instant, perhaps he might be willing to talk to Knightly now. Knightly hoped that Daniel would *want* to speak with him, if only to make absolutely clear to his former mentor why Knightly should bug out and avoid whatever complications—or danger—made it necessary for Daniel to ditch him back in Tripoli.

Knightly had thought about it. Daniel and he hadn't parted on bad terms. There had never been any rupture in their friendship, only a slow fade. Knightly supposed that happened because of the nature of what Daniel was doing in his echelon of the service and, he had to imagine, because of the pattern and tempo of Daniel's deployments.

One thought unsettled Knightly. What if Daniel were playing with him? But he could not for the life of him imagine why Daniel would do that and he quickly put this possibility out of his mind.

It was more likely, come right down to it, that if anyone was playing with him it was Kazantzakis. He thought over the talk he'd had with the chief inspector. The policeman had treated him with courtesy. And he was intelligent. A conversation laced with literary allusion, not to mention *mantinadhes*—I mean, really! Yet the chief inspector must have seen through him. What if Kazantzakis has already found the crew that broke into his room—perhaps the same ones who toured Vasses with him that day? How long would it take for the inspector to put things together, especially if he gets them to talk about what was going on in Tripoli? If they had a connection with Daniel, as Knightly had begun to fear, they might spill it all to Kazantzakis and he would understand that Knightly was probably holding out on him. Knightly didn't want to think about it. The consequences of such a train of events could be unpleasant.

But it also occurred to him that Kazantzakis had been following a trail that led from Athens to Tripoli. *Involving a certain investigation*, he had said. This might be more than a coincidence. Perhaps Daniel had come to Tripoli from Athens following a similar trail. What if Daniel and Kazantzakis were working on the same thing? If so, and if it became apparent to Kazantzakis that Knightly had withheld information concerning Daniel, it could mean some real trouble for Knightly himself. Unpleasant, indeed.

Knightly decided to contemplate the contents of the tall glass before him instead. He held it up to the sunlight. It brought to mind the poet's words: *beer-bright Vermeer*. What a phrase! Such a concise token of the ubiquity of light in the painter and the special quality of that light! Why not turn the luminous image around? Let the quality of light that astounds in Vermeer help to render to the mind the ineffably beautiful color of this product of the brewer's own exquisite art!

It was just then, as Knightly began to fear that he would be arrested at any moment for excessive brilliance, that he began to think about Elli again.

He wondered if he had made a mistake. What if Elli represented his lost youth! Daniel, too—the search for Daniel resembled his wish to see Elli again in so far as Daniel represented for him another time, a moment earlier in his career when he was younger and so much of his life still lay ahead. He began to wonder if he were chasing a will o' the wisp in either case and refusing to settle on a single purpose just to keep himself distracted so that he wouldn't see how he was fooling himself.

"Don't get maudlin," he said to himself, looking again at the glass as its golden contents ebbed.

He wasn't fooling himself. Elli's situation was real. The problems she was facing with Giannakis were very real, indeed. Knightly wanted to help her. He had been thinking about it as he drove this morning and he had determined to do whatever he could for her when he was finished in Athens and returned to her in Kremni. But what could he do? Just be there. How about that, for a start?

Then he thought about Giannakis. He felt a deep sadness for the boy. Giannakis was utterly unresponsive and his spirit seemed far away. How could he be reached? He needed to talk with Elli about what treatments they had tried. He was sure Elli tried everything, not to mention that her sister would not have let the situation simply stand if anything could be done.

Knightly remembered he had once known a boy in a similar condition, when Knightly himself was young. It was the older brother of a couple of friends of his. This older brother had blown his mind out. That was how everyone in their little town put it—"he blew his mind out on drugs"—which sounded suspiciously like a line from a Beatles' song, if not just an echo of the Sixties in general. People had said it was LSD.

Knightly wondered if that was possible. Or was it just a generous amount of dope-smoking, perhaps tag-teaming with a psychological breakdown? As Knightly recalled, the man who was father of his friends and their older brother was, well, strange. He could not remember the man without having a vivid picture of Mr. Giulini scowling and looking miserable.

Reed Giulini. That was the older brother's name. He had been incredibly popular in school. Tall, good-looking, smart, a tennis star. He also played the guitar and sang. So he formed a group with another friend and the two most beautiful girls in town. Knightly recalled that this feat alone made Reed into a kind of god for him. The two girls sang and the two boys played their guitars and sang along as well. Their versions of Simon and Garfunkel tunes were wildly popular.

Then something happened to Reed. He went away to college and came back a changed person. He would wander the town, up and down, staring straight ahead, never interacting with anyone. Knightly remembered the shock when he ran into Reed one day. He greeted him but Reed did not answer. He just looked past Knightly. Knightly recollected that Reed's eyes had dark circles around them. Reed seemed zombified. Knightly asked his friends what was wrong. They wouldn't talk about it. Their feeling of shame was palpable, Knightly recalled. He stopped asking them what was wrong with their brother.

Was it drugs that ruined him? Or an underlying emotional condition? Some of both? Reed's sister, the second child, the only girl in the family, suffered from anorexia, as it turned out. And the father was, as Knightly couldn't help remembering, something of an ogre, who likely suffered from symptoms of his own. Hardly a scientific study. But Knightly couldn't help remembering the zombie-like face of Reed Giulini when he thought about Giannakis and the boy's catatonic look.

What about Giannakis's own father, then? Was he another Mr. Giulini, lurking in the shadows? Where was he, when it all went down? *Where the hell was he now?* Was Giannakis's father still living around there? Or somewhere in Tripoli? Why couldn't Elli even talk about him? Perhaps it would just take time for Elli to open up and tell him what had happened. Knightly hadn't been around that long, after all. And then he had left Elli to go chasing after "someone to be named later." Knightly felt guilty. Elli had been understanding when Knightly had told her he had to go to Athens. But she had also fallen silent. Oddly, though, Knightly couldn't escape the feeling that Elli's silence had more to do with something else—something she herself was not telling Knightly—than with anything that he was doing. Knightly made a note to himself: call Elli tonight.

Knightly looked around at the people on the street who were passing by his table. He reminded himself that he was supposed to be on the lookout for Daniel. Even though Daniel was the one who was supposed to find Knightly. Never mind that, keeping a sharp eye out for Daniel gave him a chance to do some dedicated people-watching.

The human traffic on the pedestrian way went by in a constant stream. The metro station was just over a block from here and it disgorged in a steady pulse all kinds of metro riders—office-workers, clerks, professional-types, shoppers, students, young kids and pensioners. The people coming back from work passed by in various states of dishevelment, some hiding their weariness, walking as quickly as they could to reach home. The shoppers were of all sorts and carried bags of every description, from the department store habitués to the old ladies who carried bread and produce in cheap plastic bags worn thin as their stockings. Couples of every size and shape passed by, young and old, walking hand in hand, and even the youngest couples looked for all the world as though they had been at this kind of thing forever. And then there were the beauties, tall, long-legged women, with magnificent dark hair—or dark hair dyed blonde, the latest thing, so much the rage these days in fact that Greece was in danger of becoming a nation of yellow-hair. *Tell that to the Germans.* Many of the gorgeous women passed by him with features so fine as to make the ancient statues of Aphrodite or Artemis weep with a helpless envy and this made Knightly sigh with a helpless wonder. And then there were the beautiful men, sometimes in pairs, sometimes walking alone, going wherever they were wanting to go.

It amazed Knightly how steady was the stream of people as it flowed down the street. Aside from the obvious differences in size and scale between village and city, here was the main difference, as Knightly saw it, between what he had just left in Kremni and what he found here in the capital of the entire country and its megalopolis. In this neighborhood and in others repeated throughout the city there was the incessant and wonderfully variegated flood of human beings, while in the village one saw in the streets the same people as the day before, hence the ability—and the need—to inventory their goings-on in religious detail. The human surfeit and multiplicity of the city by contrast bred an anonymity.

He thought of what he had just seen on Syngrou Avenue, only a few blocks from here. It wasn't just the dirt and noise and commotion. In the short time he had walked on Syngrou he had seen at least two or three pairs of men who were pushing shopping carts filled with junk. They had been collecting cans and bottles, but one of these teams had managed to pack the small cart with a surprisingly bulky payload—the guts of a metal box-spring and the baffles of a cooling unit off the back of a refrigerator stuck into the air as the two men pushed and strained to keep their ship upright, negotiating both street and sidewalk on their journey through the city.

These men were immigrants, *metanástes*. They were of a fit age, probably in their late twenties or early thirties. One pair had looked like Pakistanis, another was clearly African, from Nigeria or Kenya or Angola or maybe Somalia. What appeal could this life have for them, Knightly wondered, or did these men simply appreciate the chance to barter and trade even at the margins of the economy and of Greek society? Wouldn't they prefer to do anything in their home country rather than be forced to do this? Or is this precisely the sort of activity they would be pursuing at home? Knightly had to remind himself that everywhere in the developing world (or *the world in transition*, as some colleagues now called it) the margins were well populated. And not only in the developing world.

Besides, these men may not have packed themselves off to Greece because they had dreamed of scrounging through the discards and trash of others in hopes of finding something to sell. They were likely headed for Italy or Germany or Sweden and found no welcome in those places, only a swift return to Greece, where they'd entered Europe. Or they had never gotten further than Greece at the start. Then came the question of how to manage and how to survive. What bothered Knightly was how the daily struggle of those men contrasted so starkly with the comfort, the oasis, in which Knightly found himself.

Suddenly he recalled another incident—thinking about such contrasts triggered it, between "good" areas and not so good ones, between the people who enjoy prosperity and those who struggle, between hard lives and soft—something that had happened in Tripoli on the day he had gone to see Elli. He had left his hotel late in the morning, eleven o' clock or so, to take a walk before the drive to Kremni. He had headed north up Kennedy—some called it Tasou Sichioti—and then to Agiou Constandinou. Staying on Constandinou where it branches off to the northeast, he entered an enclave of several blocks where the houses were newer and larger and each one had a big yard. By the time he reached the point where Constandinou crossed the *peripheriaki*, or ring-road, the neighborhood changed, and Knightly found himself in an area that increasingly resembled a no man's land, the further he walked.

Just before that, Knightly had happened to glance back and he caught sight of a young man, about eighteen or nineteen years old. The young man had come out of one of the large houses on the prosperous block. He followed behind Knightly but slowly. Knightly was walking at a fast pace, out of habit rather than out of any concern, and before long he saw that the young man trailed behind him. Once Knightly came into the no man's land, however, and had seen where the boundary lay between civilization and the desert, at least in that part of the city, he decided to turn around and head back to the hotel.

Before reaching the affluent zone again, he saw the same young man, who abruptly turned off the sidewalk and went into an open doorway. Knightly looked at the sign over the door; it advertised aluminum siding. As Knightly passed by, the young man looked at him. That was the uncomfortable part—the way the young man looked at him. It was fleeting and yet the look conveyed fear and hostility and suspicion, all at once. Knightly thought for a second. There was no way that kid was showing up for work. Not at half past eleven. And he didn't look like the type who needed to buy siding. Knightly also doubted that he was bringing lunch to some dear old uncle. He hadn't been carrying any bag, for one thing. Fundamentally, in the ten minutes or so he'd been walking, the boy had gone from one world into a very different one. He hadn't been carrying anything when he went into the shop. But Knightly had a feeling that he'd be carrying something when he left.

Drugs again. *Jesus, you're seeing drugs everywhere!* But Knightly had had this encounter before his room was broken into and before he went to Kremni and saw Giannakis and heard about his story. It was a chance event that put Knightly in the path of the young man who had left his house for a casual stroll and to refresh his supply, if that's what he was doing. Chance—that only means I don't get out much, Knightly thought. What stuck with Knightly about the whole thing was the incongruity. The young man with whom he'd happened to cross paths was from a cushy suburban-style development but nevertheless the boy seemed to be subject to a need to escape the bubble. All the benefits and material comfort piled up for him thanks to his privileged place in the world could not satisfy certain inner needs and finally they left him empty. He went to the shop that sold aluminum siding to buy something else to fill the void.

Or was it simpler than that? People love to party. Rich people party richly with things that cost. But what's the cost, in fact? Answer that, Knightly said to himself, and win a medal. Or just look at Giannakis, he thought. Maybe the answer *was* simple, at least as to who pays for the problem.

The search for Daniel had yielded no results. Knightly looked up and down the street one more time. No sight of anyone who looked like Daniel. Not that he was about to give up on the strategy he had chosen. He thought about some of his other favorite spots in town. *Hypocrite! You fret about drugs in society and then stumble from one beer joint to the next.* Yeah, right, he thought. As a matter of fact, as much as Knightly appreciated the fruits of grain and vine, the thought of having another beer did not appeal to him right now. Later tonight, he could go to the Scholar's Pub—an all-Irish place he loved—and have a good meal and try once again to make himself conspicuous and available for Daniel to contact.

Knightly looked up at the apartments over a number of the storefronts that lined the street. Many of these second-story flats were decorated on the exterior with elegant trim and most of them had balconies. What a great place to live, Knightly supposed. Music floated out of the windows of one apartment. Piano and voice. It sounded like a lesson. Knightly looked up at another apartment and saw a man who was standing on his balcony. He had filled the entire space with plants and some flowers and even a couple of large bushes. The man held a watering can and was pouring carefully into each plant and flower-pot. Knightly watched the man for a while, before getting up to leave. He found himself wondering if the man was himself a villager—he looked as if he was about middle-aged—and whether he was missing his garden. Like so many who came to the city, perhaps, he had also felt compelled to come, but at the same time he had tried to bring something that was of the essence of the village along with him.

2.

She had been sitting on the balcony for an hour. Or more than that, she didn't know. It was easy to lose track of the time out here. The street below was quiet, usually, but now it was utterly devoid of any traffic or noise, since it was still the afternoon siesta. They had picked an apartment in Mets, one of the nicest neighborhoods in Athens. That was funny—quite a change from the places she had been forced to live in. But that was largely the point. Get as far away as possible. Also, hide in plain sight. They tried not to be conspicuous. Yet they didn't go out of their way to avoid their neighbors. There was no need. They blended in well enough, she supposed. And the people who lived around here were good people, for the most part. They weren't looking to make trouble for other people, whether out of spite or for the sake of their own twisted amusement or for any profit they might get out of it.

Daniel was inside. She wondered if he was still asleep. Probably not. He never slept more than twenty minutes in the afternoons and he often dismissed the custom altogether. Even on the hottest days. This day wasn't one of those unbearably hot ones, but it was close. She was happy to sit quietly where there was shade. They had filled the whole space of the balcony with plants and even a couple of tall bushes. It made good cover, Daniel had joked. It also eased her spirits, soothed her. And it gave her a shady place to sit before the sun finally went down, giving up its brutal war on the innocent inhabitants of this southern country.

It also gave her something to do. They had decided that she should not be forced to live as a prisoner in the apartment and yet she did not invite trouble by going out a lot. She would walk down to the square, especially in the morning, when there were not so many people out, and the neighborhood was only slowly coming to life. She would visit the bakery. She felt as if the girls who worked there could be her cousins. And she would buy a few groceries in the market. Then she would allow herself the luxury of wandering for a few blocks, checking out the store windows, taking in the peaceful aura of the place as the day came on and life returned to this part of the city.

She spent a lot of time in the apartment but the balcony helped her not to feel as though she were trapped in a cage. It made her feel at home. She liked tending the plants, watering them, pruning them, singing to them. They grew lavishly and it gave her a feeling of satisfaction, even if she knew it had less to do with anything she did than with the simple power of Nature to burst forth wherever it was given the invitation. It was like that where she came from.

Her home was in Moldova. She came from a town in the south of the country. If Moldova is the poorest country in Europe, she thought bitterly, then she came from the poorest part of Moldova. Some people grew grapes and made wine. There was money to be made if you did that. Nobody made wine where she was from. They were farmers and the economic blight the country suffered after the collapse of the Soviet Union hurt farmers, too. Two summers of disastrous weather turned a situation that was bad into one that was worse. For the people in her town and in the other villages, it began to feel you were breathing in poverty itself every time you drew a breath of the very air around you.

Her father owned a coffee house in the town. She and her sister worked there. They served the people who came to her father's café. She couldn't call them customers because they rarely paid. Not out of choice. They simply couldn't pay. Rather than leave her father embarrassed because he owned a coffee shop where no one came to sit and pass the time and drink coffee, some people that they knew would come. They sat and drank coffee and passed the time. Those who were regulars and came most often drank the least coffee. It always amused her how some of them could sit for two hours or more and when they finally left the place you would see that the one cup they had paid for, or that her father had just given them, still had a small amount of coffee left in it.

The woman who took her and her sister away was an evil person—one of the most evil people, she believed, that she would ever meet. But the woman's timing, whether the woman herself knew it or not, turned out to be perfect, Ariani had to admit. At that time, she herself was barely seventeen and Irini was not yet sixteen. They were both in school but they had no plans. Maybe in a year or two they would have figured out what they wanted to do. When the woman arrived, dressed in her beautiful outfit, and full of excitement and big promises, they were taken in—two girls from a poor family who did not know what they were going to do to help their parents or make a way for themselves in the world. It was common for people to leave the country and work elsewhere. Many went to Moscow or to the Ukraine. Many went to the West. She had heard about a whole group of girls from a nearby village who had gone to Poland together. Those who worked abroad sent money back home. The families who got money this way were the envy of everyone else.

The woman who tricked them was even a Moldovan herself. She was from the capital but some women in their village claimed that they knew women in one of the neighboring villages who knew her. She spoke well and she wore beautiful clothes. *How stupid we were! We didn't realize that this new suit of hers was probably the only one she owned.* Now Ariani knew about those kinds of tricks. The fact that she spoke so confidently seemed to show that she knew what she was talking about. She told them that they would be working in a big beautiful house. They were going to Germany, she said. *The Germans are wealthy, you know.* She told them the house was in Hamburg. The house was so big, she said, they needed a staff to manage it. She and her sister would be trained as maids. *Your mother and father tell me you are good workers. That is all I need to know. You will be paid sixty euros a week plus room and board. You can send back to your parents what you want and keep the rest. Think of how much you can save! Then you can come back here or stay in Germany, whatever you like. Go back to school or get a better job right away, if you can. Look at me, she said. With a little money and a little more education you can find a really good job, like the one I have....*

She called the job that she had "employment recruiter." She said nothing at that first meeting about buying and selling human beings, about slavery, cruelty. Nothing of the truth of what she was doing as a "job." She told them to think about it, Ariani remembered. When she left their house, she got into her car, which was brand new, and drove away, leaving them to think about her offer and how soon it would be that they would have everything she had—the fashionable clothes, the car, the smart way of talking, the money. She was smart enough. She didn't leave them to think about it for too long. She came back the next day. She told them that she had gotten a phone call from an office her company had in Germany. The people they would work for were eager to have the new help arrive as soon as it could be arranged. Had they thought about it, she asked? It was a big step, she understood. But these kinds of opportunities don't come up all the time. And Germany isn't that far away. Were they worried about being homesick? They could come home at some point, if they wanted. She was sure that something could be arranged, once they had started working for their new employers. She said that the important thing was not to let this chance slip away.

Ariani recalled the scene in her parents' kitchen, where they sat with the woman who was offering to take them away from the miserable poverty of their country and give them jobs in a rich country, the richest in Europe—jobs that would give them a start in life that they would never have otherwise. Ariani remembered how Irini did not know what to say and how she herself asked if they could please have just one more night to talk with their mother and father and decide by next morning. It was only afterward that Ariani understood how angry the woman had been about this. She hid it well. She smoothed down her skirt as she got up, and told us that we could have one more night. But she needed an answer by tomorrow. Or else she would have to move on to the next people on her list. And then she looked at the two of us. It was a candid look, but mixed with tenderness—only one who is like the most poisonous serpent, whose fangs are dripping with the vilest hatreds that the earth has by some monstrous and cruel mistake put forth, could have put on such an expression that was so full of deceit. *I like you both. I like your parents. I don't want someone else to get the opportunity that rightfully belongs—to all of you.* She told them she would come back the next morning. And she did. And they went away with her.

Ariani looked at the plant at the far end of the balcony. It was an orange tree they had bought. She could barely see through its thick leaves because it was growing so vigorously. It reminded her of home. Not that they grew orange trees back home. Everywhere back home there was green, green. Where she came from was poor but that did not mean it was not beautiful. The fields that the farmers planted would produce a little or a lot, it did not matter. The fields surrounding her town were beautiful always, no matter what. In every season, the fields showed their beauty in a different way.

She and Irini would walk out of town to pick flowers, whatever happened to be in season. Lilies and peonies in spring, in summer lilac and lavender, daisies and sunflowers that would last into autumn. Her mother would decorate their house with the flowers and the coffee shop as well. They would go out to pick sour apples and berries for their mother to make into small tarts—some for the café, and some for themselves.

In the winter, she would go out with Irini or she would walk alone, across the frozen streams that cut through the fields. The brittle meadow grass and broom would crunch under her feet. She remembered her favorite place to go. She had only discovered it a few months before she left her home. It was a farm about two kilometers from the village and the old farmer who owned it had a horse. It was the most lovely chestnut color she had ever seen. Why do you have him? she had asked the old man one time. No good reason, he said, I just like having him around. And he had laughed. It struck her, because she rarely heard anyone laugh like that. She was more used to hearing people laugh at the end of a story that made someone else look ridiculous. Stories about disasters that could have been prevented, if only someone had not been so foolish. Her father did not laugh at those stories, it was true. Then again, she had rarely seen her father laugh at all. Especially in the year before she and Irini went away.

The man with the horse would laugh out loud, and not because he was inspired by another person's anguish or embarrassment. His eyes twinkled when he laughed, as if they sent out a small light to accompany the sound. Daniel laughed in a similar way. She had noticed it and it made her feel that Daniel and her friend were kindred spirits. The old man asked her one time if she wanted to ride the chestnut. He had figured out the horse was her favorite. She had said *no* to the offer. She was afraid. He told her she could learn in one afternoon, she shouldn't be afraid. And yet she held back. Why did she hold back? Would it have made any difference? If she had learned to ride that horse, would that have given her reason or courage to say *no* to the woman with her beautiful clothes and her new car? Would it have given her courage to say *no* to her family?

Yet she had been touched that the old man was so open and generous and she began to think about the day she would try to learn how to ride. In the meanwhile she visited the farm as often as she could get out there. She would help the old man to feed and water the chestnut horse. She would brush him, and she would talk to him, as if the animal could understand what she said. She often thought back to those days and wondered if she would have worked up the courage to ride. She wanted to believe it could have happened, so that she would not feel foolish whenever she tried to picture in her mind later on how it would have felt, riding the chestnut horse in the fields around the old man's farm.

She heard a noise inside. Daniel was stirring. It sounded like he was in the kitchen, getting something to drink. He opened the sliding door and came out on the balcony.

"Do you want something to drink?" he asked.

"No, thanks," Ariani said.

Daniel smiled at her. He had a glass of ice water and he offered it to her.

"Thanks," she laughed. She took a sip and handed it back to him.

He was wearing an old shirt that was rust-colored, made of a kind of suede and slightly faded. It looked great on him. But what made her laugh was something else. When he wore that shirt, it made her think of the beautiful chestnut horse at the old man's farm. Was it that the rich color resembled the coat of her chestnut, or was it rather the imposing physique of this superb and lovely boy, she thought?

"Why are you smiling at me like that, Ariani?" Daniel asked.

She said nothing and he looked at her sideways as he took a drink from the sweating glass.

"We've got to talk," he said.

"I know," she said.

"I want to get you out of here." He was looking straight at her. She looked away.

"We've already talked about this," he said. "It's too dangerous. There's nothing for you to do here—"

"There is," she interrupted him, "I can get back inside. I could go back to that bastard on my hands and knees. I could cry and tell him I made a stupid mistake, make him think he's won."

"He won't fall for that," Daniel said. "That's the problem. The man is a true maggot. He has no feelings, good or bad. You can't play on his weaknesses. We've been trying to get him to take bait, but it's not easy. He doesn't react whether you put pressure on him or let him feel like he's got the advantage. He keeps his cool either way."

"So what are you saying, Daniel? How are we going to find Irini, let alone get her out, unless someone can get inside and get close to Skorpios or to someone who knows what's going on?"

"We have people on the inside. But they don't know where your sister is."

"So how long are you going to wait? What if he decides to do something to her?"

"Ariani, please. You can't go back. I need you to go home. You know it. There are those organizations back home—they're doing good work. You could help them. You aren't afraid, you would speak out. You could help them to keep other girls from getting caught up in it."

"Would I be safer there, Daniel? You know how they intimidate people, if they can't just buy you off with money. So how would it be any better for me to go home, and work with those women who are fighting the trafficking, and have the pimps threatening me and my parents?"

"You'd be a hell of a lot safer there! Those organizations have visibility. Besides, I am absolutely not telling you to stick your neck out. No matter what, I can't let you go back into any of Skorpios's places. He won't hesitate. He'll do something to you. I can't let that happen, Ariani."

And then he looked at her, in that way. *Oh, fuck.* She felt herself softening. *Why does he care?* She wanted to do what he said. She wanted him. But when she thought of her sister, alone, somewhere in one of the buildings that they controlled, in god knows what kind of condition, she could hardly fight back a wave of rage—a horrible, nauseating rage.

"I'm sorry, Daniel. I can't do it. I can't leave my sister here."

She could see how unhappy he was. He was silent, staring down at his feet.

"What if you don't have time," she said. "What if you can't get Irini out before you have to leave?"

"We could give what we have to the cops. We've got some useful information. And some people on the inside. I don't think they have that—"

"Go to the police?" She looked at him in disbelief. "You must be joking! Do you know how many of them were coming to our rooms? They got it for free, Daniel. *For free!* You know how it works. There is no way I will ever trust the police!"

"Come on, Ariani. There are plenty of good cops. Like with anything, there are the good, the bad, and the indifferent. We have contacts in the police. We know who we need to talk to."

"No," she said.

He said nothing, just took a deep breath.

"Daniel," she said, looking at him intently, "if I leave here now, I am afraid I'll lose my sister forever. And I'm afraid I'll lose you." She clutched his arm. "When would I ever see you again? Do you know when you will have to leave? In a week? When—?"

He turned to her. "In about a week, I've been told, we're back on the bow."

"Then you're gone? Just like that?"

"Probably not right away. I don't think we'll be deployed immediately. The last time was nasty, and they know it. We have some time. Not a lot of time, but some."

She had known this. He had told her. She looked at him. He did not have to be doing anything for her. But he was—even risking his life. And the lives of his friends. Trying to penetrate the evil that he had helped her to escape from and that still held her sister in a prison that was not deep underground or high up in some cloud-wrapped mountain but for all that her prison was as inaccessible as if it were two or three continents away and guarded by fierce dragons.

How different he was. The men she had known were animals. They used her and her sister and the other young women she had known to satisfy their most basic and selfish desires. Or try to satisfy them. The sad truth was that they looked unhappy whenever they left, no matter what they pretended, so that she wondered if any of them really left satisfied. Maybe it was enough for them to get rid of the sheer physical itch, even if it was only for a while. That was enough to justify the degradation these men knew the girls they visited were subjected to and to justify the sense of shame that many of them felt even as they tried to smile as they left the apartments and the brothels. Of course, there were those men who seemed to enjoy the sheer pleasure of controlling and having power over another human being. The Arab men especially were like this, she thought. She remembered once she had been taken to the yacht of a Saudi prince or aristocrat or who knows what he was. After dining with his guests above on the deck, he descended to the quarters where his bodyguards had brought her and another girl and began to commit acts of the most unspeakable kind on the other girl. By the time he got to herself, he was tired out. He tried to rouse his enthusiasm again, but to her relief she discovered that he no longer seemed to be getting the same thrill as before. He finally waved dismissively at the bodyguards, turned on his heels, and left the cabin. They were taken home.

The other girl was not well. She had to stay in bed for a week. Then she disappeared. When she turned up a month or so later, they learned that she had been sent to Saudi Arabia for a special engagement with the same man. She never recovered. Glassy-eyed, listless, she would barely speak with anyone. And, crowning glory of all, at the tender age of twenty-one, she was incontinent. She would shit and piss herself just walking from one room to another. Finally she disappeared again. The rumor went around that she had committed suicide. An unlocked door to the balcony of the apartment where she was kept and a leap from the fourth floor.

Ariani had told that story to a friend, Sharon. "Arabs are the worst. And the Saudis are the worst of them all. Despicable and vile. They're brutal pigs."

Sharon looked at her as if offended. "What are you saying? That's just racist bullshit!" And then Ariani had lost it with Sharon and suddenly found herself screaming at her friend.

"What the hell would you know? Have you ever had anyone try to shove it up you after you've been tied down? After they've made sure you're doped up? Or smacked you around? After they've asked you if you're pregnant, hoping you'll say yes, because that is one of their biggest turn-ons? Don't make me sick! Why would you ever feel the need to defend that kind of swine?!"

She had ended by sputtering and nearly pummelling Sharon with her fists. Sharon held her off and just looked at her, shocked, her face growing red. She looked straight at Ariani.

"I'm sorry," Sharon said. "I don't mean to argue with you, it's stupid. I'm sorry!" Then she took a deep breath and continued. "I know I don't know what it's been like—what you have had to go through. But you know, Ariani, I wish I could say I've been left out of the wars completely.

But it's not true. My best friend was raped when I was still living in Belfast. It changed her. She won't ever be the same. Not emotionally or physically. For god's sake, it wasn't anybody from another goddamned country that did it to her, either. At least, as far as she can remember, they beat her up so bloody well! I'm not saying it's the same as what you've been through. But the damage that's being done to women—it's all around us, Ariani. What can I say? I'm sorry I offended you. I really didn't mean to do that. I just said what I said without thinking. I'm sorry."

And Ariani had said she was sorry, too. They never fought again after that. But Ariani never changed her opinions, either. The funny thing was that it was Sharon who had introduced her to Daniel. She and Daniel were friends from Daniel's student days, when he had come to Greece for the first time. Ariani was still working for Skorpios when Sharon introduced them. It wasn't long before she and Daniel were spending time together, however, and Daniel helped her to get out of the reach of the network.

She had fallen in love with Daniel. And she thought that Daniel loved her, too—but she didn't believe he was *in love*. He wouldn't even touch her. You're just nineteen years old, for christ's sake, he would say, and I'm almost ten years older. She would tell him that was nothing. She had uncles who were twenty-five years older than their wives. He would smirk and then say, "I can't, Ariani. I would feel guilty. I have no right to. It would be taking advantage of you. Why did I help you get free? Just to have a chance to get sex from you? How would I be any different from those assholes who were abusing you and the other girls?"

She would argue with him. "You're not forcing me and you're not taking advantage of me. It's my choice. I'm not a prisoner anymore. I can make my own decisions now. You think I'm just grateful to you because you helped me to get free? That's not it, that's not why I want you, Daniel. How long would you have to wait, to make it feel *honorable*, like you're not taking advantage of me? Six months, a year?"

He looked at her when she said this. He was telling her with his eyes, *You're crazy!* That's the first time she came really close to him. She was standing between his feet. She put her hands on his chest. He was looking at her. Then she began to undo the buttons of her shirt. She tugged and let it slide off her shoulders and down her arms. Then she looked up, into his face. "Don't make me say it, Daniel, don't make me say that word," she thought to herself. *Please.* He didn't make her say it. He kissed her instead. He put his arms around her and, slowly, as she held on to him, their clothes began to scatter on the floor and their limbs tangled in a confusion of panting, teasing laughter. It had astounded her. For the first time, she learned what it felt like to make love with someone who cared, who actually *cared* about you. Daniel was the most physically powerful, most *fearsome* man she had ever been with. And yet he was the most withholding, the most tender with her, patient, waiting for her—the most perfect.

She looked at the orange tree at the end of the balcony. She looked at Daniel.

"Daniel, forgive me. I can't leave without my sister."

"I know, Ariani. Goddammit. I understand."

She looked at him. When they talked about such things—the network, Skorpios— she could never tell exactly what he was thinking.

She leaned over, trying to look him in the eye. "Daniel?"

"Yes?"

She stood up and took one of his hands in both of hers, lifting him slowly from his chair.

"You still look tired to me, Daniel. You look like you didn't sleep at all. Let's go in and finish the nap!" She gave him a sly look and dragged him back into the apartment.

They went into the bedroom and made love as if it was the end of the world and the trumpets had just blown to announce the very last few hours of pleasure left on earth. It always amazed her how Daniel's skin could be cool to the touch and yet she could feel inside him a core of fire that seemed to be hotter than sin itself. A dew would form on his forehead and just when she was about to scream a drop or two of the beads of his sweat would fall on her and she felt that she was melting away as she came and he would come at once and their arms and legs would tighten around one another and then relax and gradually come apart as they lay close together.

They lay that way for a long while, breathing slowly. Then Daniel looked at her and said, "What am I going to do with you, Ariani?"

She looked at him through eyes that were half-closing. He realized she hadn't slept at all that afternoon or the night before. What am I going to do with you, he whispered in her hair. Ariani was already asleep, her head on his chest, the side of her body rising, falling, slowly, almost imperceptibly. Daniel held her close to him, smelling the sweetness of her hair, her skin, the sweetness of her exhaustion. He lay there on his back, and as he stared at the ceiling, he spoke to himself again.

"…and what in the name of god's green earth am I going to do about you, Will?"

3.

KNIGHTLY WALKED INTO HIS HOTEL AND THE FIRST THING he saw was Kazantzakis. The chief inspector was sitting in a corner of the hotel's main lobby, ensconced in one of the leather-upholstered armchairs that surrounded a large glass coffee table rimmed with marble. Kazantzakis sat with one leg crossed over the other and he was staring at the door of the hotel. Directly at Knightly, that is, as he walked in. The impact was sudden and heart-stopping. Knightly felt as if a bull's eye had been fixed squarely on his chest and the inspector had just pulled the bow and let fly, *thwang!*

Knightly stopped in his tracks and looked at the policeman.

"Inspector! Good afternoon—"

"Good afternoon, Professor Knightly."

"This is a surprise—what brings you here, if I may ask? Is there something wrong?"

"No, nothing's wrong. Please don't worry, your room has not been broken into again."

"Well, that's a relief," Knightly said, as he sat down in a chair next to Kazantzakis's.

Knightly wanted to sit down in order to give himself some time to think. He also wanted to break free, even for a moment, from the steady gaze of the chief inspector, in which Knightly felt trapped, despite the civility of the conversation.

"So what brings you here, Inspector?" Knightly asked.

"You will recall that I work here in Athens, Mr. Knightly."

Knightly let out a laugh. Kazantzakis was smiling at him, but not in a way that gave Knightly any comfort.

"I have a new piece of information," Kazantzakis said, " and I wanted to share it with you. I was hoping that you could comment on it, as a matter of fact."

"What is it?" Knightly asked.

"The police picked up one of the men who broke into your room in Tripoli. He was still in the city. There were two others, if you recall, but they are long gone, apparently."

Knightly swallowed, an involuntary reaction. He hoped it was discreet.

"In any event, my colleagues interrogated this man. He is a Romanian. He was indeed following you, Professor."

Kazantzakis paused, never taking his eyes off Knightly for a moment, and yet Knightly had the feeling that the inspector was watching him even more intently when he resumed.

"This Romanian claims that he had been hired to follow someone else, not you. His original assignment was to shadow another American, and in the course of tracking this first target, so to speak, he told us that he came across you. The Romanian claims that you got in the way, that is to say, he claims that he saw you following the other American and that you were trying to make contact with this person."

Knightly now felt his stomach constricting painfully, as if a small hard ball of lead had suddenly formed in his gut and was sitting there with nowhere to go.

"Of course, the Romanian had no idea about who you were. But he gave an accurate description of you, Professor," he paused again, looking at Knightly, "a very accurate description. This man and his colleagues broke into your room to get a better idea of who you were. They found nothing very helpful. On the contrary, what they found—or didn't find—in your room left them somewhat perplexed, I believe. You were not exactly what they were expecting!"

Kazantzakis laughed at this and Knightly gave a wan smile, nodding at the inspector.

"What's going on, Inspector?" Knightly asked, trying to turn the conversation in a different direction. "I just don't get it. Who is this Romanian? Did he say what he's up to? I mean, is he working for someone?"

"Mr. Knightly, I am not concerned with the Romanian at this point. I can't really comment on the substance, but I will tell you that in all truth he knows very little. What does concern me, however, especially where you are concerned, is this other American."

Kazantzakis leaned forward and looked closely at Knightly as he spoke.

"Would you tell me once more what you have been doing in Greece since you arrived, Professor, and where you have been? I'm especially interested in the people you've been in contact with."

The inspector took out a small notebook and a pen and waited for Knightly to speak.

"I haven't really been anywhere, Inspector. I landed in Athens, got a car, drove to Tripoli, and went to visit my friend in Kremni. Oh, yes— before I drove to Kremni I made a quick excursion to Andritsena, I mean, to Vasses."

Kazantzakis looked at him with surprise. "You mean, to see the temple?"

"Yes," Knightly said.

"Why did you do that, Mr. Knightly?"

"I am a classicist, Inspector. I love that site. But, really, I just went there to clear my head. It's about as peaceful as any place I know."

This seemed to make an impression on Kazantzakis. The look of pleasure that had crossed his face, however, soon yielded to a harder look.

"Have you met anyone beside your friend, since you've been in Greece?"

"No, Inspector. Only Elli. And her sister—she has a sister, Chrysanthi, and I saw her briefly. That's it, Inspector. Oh, yes, and Elli's son, Giannakis. I met him, too. She has a son."

Kazantzakis stared at him. No other outward reaction, but the last bit of information had registered with Kazantzakis, Knightly could see.

"You did not meet with anyone in Tripoli?" Kazantzakis asked.

"No. I didn't meet with anyone. Except you, in my hotel room!"

Kazantzakis grinned at this, to Knightly's surprise.

"This Romanian claims you were following an American in Tripoli. He told us that he saw you chase him—that's how he put it—all the way from Plateia Agiou Vassiliou to Plateia Kolokotroni!"

Kazantzakis paused.

"Please, Professor Knightly, think carefully about what you are going to say. What were you doing in Tripoli on the morning you arrived? What were you doing when the Romanian saw you?"

Knightly looked straight at Kazantzakis.

"I don't know what to say, Inspector! I wasn't doing anything. I was having a coffee at a café. I was enjoying just sitting and looking at Agios Vassilios, I was enjoying being in Greece again. I was trying to recover from a mild case of jet-lag. And I was thinking about meeting my friend, whom I hadn't seen in over twenty years! That's it, Inspector. I wasn't *doing* much of anything!"

"You were not trying to meet with anyone on that first morning? Another American? Anyone?"

"No, Inspector. I hadn't set up a meeting with anyone nor did I meet with anyone. I'm here alone, and I haven't made any plans to meet with anybody, not colleagues, no one, except for Eleftheria. That's it, end of story!"

"By the way, Professor Knightly, where did you meet this woman, originally?"

"In Tripoli, as a matter of fact. She was working there, many years ago, as a waitress. I met her there, at the restaurant where she was working."

"Very good. On this current trip, you say that you have only met with this one person, Eleftheria Parthenis. This was the reason for your trip, in large part, to see her again. You were only in Kremni for two or three days, Professor. Could you tell me, then, why have you returned to Athens now?"

Knightly cursed to himself. *This man is positively a hound!* Or I'm just stupid for not seeing that one coming. Knightly cleared his throat and leaned forward himself, giving Kazantzakis what he hoped would appear as a meaningful look.

"Inspector, now this is getting very personal. I mean, it's embarrassing, really. I would prefer not to talk about it with you. As I say, it's strictly personal and it would mean nothing to you, I promise. But to talk about it is embarrassing, as I say, and even a little painful. I am in Athens, but only briefly. I am going back to Kremni soon and I have no plans to go anywhere but there."

Kazantzakis was watching him closely. Then he sat back in his chair, closing his notebook. He let out a deep breath, then spoke.

"In fact, I have no interest in prying into your personal life, Mr. Knightly. I will simply repeat what I said to you before. Please consider it carefully. If you have anything to tell me that you believe is significant, I want to hear it. The Romanian may have been spouting nonsense. But there is something else that unfortunately I am not at liberty to share with you—it has to do with the general investigation I am conducting—that makes me interested in this other American. I am not sure about you but I don't believe very much in coincidences, Professor. Two Americans, on the same morning, in Tripoli. Granted, the eyewitness is not an individual of sterling character. On the other hand, there was nothing for him to gain by telling us a tall tale, at least not a tall tale of this particular shape."

Knightly looked as if he was going to object but Kazantzakis merely waved at him.

"All I want to say to you is that I do believe you will contact me if you come across anything or have any information that would be useful or of interest to the police."

"I promise you, Inspector. If I knew anything of any importance about any matter that the police were concerned with, I would call you immediately."

"Well, Professor, thank you for your time. You still have my card?"

"I do, Inspector."

"Good evening, then."

"Good evening, Inspector."

Knightly watched as the Inspector walked through the lobby and left the hotel. He took a deep breath, stared at his reflection in the glass-top of the coffee table, and slowly exhaled. *How many ways did I blow it?* He knows about Daniel! But then Knightly realized that Kazantzakis knew very little about Daniel. At least as far as Knightly could see. Safe for now, he thought. But he also realized that he himself knew very little about Daniel, when it came right down to it. Very little about why Daniel might be in Greece and what he might be doing. The conversation with Kazantzakis left Knightly feeling strangely drained and yet slightly exhilarated. Like a field mouse that's felt the talons of the hawk and yet escaped. For a while, anyway. Knightly got up and took the stairs, but slowly, to get to his room.

Kazantzakis walked slowly to his car. He was thinking about Knightly. And the other American. Knightly claimed to know nothing about it. Kazantzakis would have been likely to dismiss the story the Romanian had told. But it connected to another piece of information that had come his way.

A colleague, an old friend of his, had come to his office recently. The friend worked in an elite unit—the anti-terrorism unit—and he had a question. He had begun by quietly closing the door, turning to Kazantzakis, and telling him that the conversation they were having was in fact not taking place. "Remember that," he said. "Remember not to remember we're talking," Kazantzakis answered. "Right," said the other. He described to Kazantzakis the recent brutal killing of a small group of anarchists. Even Kazantzakis, with his years on the job, was surprised by some of the grisly details. "Does it match the signature of any of your gang hits?" his friend had asked. Kazantzakis had said no. "In the cases I come across, it's usually neat and clean. A professional hit is terrifying in its own way." "To be sure," the friend said. "It doesn't fit anything we've seen either." "You don't think it might have been a splinter of *Chrysi Avgi*, Golden Dawn, our neo-Nazi friends, exorcising some of their demons on those poor leftist bastards?" Kazantzakis had asked. "No," his friend had answered. "They are brutes but they don't go to such lengths, and besides they aren't so creative." Then he paused. "As a matter of fact, there was a similar attack carried out on some members of *Chrysi Avgi*. There were seven of them. It seems the attacker followed them home from one of their rallies. It was the same kind of bizarre violence. In that case, five were killed and two were left unconscious. One of them woke up with a note stuffed in his mouth: "Clean up this mess." Kazantzakis thought a moment. "One attacker?" "That is what the survivors say, in each case. And this lone attacker speaks English. With an American accent, according to the young girl who witnessed the assault on the anarchists." The two men had just looked at one another. "The violence of the two attacks is off the charts. I wondered if you'd seen anything like it. We seem to be dealing with someone who is trained to deal out a spectacular amount of punishment," the other man said. "Special forces' training? and an American?" Kazantzakis objected, "But why observe all the protocols—the stealth, the hood, and so on, and then give it all away by opening your mouth and talking to the victims? It doesn't make sense. It seems careless." "Was it careless," his friend asked, "or just reckless?"

The other American. What would be the statistical probability that the Romanian was telling the truth and had in fact witnessed this Professor Wilson Knightly trying to make contact with an American who just happened to be some element of an American special forces unit out and about doing god knows what in the sovereign nation of Greece? It all seemed too fantastic. And Knightly had insisted he had not been looking for nor had met with anyone other than a Greek woman, this "friend" of his from long ago, Eleftheria Parthenis. He was inclined to believe Knightly. But he could not shake his suspicion that what was at play was perhaps not sheer coincidence but rather the slow agglomeration of facts that marked the beginning of any sub-plot of a story. Two or three facts. But a beginning. If this gossip about Knightly and the "other American" were not nonsense or coincidence and Knightly were involved in some way, Kazantzakis was also tending to think Knightly might know something, but did not know what he knew. After all, what could a professor of classical philology possibly know about the activities of a clandestine warrior, not to mention of incidents of the sort of shocking violence he had discussed with his old colleague?

Kazantzakis reached his car. He got in and thought to himself, *Why am I being so easy on this Knightly?* Because Knightly is an honorable man. It sounded ludicrous, when he said it to himself. Yet he believed it. He was a good enough judge of character. And he had deduced that Knightly lived by a code whose central value was to treat others well. Knightly was discreet about this Eleftheria woman, for example, and he seemed considerate of her as well. So what if he felt he were protecting someone? Kazantzakis felt the professor would admit that he had a duty to speak the truth. But it would be difficult for Knightly to balance this duty and the duty to a friend, not to expose that person to any trouble or danger. "I have to trust," he thought, "that for now Mr. Knightly will know the proper balance between those two competing claims. For now—"

Good god, you've gone soft! Kazantzakis laughed to himself as he got into his car, started it up, and pulled out into the street. Traffic was light, mercifully. He was half way home before he realized he was thinking of Knightly again. He realized that he was genuinely fond of the man. On the basis of only a couple of meetings and in spite of the improbable story that was unfolding around and uncomfortably close to this professor from America. It dawned on Kazantzakis that what appealed to him about Knightly was, to some degree, that he was a professor. A teacher and scholar. A philologist. Kazantzakis felt a touch of envy toward Knightly—not the bitter kind, the jealousy that makes enemies, but the sweet envy that inspires admiration. Kazantzakis admired Knightly for the path he had taken. Knightly had decided at some point in his life, apparently, to devote himself to the study of languages and literature. That he chose the ancient languages, and in particular the history and culture of Greece itself, intrigued Kazantzakis even more. What compelled his choice, what passions moved him to choose such a path, one that would be rich in the rewards of the spirit but grudging of money and fame? Not that a policeman can expect very much in that way, either, Kazantzakis said to himself. But it wasn't always the case, he thought, that he was going to be a policeman.

Kazantzakis envied and admired Knightly because Knightly had taken a path in life that was for Kazantzakis a road not taken. Kazantzakis began to think back. To the time he was at university. He remembered the day he left Crete. It had been a very hot summer. The long boat trip to Piraeus and then getting the train from the Larissa Station that would take him north to Thessaloniki. He had one suitcase and enough money to buy the sheets that would cover his bed. It had nearly killed his mother that she was not coming with him and helping him settle in. But he had refused any help. He was going away and he would have to be capable of taking care of himself. He was striking a blow for his own freedom. He would have lost the argument, of course, if the city of Thessaloniki had not been so far from his island. He felt just how far away it was on that first night, when he finally arrived, exhausted, and lay on his bed, staring at the ceiling and contemplating for the first time just what freedom felt like.

It was September, 1974. It was just after the Colonels had been deposed. Just as those were heady days in Athens, there was great excitement in Thessaloniki, too, and especially at the university. Politics was very much in the air. Like every young person, Kazantzakis was looking for something to believe in. Or was it for something to disbelieve? Politics had in fact invaded the campus and the various parties had begun to stake their claims and cultivate their followings among the students. Kazantzakis tried and investigated them all. His early excitement soon gave way to repeated bouts of disenchantment. He saw too much that was self-serving and self-aggrandizing, at the highest levels of the parties and also at the local and parochial levels. In all of that, he had found more than enough to disbelieve.

Kazantzakis decided to throw himself into his philological studies. He loved the classics but he felt drawn to the poetry and drama and prose of other periods of Greek literature as well. Here was a calling, he thought, that would enable a dispassionate seeking after truth. He would become a scholar and a writer who would study the people and events of earlier times and of his own and he would bear witness to whatever he saw in those people and those events. When he was about to finish his degree, one of his teachers told him that he should continue his studies and pursue a doctorate. He had come up with a provisional title for his doctoral thesis, "Concepts of Fate in the Poetry of Seferis and Elytis."

And then the disaster. It was a rainy afternoon in the city. He had come back to his room after spending most of the day at the library. He was almost asleep, drifting somewhere between consciousness and an uncomfortable feeling of oblivion, when he was jolted awake by a knocking at the door. Someone was telling him he had a phone call. He walked down the hallway and saw the small table that was set up in the hall for the phone and the receiver resting on the table. He picked it up. It was his uncle speaking to him. From Crete. His mother was beside herself, she could not come to the phone. *I'm sorry, Aris. Your father*—his uncle was clearly struggling with the words. *Aris*—the old man was screaming in order to force out the words.

Your father has died.

The next morning, Kazantzakis set off for Crete. He returned home for his father's funeral and he never went back to Thessaloniki. His mother was bereft, left alone and without support. To make matters worse, Kazantzakis had two sisters, one older and one who was younger. Neither were married yet. There was too much responsibility for him at home, now that his father was gone. He could not return to his studies. At the funeral, a friend of his father's came up to him and put a hand on his shoulder. You can become a cop, Aris. Just like your father. His father had been a policeman as was this friend of his. The older man had looked at Kazantzakis with a smile that did not grow too wide, under the circumstances, but nevertheless was full of a genuine affection. *Like father, like son.* His father's friend looked at him. And that is what Kazantzakis did. He went to the academy and he became a policeman.

Old Time, aging mercurial thief, sometimes his treasures will yield;
but Death, ever young, greedy one, never gives back what he steals.

Should he go home? Kazantzakis thought about it while he parked the car and decided against it. It was almost seven o'clock. But why go back to an empty house?

He decided to go for a walk around the neighborhood. He walked slowly, passing by the small shops, the newsstands, the *kafeneia* and eating places, that lined the streets, one after the other, of this neighborhood he loved. It had taken them so long to be able to afford to move here. Well after the children were born. Why?

If she were still here, he would go home. He would have gone home and she would have greeted him, as usual, and he would have entered a house full of life, flowers in the hallway, flowers on the table, the kitchen redolent with an afternoon's cooking, the food almost ready. Her face, lit by a slender smile. Why, why, why? He had asked himself *why* and he still asked himself every day why she had to be the one. Why it had to be her.

He met her while he was still in the police academy and they were married in scarcely more than a year. Their first child was born a year after that. A son, Petros, and then a year and a half later, a daughter, Antigone. Once he had met her and she agreed to marry him and be his wife, she gave him so much and did not stop until his life was full of happiness. At every time of year, the house was decked out and ringing with laughter or spiced with quarrels over the business of the day or graced with the latest accomplishments of the children as they grew and as they traversed the rites of passage that arrived, one upon another, through the years.

The lump in her breast had come as a total shock. One day had the power to change everything. It seemed out of all proportion. Never mind about fairness. The very idea that one day it could be fair sailing and clear skies, and then one more day, just one more day, the earth and sea and sky could change places, everything upside down, wrong way around. Stopped. Ended. Or about to end.

The disease was cruel with her. It wasn't only the shock it delivered at the beginning that was awful. It was the terrible speed of the disease and the direct path it took to keep ahead of even the most grim prognostications of the doctors. She was too young, too healthy and vital, he would say to them. They would say nothing in return, after a while. Only the disease would roar, with a savage pride in its power. It waited for nothing, it was impatient to run its race. It devoured her body in a matter of ten months. All of her substance, all of her vitality. All of her, except for her spirit, which she kept inside her and whole, until she died, but at that moment which Kazantzakis would never forget but which he could not bring himself ever to remember perfectly, even that was lost to him, her precious spirit, which she had kept whole and protected against the unstoppable, vicious disease but which in keeping it whole she took with her when she fell asleep for that very last time, aided and comforted and carried away under a lethargic cloud induced by heavy doses of morphine.

Aphrodite. *It had taken us years to make that home. To find one we could afford.* They had looked for years, finally settling on a moderately-sized apartment in Pangrati, which was, along with Mets, on its southern edge, one of the truest neighborhoods in Athens, full of life but with a casual and unforced charm, living as if it were a village in the heart of that enormous city. Their home had been filled by her presence, while she was alive, and by the children's, before they left. Now it was full of a pervasive and unnerving quiet that he had to expend great amounts of energy to dispel and drive away. Put on the stereo, put on the tv. Why, for whom, who will listen? Long walks in the neighborhood were better than going home to confront once again the great loneliness that waited for him, steadfastly, every day and every evening.

Petros, their son, was in the navy. Kazantzakis was incredibly proud of his son. He was an officer. Kazantzakis looked forward to the times when Petros was in Athens and was able to visit or they were able to rendezvous somewhere for a meal. It was like manna to him, every time he saw Petros, but the boy—he was no longer a boy. *And he had given up childish ways.* He had his own path to follow.

It had been different with Antigone. She had been studying in the United States when Aphrodite became ill. She was working on a Ph.D. in classical philology—she was almost finished with her dissertation, in fact. Classical philology! The daughter had taken up a path that returned to the dreams of her father. But she came home as soon as her mother was diagnosed with cancer. Antigone had proven to be not only the good daughter, faithful and selfless, but a gifted caregiver as well. How often Kazantzakis had thanked the stars for her presence. As Aphrodite became weaker—toward the end, the disease left her utterly without appetite, and she became emaciated and extremely frail—while it seemed to cause Aphrodite deep pain that Kazantzakis should see her when she was at her worst, in some way that was difficult for either of them to speak about, Aphrodite held nothing back from her daughter. She opened up to Antigone and allowed her daughter to share in her weakness as the disease destroyed the last fibers of her body.

When Aphrodite died, Antigone told her father she had made a decision: she would stay in Athens and take care of him. She was so adamant, and so loyal, it required all of his powers of dissimulation, even as it broke his heart, to tell her that what she had decided to do was unthinkable. He was not going to let his own daughter forsake everything she had done, that had led her to the very thing that he himself—her own father—had once dreamed of accomplishing. He told her flatly that he would not let her throw her career and all of her wonderful promise away. Besides, what was there to take care of, as far as he was concerned? He would eat, work, sleep. He would carry on. He sent her away. She returned to the States, to her school in California. She finished her degree and was hired immediately as an assistant professor of classics. Kazantzakis was so proud, when he read on his computer screen the e-mail she had sent him about winning the job, he leapt from his chair and, raising both of his hands toward the heavens, he told Aphrodite the news! Sinking back in his chair, he thought of his good fortune. And he thought of how much he missed his wife and his daughter.

He had reached Odos Imittou. He walked a couple of blocks and saw he wasn't too far away from one of his favorite theaters. It was summer—the season of *therino* cinema—and the films were playing outdoors, on the roof-tops. He walked up to the theater. There were two films playing, one at 8:30 and the other at 11:00. The earlier show was *An Affair to Remember.* Cary Grant and Deborah Kerr. He looked at the posters displayed in the window. He had seen the film and remembered liking it very much—a classic, after all. As he looked at the poster, the scene that came to his mind was the moment when Cary Grant waits for Deborah Kerr at the top of the Empire State Building, where they had agreed to rendezvous, a promise she does not keep, because she has suffered a terrible accident on the way to the meeting, but Cary Grant of course has no idea what has happened to her and can only think that she has abandoned him. Much as he liked the film, Kazantzakis thought he would skip it this time around. The other film was *Cape Fear.* Interesting program, Kazantzakis thought. A good balance, the bittersweet romantic escape, on the one hand, and, on the other, an intense brush with the darker side, the sinister. Since he had ample opportunity to partake of the sinister in his own line of work, he decided to forgo the other offering of the *therino* as well. Maybe he would check again next week to see what was playing.

He decided to eat something in one of his usual *psistarias.* What would it be tonight—grilled chicken, or pork? Perhaps *kleftiko*—pork thrown on the spit and roasted as if for the bandits. Kazantzakis smiled. That almost sounds like a walk on the wild side of life. Let's have the police inspector eat like a bandit! He ordered and they brought him his robber's portion. No need to return home, he thought. When he finished, he got up and paid. Then he found his car and drove back to headquarters to work the rest of the evening. Better to go back home when he was good and tired. Then he could just wash his face and teeth, get undressed, and go straight to bed. No sitting around with too much time on his hands. Time to sit and listen to the ample quiet of the apartment that he shared with himself and with himself alone. Perhaps that was the other thing that he envied about Knightly. It seemed that Knightly, too, was alone. But now Knightly stood on the verge of some new beginning, as far as Kazantzakis could make out. There was a relationship that held the possibility of starting anew. Kazantzakis simply could not imagine that for himself. He was older than Knightly by perhaps five years or so. But it wasn't only that. He did not think he would ever want another relationship to replace the one he had had with his wife. The deep silence of the apartment where Aphrodite had once lived with him and that he now inhabited in splendid isolation felt to him like a permanent state. Kazantzakis entered the police building and took the elevator to the floor where his office was. He sat at his desk and opened the file that had been waiting for him there.

That was how it was and how it would be for the rest of his days. He could accept it far more easily than he could ever accept the unspeakable fact that his beloved Aphrodite had been taken from him and from his children in the first place. He would eat, he would work, he would sleep. What more, after all, did he need?

…but Death, ever young, greedy one, never gives back what he steals.

4.

"THIS IS KILLING ME," HE CURSED. *THAT SON OF a whore! What is he thinking about?*

Panos threw his cigarette to the sidewalk and ground it out with his foot like he was killing a bug. He had hardly slept all night. He was where he was supposed to be. He looked at his watch. He had been told to wait for a call he'd be getting at seven a.m.

Five minutes to go.

He had been up all night. He had been told to watch some girls, along with another guy, a regular, who was his same age. Panos had worked with him once or twice before. They played cards in a room on the first floor of an old apartment building that Skorpios had an interest in—he had helped the owner buy it, was the story he heard—while the girls worked in rooms on the two floors above. Panos had left the place after four in the morning and had barely gotten to bed when his phone rang and he was told to go back out. *We got another job for you, Panos. Get your ass back out on the street and wait for the call.*

That was fine—no, it wasn't fine, really, but he didn't care, he could take it. The problem was it had been three nights like this in a row. Just what did the old bastard think? Was Skorpios jerking him around? Or was this some kind of a test, maybe? Was it a test to see how loyal he was or how much he could take or some bullshit like that? Fuck—he could take it. Just better be something in it for me, that's all, Panos thought to himself.

He yawned. His phone rang. "Yeah, I know where that is. Right, just off Syngrou. Yeah, I'm almost there now. I'll see you in two minutes."

Panos snapped the phone shut and headed down the avenue. It was Takis. He was pretty high up. He wanted him to go to a club that was just off Syngrou, it was called *Kerasia*, "Cherries." Panos knew the club. Shit. Takis. He's pretty high up, he knows Skorpios pretty well, he thought. Maybe there is something for me in this after all.

As he got close to the club, Panos couldn't help chuckling to himself. There were some swanky hotels on Syngrou just before you turned off on the street where the club was. It wasn't that the *Kerasia* was a dump or anything. But it wasn't the greatest kind of a place. That is, it was pretty obvious once you were in that you could get hooked up pretty easy. Get whatever you wanted, basically. Right around the corner from someplace decent. That was kinda funny.

Kerasia. What a stupid fucking name. The club was called "Cherries" because the owner was from the Peloponnese—from Tripoli—and that place is famous for cherries. How the fuck did Skorpios get hooked up with a *malaka* like that? Goes to show you don't have to be all that smart. Just hang around long enough. That's just what Skorpios did himself, probably, right? Hang around and save your money until you can buy things for people. Then you squeeze their fucking nuts so they do whatever you want. Doesn't take a genius to pull that off. Maybe some day the kind of set-up Skorpios had, he could have something like that, too, Panos thought. He wasn't young, but he wasn't too old, either. Doesn't take a genius.

Kerasia. That was one of the clubs Skorpios liked to hang out in. There were others. He had heard that. That wasn't genius, that was just smart. Don't stick to one place. Keep on the move. *Don't be predictable.* That's what Skorpios himself said once. Panos had heard it. That was the one time he had actually seen Skorpios in person. He was there, not close to him, but close enough to hear the old man saying those very words. *Don't be predictable. The minute you get predictable, that's when you are gonna get nailed.* That's what the old man said. Not genius, but smart.

Besides, the more clubs, the better. Skorpios probably liked being the big-shot. He could show up in one of these clubs and watch people fall all over themselves trying to impress him. He was the *nonós*—the god-father—just like any kid gets when he's christened—only Skorpios was a "*nonós* of the night." And he takes care of their problems, so people fall over themselves to make him feel special whenever he shows up. You don't look around for a table when you're a guy like Skorpios. You got a table—fuck, you got your own booth! Right this way. Here's your place, Mr. Skorpios. That wouldn't be bad, Panos thought, being a big-shot like that. Hang in there long enough, you might get it. You probably deserve it every bit as much as that skinny old man. Fucking ugly bastard, too. Skorpios! Like a fucking lizard.

Kerasia! What a stupid fucking name for a club.

And there it was. Two and a half blocks down the street, the second or third door on the block. The entry was street-level. Above the door, there was a white plastic sign that said, ***KERASIA***, with a pair of cherries next to the name, all of which at night would be lit up brightly in neon, red for the letters and red for the cherries.

Panos went inside. The club was dark, dark enough that he had to wait a minute inside the door-way for his eyes to adjust. When he could see again, he saw a large room with chairs and tables set up all around on a red carpet, and a bar that ran the length of one wall. The bar itself was solid cherry-wood and it was lined with bar-stools that had seats covered in red vinyl. Along the side of the far wall, to the right of the bar, there were five or six booths, the last one of which had red velvet curtains screening it, though the curtains were drawn back. He saw Takis, who was sitting there and facing out, toward the door. He was talking to someone opposite him. Panos walked over to Takis slowly. The bartender was looking at him as he went by. So was the guy at the far end of the bar. The guy was just sitting and smoking, watching him as he went toward the booth with the curtains.

Takis was looking at him as well. "Panos, you're on time. Good. Come over here."

Takis beckoned him, circling with his arm. "Come on—come closer, come over here." The guy at the one end of the bar was watching him closely. There were a couple of other heavies in the club, two or three at least. One sat at the other end of the bar, closest to the booth where Takis was sitting. There was another one at a table not too far away, sitting by himself. These guys were protection and not just regular customers, he could tell, because they were trying to look like they weren't doing anything. Like they weren't here for any reason, just to sit and have a drink. But as actors they were shit. They couldn't act their way out of a plastic sack. One or two of them didn't even look Greek. Albanian, maybe.

Panos came near to Takis, close to him but not on top of him. He glanced over to see who was sitting opposite Takis. He saw a smallish figure in the shadows. He froze. It dawned on him who this was. Skorpios.

"We have a job for you, boy. Are you ready? How is your car running these days? Is it running okay?" Takis laughed as if he had said something amusing.

"My car's working okay. Sure, I'm ready," Panos said. "Just tell me what the job is."

Takis looked at him closely. "It's simple. We just need you to transport one of the girls. Give her a ride. From point A to point B. Simple, like I said. Can you do that?"

"Sure, I can do that. Just tell me where and when."

"That's good, Panos. Good. I'm talking about now. I want you to take off now. Take Messogion outta town. You'll get a call in about ten minutes, not much more. They'll tell you where you gotta go. Okay? Didn't I tell you it was simple?"

Panos was about to say something when he noticed the figure in the shadows stirring.

"Takis is wearing you out, eh, boy? Can you take it? Whaddya say, eh? Is he gonna wear you out or can you take it?"

"Sure, I can take it. He's not wearing me out, Mr. Skorpios. No problem. I can do the job. Like he says, it's simple." Panos felt like an idiot, parrotting what Takis and Skorpios had just said to him. He also flinched saying "Mr. Skorpios." What the hell was he supposed to say? He figured he was okay, even if it sounded stupid to himself what he had said. He guessed the rule was that if you knew Skorpios well, you said *Skorpios*, but if you didn't know him, you said *Mr. Skorpios*, like he himself had just said it. Skorpios didn't seem to react, either bad or good, when Panos said what he said.

Takis spoke to him. "Okay, that's it. Get going. Get in that fucking car of yours and you'll get the call, like I said. They'll tell you where to pick her up and all the rest."

Panos was about to go when Takis called out to him.

"Hey, I almost forgot. Here—" and he handed Panos an envelope.

"It's a little early but, what the hell, you have earned it, my boy. Okay, now get out of here." Takis was finished with him, it was clear, as he turned toward Skorpios. But Skorpios gave him a final glance. For a second, Panos almost thought the old man smiled at him. It was probably closer to say that the adductor muscles attached to the old man's lacertilian upper lip remembered for an instant what a smile might have felt like. But it was a vague memory, at the most, and the attempted smile failed abruptly. It wasn't a smile at all, Panos thought. More like a grimace. Or not a grimace, but more like a snarl. The way the old man's lip had moved vaguely upward was more like an adder or asp, coiling, replete with poison. Like a scorpion's tail, arched, poised, ready to snap and deliver the sting. Sting, and hurt. Ready to kill.

Panos was shaking when he got outside the club. Fuck me, he said to himself. When am I going to stop taking this shit! Fucking Takis! *If your car is running these days—what an asshole.* Panos looked in the envelope. *What the fuck—?* He whistled. This is twice as much as usual. Not bad. Maybe that's it then. They're jerking my chain just to see if I can take it. Maybe I was right. You just gotta hang in there. You do your job and save as much as you can, and eventually you get to the point where you can go into business for yourself. How sweet would that be, to be giving orders to fucking Takis for a change? *Hey, Takis, if your stupid car is running these days, go do this bullshit errand for me. And while you're out there, go blow yourself, you fucking moron!"*

Panos found his car, right where he'd left it. He got in and took off immediately so that he would be where he was supposed to be when he got the call that he was supposed to get in just about ten minutes, not much more.

5.

HE GOT THE CALL AND IT WAS JUST ABOUT ten minutes later, just like Takis had said, or at least not more than fifteen. He had taken Konstandinou, Vasilíssis Sofías, then Messogion. He was past Nea Psihiko and nearly to Ayía Paraskevi, heading east, when he got the call. He didn't recognize the voice that was talking to him. But the guy, whoever it was, did say that he was supposed to be picking up a girl. And he told him to go south. He gave him directions to a place in Kantza and then hung up. That figures, Panos thought. It wouldn't be a neighborhood like Gerakas, probably, where Skorpios would have a place where he was keeping girls. Kantza. Okay, I know that area a little bit. This should be easy. He settled in as he drove through Ayía Paraskevi and headed toward the highway.

He found the place in Kantza without any problem. The building was set apart from the buildings on either side of it. It was a graceless concrete structure—an ugly, blockish, sulking monstrosity of a building, like an overgrown bunker, really. There was one door, in the center, leading in. Panos went through it. He turned down the hallway to the left. When he came to the first apartment, the door was open. A man he had never seen before was sitting at a table. The man got up leisurely and walked to the door, where Panos was standing.

"What are you here for?"

"The girl," Panos said.

"Right. She's all ready for you. Come on, I'll show you where the stairs are."

The man took Panos to the end of the hallway. He opened the door and pointed up the stairs.

"Two floors up. She's in 308. She's in there waiting for you. She'll tell you where you're supposed to take her."

Then he gave the door a push as Panos slid by him. The door closed and Panos could hear the man walking back down the hall. He had walked up one flight of stairs when he heard an enormous crash outside the building, out of nowhere. The noise startled Panos. It sounded like someone had lifted a big trash can over his head and thrown it down on the pavement, *bang!* It made Panos nearly jump out of his skin.

He reached the top of the stairs and opened the door to the third floor. He looked down the hallway. Light was coming into the hallway through an open door. He walked toward it. 302…304…306. That was it, the door that was open. He went inside the room. And he saw the girl. She was lying on the floor. She wasn't moving, not a bit. *Shit!* She was dead. It wasn't just that she wasn't moving. She had a huge hole in her chest. Blood was seeping out of it still, a dark pool of it forming underneath her. She was pretty. Her eyes were open, but glassy. She was staring at the ceiling, or that's what it looked like she was doing, at least. Looking straight at heaven.

Panos recognized her. That was the girl he had taken on the errand a couple days ago. He had been told to take her to a pawn shop. She came out of there with a small package. She didn't say what it was. Maybe she didn't even know, because she didn't open it. It was tied up with cord. She was out of there so fast, it must have been waiting for her to pick it up.

Panos had seen her give the guy inside the store some money. Then she came back to the car and put the package in her bag. He had brought her to another place, not this one. But now she was here. She was most definitely here. And she was dead.

She was beautiful. He remembered that from the other day too. Beautiful like a wild creature, all legs and arms. They were sprawled on the floor, like she had tried to run away, right before she got hit. It looked like she had tried to grab something with her fists, hold on to it, squeeze it real hard, but then she just let go. She looked like she had wanted to say something at the end. It was horrible. Whatever she was trying to say and it couldn't get out. It looked like it got half-way out of her mouth, and then stopped. It was frozen there on her face, whatever it was she was wanting to say. Frozen, just like that stare, her eyes, pointing straight up, like she was looking at the sky right through the ceiling.

Panos sensed someone else was in the place. Another man. He had come out of the next room, but he had come out so quietly Panos hadn't even heard him. The guy stood over the dead girl, with his legs spread apart, because he was being very careful not to step in the pool of blood that was still spreading out around the body of that poor girl. The man looked at Panos. He had a gun in his hand. It was an automatic. He couldn't tell what kind. But it looked like a good piece. The man raised the gun, holding it just over the body of the dead girl, and he fired it straight at Panos.

It hit him in the chest like a hammer. *Oh, fuck—no!* Panos looked down to see the hole in his chest and it was there all right, a big fucking hole. *No!* Panos felt himself crumple. His knees hit the floor. It felt like someone was reaching inside that hole, jamming a hand in and grabbing at his throat, his windpipe, trying to pull it right out of his body. His chest was burning. He couldn't breathe. He tried to gulp down breaths of air, he just couldn't do it. He was lying on the floor, he could tell, when the room started to go dark. Then he couldn't see anything. He couldn't feel anything. He couldn't breathe. He could feel that he was passing out. But he couldn't feel anything else anymore and he couldn't hear a thing anymore either. He couldn't breathe. *No!*

The other man was still standing over the dead girl. He was wearing gloves, but he took the additional precaution of wiping the gun with a white rag. He put the gun in the hands of the girl, pressing her fingers gently around the handle and trigger. Then he walked over to Panos. He bent down and put his hand in one of the dead man's pockets. The man took out the envelope, looked inside it, quickly counting the money. He grunted with satisfaction. Then he bent down again and gave Panos a gun as well, putting it in his right hand, which was stretched out toward the place where the girl was lying.

Then the man left the room.

—•—

Takis's phone rang and he answered it.

"You done? Good. You use her gun? Right. Now clear outta there. What? You already out? Good."

He closed the phone and looked at Skorpios.

"It's done. They're both toast. The slut, and that little smart-ass, too."

"Are they outta that building."

"Yeah, they're out."

"Good work, Dimitrakis," Skorpios said.

"They used the gun we had her pick up," Takis said, "Let the cops chase their tails over that one."

And he laughed.

Skorpios nearly laughed, too, but the sound coming out of his twisted lips seemed more like a hiss. His face was red. It was hard to tell. Takis wasn't sure if he was glad or pissed off. The only thing Skorpios said to him, in fact, was "Let's see what the little whore will do about it!"

Then they sat in silence for a while, before Takis took off, leaving Skorpios in the booth with the red velvet curtains, sitting alone in the shadows.

She was sitting alone on the balcony in the dark. Daniel was inside, cleaning up after dinner. She was looking at the sky. The curtains behind the glass door of the balcony were drawn. There was no street light outside their place. Just one on the next block. It was dark, comfortingly so. She could see the sky clearly. She looked up at the stars.

She was thinking of her sister, of Irini. Where was she? She was worrying about how they were going to find her. She could be anywhere. Skorpios had access to many different properties. He was constantly dumping some and acquiring others. Or he would use buildings that belonged to others who were beholden to him. Irini could be anywhere in the city, somewhere in or near the heart of it or somewhere on the outskirts or in any of its neighborhoods.

Ariani was looking at the stars when suddenly one of them blazed up and, as she saw out of the corner of her eye, left a thick streak behind it as it fell across the sky.

A shooting star! It was beautiful and yet it sent a chill through Ariani.

Irini.

Ariani thought of her sister. She thought of her sister the way she was when they were both young. She thought of a summer night, one in particular, when they had been out with friends, on a night like this one, and they were sitting in a field, just outside the town, looking up at the sky and gazing at the thousands of stars that were spread far and wide, high over their heads, each one blinking in such a way that even if their light was muted by distance they still appeared to be lit from inside with an intense fire.

It was Irini's birthday, in fact, and they had wandered into the field. They were feeling a strange sense of freedom because of the day's celebrations. They sat in the field and watched the stars with the usual wonder when one had suddenly moved. It made a quick silvery arc, downward, a brief smudge on the blackness where the star had been a moment before. One of the girls said, "That means someone is going to die." Another said, "When you see a falling star on your birthday it means you are going to die." "It means your soul is going to leave your body and fly through heaven!" And what began as a story meant to tease and delight became a joke meant to frighten, and then a cruel one, at that, because Irini believed it at once. She became obsessed with the idea and started to cry uncontrollably so that the other girls, including Ariani, became panicked and tried desperately to console her. Ariani tried to convince her that they were only joking. Every time Irini became reasonable again, however, she would think about the dire omen they had just seen and she would begin to sob all over again. The problem was that the story they had made up about the shooting star resembled far too closely the kinds of stories Ariani and Irini had heard all of their lives from certain women in the village, charming stories to be sure but stories in which superstition and the uncanny were given full rein. Indeed, their mother was upset when they got home and she saw that Irini was inconsolable. But she was angry because the girls had announced the significance of the evil omen to Irini so bluntly and not because her daughter had been terrified that way by mere nonsense.

Now Ariani had seen a star falling across the sky, flaring and vanishing all in one instant. What might it mean? Perhaps it did not mean anything at all. Or it merely focused for Ariani all of the worry that she carried for her lost sister. Or was it the last trace visible within this earthly world of her sister's very soul? The idea made Ariani shudder. Ariani thought of how Irini had trembled that night, unable to escape the fear of a sudden death with which the star had suddenly threatened her. She thought of her sister now, wherever she might be. Was she afraid? Or was she free from any threat, though Ariani had no way to know it?

As Ariani sat and thought about Irini, she began to think about their mother as well. She thought about the day that the woman took them away from both their mother and father and from their home. She thought about the scene in the kitchen, where all of them had been sitting when the woman arrived. When the woman came into the house, she found them there in the kitchen—the parents, and the sisters, and one of their aunts, their mother's older sister. The woman was pleasant but made it clear that she had no time for a chat and got the girls up in order to get them out of the house. Irini clung to her mother's neck, crying, and Ariani herself felt the tears running down her face but tried to fight them back.

Ariani tried to remember her mother's face. She tried to recall the expression that her mother had on her face at the moment just before they left the house. She could remember it clearly. But for that very reason, that she could see so vividly in the eye of her mind her mother's face as it had been at that very moment, she had forced that image to become blurred and indistinct. Her mother had been crying real tears and those tears were welling up from a deep fear inside her mother's heart. But what Ariani had realized sometime later, what made the moment so painful to recall, was the suspicion in Ariani's own mind—a horrible, haunting fear of her own—that her mother knew where her daughters were going. What kind of work it was that the woman was really offering. Her aunt knew. Ariani was now sure of that. And her aunt was consoling their mother, of course, but also compelling her to accept the new conditions of their lives that would mean some kind of material gain for the family as a whole. Yes, at a cost, yes. But at what cost? Or to put the matter more truly at *whose* cost? Their mother had been overwhelmed, she felt sure, by how quickly events had moved and by the cleverness and guile of the woman and by the hardness of her own sister, their older aunt. *She* knew. And she tried to make sure that their mother barely knew. But the tears that burned their way down her mother's face that day were the marks of a torture that her mother was just starting to apply to herself for her own weak will and in-decision. And for her own complicity in her daughters' fate.

Their mother had known. Or did she? Ariani did not want to believe that she did, of course, but she was also tired of fooling herself as much as she was furious that they had been fooled. She wanted to cry. She missed her sister and she was sick with worries about what was happening to her at this very moment. She just wanted to wail and curse at the stars themselves for their uncomprehending distance and their failure to provide a light that would lead a way out of the terrible darkness of their lives. But she couldn't cry. It had been too many tears already that she had cried, for the first month or two of their journey into the moveable prison of the trade in sex-slaves. Then the tears just dried up. All that was left was the dread and concerns that begged for tears to wash them away. Or what was left after that was the anger. The anger and a thirst and hunger for vengeance that all promised that they would taste more sweetly and with a finer savor than any tears could provide.

Ariani sat on the balcony and thought about her sister. She looked up at the stars. It felt to her that the stars were infinitely far away, on this night anyway, as serene and still as it was. Infinitely far away.

6.

As he stepped from the quiet street into the brightly lit entrance of *The Scholar's Pub*, Knightly felt as if the noise from the place went barrelling past him, flying into the night either to escape the roar of the bar or else to find another establishment to inhabit for a while and fill with its cheerful chaos. He usually came to the pub for lunch, when the place was empty and quiet. Apparently, the pub was popular at night. A soccer game played on a mammoth tv screen that was set on one wall. The bar itself was crammed with people, most of them young men, but there were girls with many of them, too. The staff was all Irish, or so it was advertised. The crowd was a motley, distinctly international, even at a casual glance. Plenty of Greeks as well.

Knightly found a small table by the wall opposite the tv and the soccer game. The waitress came over and asked if he wanted a beer.

"Guinness, please."

"Great, I'll get that for you," she said. She was Irish, for sure.

The Guinness arrived. Knightly contemplated it for a moment before he took a sip. He considered whether, if he proceeded with ritual slowness, all of the difficulties he was facing would sort themselves into a proper order, as if by magic. The Guinness was delicious, as usual, but no magic occurred of the sort he was hoping for, at least as far as he could tell. He had been trying to calm himself, ever since the interview with Kazantzakis, but nothing had worked. He tried resting in his room, he tried reading. When he had found he couldn't stop thinking about what Kazantzakis had said to him, he tried going for a walk, taking the long way round to the Pub, through the Plaka, to Syntagma, then all the way down Ermou to the side-street where the pub was situated.

He thought about what Kazantzakis had said. What was it, exactly? That the Romanian claimed he had been following "the other American" when a second American appeared. Professor Wilson Knightly himself. Described to a tee. *Oui, c'est moi!* Shit. Why did the Romanian have to be there? But what was truly upsetting, more than being exposed himself, Knightly realized, was that the Romanian confirmed what Knightly had suspected—or feared. Daniel was in Greece but not on holiday. He was working. Knightly doubted it was official. The Romanian didn't seem up to the level of a state-agent. Not to mention the odd crew that Knightly had encountered at Vasses. Organized crime, then? Everyone knew that Romanians and Bulgarians were doing a brisk business in Greece, in prostitution, drugs, arms-dealing. The Albanians were almost old hat by now. And it wasn't just Greece that provided the booming market, but the rest of southern Europe—the rest of Europe—as well. Just how would Daniel be caught up in that? Knightly felt the absurdity of it. Daniel had been well trained to fight, to kill. To survive. Yet Knightly found himself worrying more about Daniel than about himself.

Knightly thought about Kazantzakis. He had to admit it, he liked the inspector. There was something courtly about him. But there was also a growing possibility, Knightly was all too aware, that he might be getting himself into real trouble. Should he just be honest and confess to Kazantzakis?

But confess to what? The simple fact was that he had not met with Daniel and he had not spoken with him. In all truth, he knew nothing. As soon as he knew something—anything concrete, that is—he would tell the inspector. Or at least he would be in a better position to decide what he might tell the inspector that might be of some real value to him and at the same time not be damaging to Daniel in any way.

He looked around the pub. *Couldn't you make it easy on me and just walk in, Daniel, old boy?* Knightly laughed. But the inspector had been serious. Something had happened, it was clear, that was no laughing matter. What if Knightly were going too far? He had no idea what he was getting into or what this was all about. The inspector had a good idea. And Daniel surely knew even more. Knightly admitted to himself that he was out of his depth in chasing after Daniel. But perhaps that is exactly why he wanted to pursue it. Finally. To be out of one's depth! How many chances does a person get, in an average lifetime, to go running at full speed and break out of the comfort zone? In the lives of many people—never. This might be the one thing that was morally indefensible, then: to come upon an opportunity to do something that meant one had to run a real risk, to face a situation that seemed to test body, mind, and spirit, perhaps even to taste real danger, only to decline the offer and to shrink away.

The waitress came back and asked what he would like. *A burger and fries. And, yes, another beer, thank you. Kilkenny's, please. That would be lovely.* Oh, now you are really stepping out, aren't you, lad? Now you're courting true danger! Knightly laughed at himself. Okay, it's all warmth and comfort now. But who knows what's coming. *Better to keep my strength up.*

Knightly looked around the pub. How many times had he been here? He had been here many times but it had been Daniel who had introduced him to the place. It was when Daniel was spending a semester in Athens and Knightly was on sabbatical so he came to Greece and they met in the city. Daniel had said the pub was one of his favorites.

And how many times, Knightly mused, had he been to Greece? The thought struck him. How many times had he been to Greece, in fact, without ever trying to get in touch with Elli? Many, many times. That one stung. He shook it off. He remembered how he had come to believe that she had forgotten him. He recalled how much that hurt. He would have been glad to look her up. But it wasn't in the cards, he had convinced himself of that. Or was that conviction, once again, just a lack of courage?

And he had met someone else. Maybe too quickly. He began to realize—was it really for the first time?—that the experience of meeting Elli had made him feel afterward how empty life was without a relationship of the same quality and intensity. He had not felt the lack of such a relationship as acutely until he had known her. Was that why he felt so alone when he had gotten back to the States? Was that why he tried so hard to find someone else? Or was it just in the natural order of things that, at that time in his life, he should look for a mate and think about starting a family?

Uncomfortable thoughts. He hardly knew which was worse, thinking along such lines, or thinking instead of Kazantzakis beating him with a rubber hose and giving him the third degree as he sought the precious information he seemed to want from him.

The food came and another beer and Knightly lost himself in the pleasure of the moment. When he finished, the waitress came over to take his plate.

"Would you like anything else?" she asked.

"No thanks," Knightly said.

She smiled.

"Wait a minute," he said. "Would you mind if I asked a stupid question? You get Americans in here, but maybe not that many? I'm just wondering if by any chance you've seen a particular guy—an American, I mean. Tall, curly hair, but cut short now, late twenties, good-looking guy. Have you seen anybody with that description?"

She just laughed. "Look around you," she said, waving her arm. "Do you think I'd remember if that guy you're talking about came in here?"

Knightly could feel himself getting red. "Right, silly question, I'm sorry. How would you have noticed! It's just that I'm looking for an old student of mine. I heard he was in Athens. But I haven't been able to track him down."

She smiled again. "Well, I'll be on the look-out from now on."

"Thanks," Knightly said. He looked at her for a second. *Why not make matters worse?*

"Say, if you don't mind me asking, what is your name?"

"I don't mind at all," she said. "It's Sharon." She turned and walked away.

Knightly looked around at the crowd that filled the pub. It was a young crowd. Lots of kids in jeans, funky shirts, white cotton, tee-shirts, sweat-shirts. Some gelled hair. Some tattoos. A piercing here or there. Plenty of people smoking and everybody drinking. Laughter bursting and peeling out of one cluster of customers and then another. The whole place rang with a brightness of spirit that seemed completely out of line with what one read in the newspapers about economic crisis and a country on the brink of social revolution. Okay, they weren't all Greeks. But many of them were. And was it so much better where the others had come from—Italy, Spain, Ireland, England? Was it just a brave face that people wanted, or needed, to put on? Or was this the one sort of pleasure these young people could still afford? Or were these the lucky ones, the children of wealth or of those who were wealthy enough. Of those who were going to ride out the storm, no matter what sort of complaints they might give voice to, both parent and child, in the meantime?

The waitress—Sharon—came back with his check.

"Thanks," Knightly said. "I really enjoyed that."

"Thank you," Sharon said. "I'm glad you did. Good night, Professor."

"Good night." He watched the girl as she walked away.

Professor? Smart kid. She must have gathered that from what he had said about looking for a former student. He looked at the bill. It was what he expected. Knightly put his hand in his back pocket to get his wallet. As he fished it out, he happened to look at the back of the check. Wait a minute. There was writing there, in small letters, in the same black ink and, so far as he could tell, in the same hand as the figures on the bill itself:

The handwriting is on the wall, old man.

What the—?! Knightly thought to himself. *Old man? Wow—was I that obnoxious? Or is this a joke, is she yanking my chain?*

He looked over at the girl, Sharon. And, though he may only have imagined it, he thought that he saw her glance up at him when he looked over at her. What was in that look he could not say exactly. But it was one you'd classify, he said to himself, as a *significant* look.

He left money on the table and got up to leave, taking the bill with the writing on the back along with him. *The handwriting is on the wall, old man.* He thought about the cryptic message as he left the pub. Was it a message? He thought a minute. Just before she had brought him the check, hadn't he seen her over there, over on the far side of the restaurant, beside the bar, talking on her cell-phone? He suddenly remembered thinking that it was strange. The place was busy and she's taking time out to talk on her cell-phone to some friend of hers. Then she delivers a message. If it was a message.

A message from Daniel?

He stopped on the sidewalk outside the pub. He looked at the back of the check again. At the message. He was sure it was a message now. *God damn it*, he muttered. *It's a message from Daniel. He's directing me to a place. And I know where he means.*

———◦◦◦———

"Hello, Elli?"

"*Nai*, yes?"

"It's me."

"Will! How are you?"

"Fine. I'm in Athens and everything's fine. I might even be making a little progress. Anyway, I just wanted to check in and see how you were doing."

"I'm good, Will. I'm glad everything is going well there. Do you think you can come back in a couple of days?"

"I made a promise."

"You don't have to promise anything, Will—"

"No, really, I only need another day or two. Besides, I want to get back there. I want to see you and spend some time, you know...."

"Sounds good to me. But I don't want you to feel as if you're under pressure."

"I don't feel that way, believe me. Except the kind of pressure I put on myself on a regular basis—no, wait, that's a joke!"

"A lame one!"

"Aha, so you miss me, too. I knew it!"

"Very funny, Professor Knightly."

"Don't pull rank on me, Elli. Say, Giannakis—how is he doing? Is he doing okay?"

"He's doing fine, Will. Thank you for asking. We are all doing fine here."

"Elli, I do miss you. I'm looking forward to seeing you again. It's a bit of an improvement, you have to admit, that it will only be a day or two, instead of twenty-five years."

"Ha! We can agree about that. I miss you, too, Will. I'm looking forward to having you back here. You can stay with us—forget about Tripoli—we have the extra room. It was my mother's. That room is yours."

"That's very kind of you. Okay, you've got a deal. Take care of yourself, Elli. I'll see you soon."

"Thank you for calling, Will. Goodbye."

"Goodbye," Knightly said.

As Knightly turned off the phone, he tried to picture her. He had heard voices in the background. That would be Thalia and her husband, who owned the bookstore where Elli worked. He remembered—she had told him she would be working late that night. They were taking inventory. She was probably just getting ready to leave the shop and go home. To Giannakis. Chrysa would have had him over, given him dinner, and walked him back to Elli's house. And that's where Elli would find him. Knightly thought about the way that Elli took care of her son. He thought about how much patience she showed in dealing with his affliction—but she would not like him expressing it that way. Giannakis had emotional and physical problems, Elli was helping him live his life. The problems were there and they faced them together. What affliction? She never complained. She worked to support them both and she depended on her sister to help her make the situation workable. Affliction? Knightly had not seen Elli show anything other than her strong and positive side. She was hiding her sadness from him, perhaps from the world as well? Or had she fought her way to some higher perspective, so that her misfortunes, and her son's, lost the significance they might have for someone else? Or did she simply love her son in a way that made those misfortunes trivial by comparison?

Knightly admired her and wanted to understand how she lived with a situation that would sorely test the courage and endurance of other people—including himself. He wished he were with her now. But he was consoled by the fact that he had found out that he had been on the right track, after all. It seemed that Daniel was in Athens, in fact, and that Knightly was only a step away from meeting with him. Should he go now? No, not now. He had decided to wait for the morning. But he would set out at first light.

—✶—

"Hello, Athena? Yes, this is Kazantzakis. How are you? Good. Yes, I'm fine, thank you. I just wondered if you had anything new? No? No, nothing here either. Except for one thing. Skorpios is doing some weeding out, some folks he's not too sure of, it would seem. The kind of thing we saw with that hit in the warehouse. Right. He's probably been doing it all along, but now he's doing a little more of it. Maybe we're putting some pressure on him. I think he's not liking it or at least he's building a fire-break, so we don't get too close. But the thing is that it's not just us, apparently. What we're hearing now is that somebody else is gunning for him. A rival? That would make sense. But it's not clear that it's someone who's in the business. For one thing, some of Skorpios's delivery boys are getting hit—yes, the ones he's not taking out himself—but nobody seems to be interested in making a move or taking any of the action. Right…it's not clear at all who is going after his network or why. But somebody else is putting pressure on him and he seems to be feeling it. Anyway, we're working on that, too. Listen, before I let you go, I want to ask you for a favor. Would you look into something for me? There's a woman, her name is Eleftheria Parthenis… right, exactly—she's the friend of our Mr. Knightly. Would you look into her situation for me? She's living in Kremni right now. She's originally from there or from some other small town around there, but she also spent time in Tripoli. She worked in the city for a while, according to Knightly. Just see if you can find out anything about her—I mean, if there is anything to find out. Thank you, Athena, I appreciate it. Yes, yes, thank you, and to you, too. I'll be seeing you in a day or two. Goodbye."

———◦∿◦———

Elli said good night to Thalia and left the bookstore. The night was warm. She walked down the street, passing by other stores—a camera shop, a video store, a butcher's shop, a bakery that specialized in cheese pies, another bakery that sold sweets. When she looked up, above the roofs of the houses that began where the businesses left off, she saw the sky was filled with stars, each one pricking the canopy of night with its singular light.

She passed by the school, the soccer field, a small playground, the community center. Then the cemetery. She thought of her parents. That must be a particular stage of life, she thought, when you pass a cemetery and what comes to mind are those very people who brought you into the world and who gave you life. Her own parents were not here, of course. They were in the cemetery in her home town, and Chrysa's. Who was lighting a lamp for them? Who was keeping their graves? There were some friends of her parents who still lived there, either older people who were still alive or their children who would remember her mother, especially, and they would tend to things, checking the oil in the little lamp, lighting it along with the incense, keeping the tomb itself clean from grass and weeds and dirt. It was difficult for Elli to think about because she felt guilty that she was not there to do it. In fact it wasn't just guilt. She wanted to do this for her parents. She differed with Chrysa whenever they talked about the subject. Chrysa was realistic about it. She would point out that friends in the village were seeing to the graves. They would go up to the village themselves whenever they could. That was enough. But Elli could not feel comfortable with the situation like her sister.

How would Will feel about it? Would he take her side, or at least understand why she felt that she should be the one to offer the rituals of care and respect to her parents, or at least to their last resting place? She felt sure that he would understand her. She missed him, she realized, as she thought about this. All the qualities she had seen in him long ago. Kind, accepting, caring. They were still there. Only more so, or she herself saw them more clearly now, after the passing of time. He was sensitive and strong, she thought. She felt lucky and grateful to him that he hadn't run away screaming when he saw what her situation was—that she had a son, and that the son was in fact a young man in Giannakis's condition. How nice it would be to have the help of someone like him, to have his support, from morning to night, day after day. But she worried about whether he would want to be involved at all, if he had time to think things over. Would it seem to him, once he reflected on it, that it was too much to take on? She hadn't wanted to think about this, but she was afraid that he would politely tell her "so good to see you," then run away as soon as he could.

And it wasn't just that. The worst part about not seeing each other for so long wasn't simply that so much time had passed, which felt like time that they had lost. It was all the history that they had each created, but separately from one another, that they hadn't shared.

She wondered what he was doing in Athens. Though she was mildly curious she really didn't care. If he said that he had something there he felt he had to do, that was enough for her. She didn't want to pry into his affairs. It was his business and as long as he was safe she didn't mind that he was doing it. Perhaps she didn't mind because she doubted that there were many dark secrets that he was hiding from her. Even if there were, she might still feel the same. This was a difficult thing for any couple to deal with, she felt, and especially for two people who had been separated for a long time. How do they come to share all of what they have been through? Should there be no secret places, or should everything be said, everything brought into the light? How do two people handle the fact that there might finally be secrets that the two don't share, from the time when they were leading their separate lives?

She was home. The lights in the house were on. She stepped up on the porch and leaned over to look through the window. Giannakis was there, sitting on the couch and looking in the direction of the television. She stood and listened. There was no sound or light coming from the tv, it was not turned on. If she went in and turned it on for him, she thought, it might upset him. It was a strange thing. While Giannakis was normally passive, the one thing that seemed to trigger a response, and a strong one, was when he was sitting in front of the television and someone changed it. Either turning it on, when it had been off, or vice-versa. It was very odd. They had had some severe flare-ups over this kind of thing and it had been hard to calm him down afterwards. Elli was almost grateful for these eruptions, as perverse as it was, but that was only because during these tantrums it felt as if they were making contact at last, even though the interaction was purely functional. She longed to communicate with Giannakis. She longed to have him react to her, to respond to something she said or did. Anything. But she knew the longing was fruitless and it led to such a painful feeling that she quickly put it out of her mind.

Elli went into the house. She walked over and stood next to the couch, where Giannakis was sitting. She put her arm on his shoulder and told him it was time for bed. He said nothing, but slowly got up and followed her to his bedroom. Chrysa had already gotten him into slippers. Elli helped him take them off, then she helped him take off his shirt. She folded it and put it on a chair next to his dresser as he took off his pants and got himself into bed. She came over to him and bending down she kissed him on the forehead. *Good night, Giannaki mou.* And she turned off the light.

She washed herself and brushed her hair in a perfunctory way and then went into her own bedroom. She undressed and put on an old tee-shirt—it was very old, one that Will had given to her many years ago, during the summer when they met. It had been one of his. It was for a sports team she had never heard of. The Boston Red Sox. She had kept it.

Then she climbed into bed. She must have been more tired than she realized before she lay down. A feeling of exhaustion swamped her senses, washing over her like a drowsy wave. As she drifted away, she thought of her son. Giannakis was probably already giving in to sleep, or at least that is how she pictured him, falling asleep just as she was and finally at peace with the world, lying in his bed, in the very next room to hers. She fell asleep within a moment, even as she was giving thanks for what she felt deep in her heart as a kind of miracle, that her son was alive, and for the fact that, despite his being broken in spirit, all of the ordeals his body had suffered he had survived.

7.

It was going to be a long night. A night without sleep, for all of them.

Mac was standing next to the hallway that led out to the door; he was holding a short-barrelled shotgun. Tex was on the other side of the hall, his hand resting on the butt of the Glock jammed inside his belt. The others sat around a table at the center of the room. They were all waiting.

Daniel looked around at the men assembled there. They were hand-picked from squads he had led in the past. A couple of them had come to Greece with him after their last mission. Rest and relaxation. That had been the plan, at any rate. But things had turned out differently. The others had not been far away, when they were needed. He knew these men well. He knew he could depend on them and they trusted and respected him. They were like family. By a long and harrowing process, a strange journey that literally had spanned continents and oceans, these men had become like brothers to him.

There was "Tex." Infantry, rifleman. Technically, a weapons specialist. In cold fact, he was a sniper of surpassing skill. He was a Texan, hence the nickname. Where all of the team had them, Tex was the only one whose nickname was obligatory. This was because of his given name: Warwick

Smith. *Jesus Christ, one of his buddies had said to him, what the hell did they go and do that for?* Meaning his parents. He explained how his mother had a cousin who lived in Rhode Island and she went to visit once. It was the only time she ever left Texas. So she named him—that. At which point he had solemnly declared to the group that he'd be much obliged if they would forget about the other name. It was just Tex, y'understand? And then he added, without much of a smile, that if anyone forgot and called him by that other stupid fucking name he'd give 'em an exit wound the size of West Texas. Since the rest of the squad knew very well what he could do, how he could kill with complete surprise at stunning distances, they were ready enough to respect his wishes as to the moniker.

Then there was Ricky, aka "Mex." Enrique Gonzalez. His parents had come to the United States without documents, working in Phoenix and sharing a small apartment for years with one of his father's brothers. His mother found work as a maid and his father in construction until they had enough for a place of their own. They applied for citizenship and finally outlasted the long arduous process of obtaining it. Their son proved an excellent student at every level and as he was about to finish high school he succeeded in getting into West Point. Two years after receiving his commission, he joined the Army Rangers. An engineer by training, Ricky was an expert in demolitions. A genius both in constructing things and in bringing them down with a bang. When he served as spotter for Tex, at which he was also skilled, he was given that name "Mex." Hence, the team of "Tex-Mex." It was a bit of nonsense each of them could have done without. As long as no one uttered the name Warwick, however, it passed without a fuss.

Michael MacGregor was another weapons specialist and an expert in hand-to-hand combat and martial arts. Mac or Big Mac or Mikey grew up in Los Angeles in a neighborhood that was poor and black. He found refuge in a gym that was four blocks from where he lived. He always said that the streets taught him speed but that it was at the gym that he learned discipline and that his first teacher, who gave lessons in karate to the kids in the neighborhood, had showed him the path to the true arts of self-defense and self-knowledge. Unbelievably quick and unbelievably tough, nevertheless Mac was mellow and soft-spoken. It was his nature, they all said, and the result of what it's like to be the guy that no one in their right mind would ever pick a fight with. The famous story about Mac related to the time he was on "special assignment" in Idaho. That is, he was on leave and picking up a few bucks assisting the state police. He had gone into a bikers' bar with a couple of troopers who were operating undercover. They saw their mark about to leave the place and so they got up to follow him out and make the arrest. They didn't know it was a set-up. Mac got out the door but three beefy members of the gang stepped in front of the two troopers to keep them from going out. The two troopers were no slackers, however, and they had the bikers subdued and cuffed in what one of them later claimed was roughly sixty seconds. When they scrambled out of the bar to save Mac from the ambush, what they saw to their astonishment was Mac, cool and collected, putting cuffs on their suspect. On the ground all around Mac were the bruised and broken up bodies of six of the gang's nastiest enforcers, who were lying there moaning and groaning and leaking blood and bodily fluids and pure wasted nastiness.

Carl "Doc" Hofstadter, aka "Tank," had finished three years of medical school at Harvard when he decided to enlist in the army and he too had entered Ranger school and passed the course. With an intellect that was unusual even among the gifted individuals with whom he had served in Special Forces, Doc was a fully trained combat medic. He was also the strongest man that anyone had ever seen. Solidly built, only slightly above average height, he was physically powerful in a way that beggared description.

The story that the guys loved to tell about Doc concerned a time when he was in Paris on a team that was tracking a terror suspect. The team had finally cornered the suspect when a desperate chase ensued and the bad guy ran down into a Metro station. His timing seemed to be perfect. A train was about to leave and the creep jumped on just as the doors were closing. Several of the team members were close enough to see a grin on the face of the terrorist. But what the guy hadn't seen was that Doc had been only steps behind him. There are at least four Deltas who have sworn to seeing the following. Doc thrust his hands in between the doors of the train, which were fully closed, and just as the train was starting to move, he pulled the doors open, grabbed the grinning asshole by his collar and hauled him off the fucking train. "Passengers will please keep clear of the doors when the train is in motion…" *Right!* An alternate version had it that Doc simply picked up the train—or at least the single car in which the suspect was located at the time—and shook it until the fugitive tumbled out onto the platform.

Doc was mild-mannered and gentle like Mac and the two were indeed close friends. He himself sometimes referred to the two of them as the German-Scottish alliance. The men they served with took their side in any argument, whatever their side might be, out of respect for their spiritual refinement, it was insisted.

William "Radio" Chen grew up in Boston. His grandparents came to America from China and worked in a restaurant in the city's Chinatown. His parents went to college and entered the professional class, so that Bill had all the advantages of a middle-class upbringing. He was majoring in electrical engineering at MIT when the Towers were taken down on September 11, 2001. When he graduated with his Bachelor of Science degree, he had job offers from three different companies. A few days before his graduation, Bill's father asked him which one he would choose and he told his father that he had enlisted in the navy. His father had fainted—literally fainted. Chen thought his father had a heart attack. But they reconciled nine months later when Bill had not only passed through basic training but had moved on to training for the Navy Seals—their notorious "hell week" and beyond. He had been a competitive swimmer throughout his school years and an avid sailor as well, especially during his undergraduate career. And he knew how to disassemble, reassemble, and operate any communications gear that his training officers had been able to throw at him. Wet or dry. He had been on a couple of missions with his first Seals unit when he was drafted by a "special activities" commander who had heard about his combination of uncanny technical abilities and superior physical endurance. He served under Daniel on two missions and they became fast friends. At the moment, "Radio" was acting as sentry and look-out on the roof of the building across the street from where his friends were meeting.

These were the men who made up Daniel's team. His official un-official team. They were his *dictyo*, his network. The group was an anti-*dictyo*, really, since he had called them into being in order to fight and to bring down a criminal ring that was dealing in prostitutes and drugs by means of a network that spread through a decent-sized portion of Greece and emanated from the figure of Skorpios. The network surrounding Skorpios had kept him safe from rivals and from the police alike. Something more lethal was needed, Daniel had decided, once he had been drawn into the fight, a unit that was incorruptible and also one that was capable of being as vicious as Skorpios himself. Or more so.

"Let's talk, gentlemen," Daniel said. Tex came over and sat down. Mac stayed by the entrance to the hall but turned toward the table where they were sitting. Daniel began the meeting.

"As you all know, Joshua and Taz are off the script. We haven't had contact with them in twenty-four. Doc, you said you spoke with Taz early yesterday?"

"Right," Doc said. "It must have been just before he took off. He said that he was backing up Joshua. 'Recon,' he said. I asked him whether Joshua talked about it with you—" he looked at Daniel—"he said 'of course we're clear with Daniel.' But he was acting strangely. That was the extent of the conversation. That's when he left."

"Right, Doc, thanks." Daniel looked at the members of his team. He knew what they were thinking. About how the behavior of Joshua had been getting stranger by the day. He had started free-lancing. This was upsetting just because he was one of their officers. But it was still more disturbing because they had learned about the missions Joshua was conducting and that these forays were becoming more and more bizarre.

"It won't surprise anyone if I say I've seen this coming. I think we all have seen it coming. But, whatever—right now the point is that we have to locate those two. Andreas is probably with them as well. If they go off half-cocked and make a big mess, then we all have to answer for it. We've got to find Joshua and Taz before they get themselves hurt, if Skorpios gets the drop on them"—he sensed the group was sceptical on this point, "or before they catch up with Skorpios and slice and dice him so that the whole shit-bag hits the fan."

Daniel stopped. A noise was coming from the cell-phone in front of him. He looked at it. It was a text from Radio: "Friendly."

Twenty seconds later there was a knock on the door. Mac turned and walked down the hall. He levelled the Mossberg waist high and took a step back as he unlocked the door. Tex was eight paces behind him, slowly raising the black Glock.

"Come in," Mac shouted.

It was Chrysóstomos. He was a policeman, a cop in the city of Athens. His cousin, Andreas, had introduced him to Daniel several years ago. Andreas had served in the army like all young Greeks, but had chosen a branch of the Special Forces and served with Daniel and Joshua as a liaison

officer when the two were assigned in the Mediterranean. The three became good friends. But Andreas had grown particularly devoted to Joshua.

Chrysóstomos came in and sat down heavily at the table. He looked
ghastly, drained. His face was pale, his eyes hollowed and red.

"Tommy, what's wrong—you look like a wreck!" Daniel said. "Talk to
us, what's going on?"

Tommy did not speak. He slid his elbows onto the table and buried his
head in his hands. The others sat there waiting for him to say something.

"It's bad, Daniel, really bad. I have horrible news. I'm sorry—" he
raised his head and looked at Daniel.

Daniel knew what he was going to say. It was what he had been afraid
of. *Irini.*

"What has happened to Irini? Talk to me, Tommy!"

Chrysostomos looked up. His voice came out flat as he spoke but his
eyes were full of an anguish that moved Daniel.

"The cops found her in a flat out in Kantza. She was shot, Daniel. The
way it looked, some stiff—a nobody, a lackey of Skorpios's, I'd be willing to
bet—shot her in the chest. But he was lying there dead, too, shot through
the chest himself. By a gun they found with Irini, had her prints on it and
apparently belonged to her. It looks like a set-up to me. But what's the difference—Irini is dead. She's dead, Daniel. Jesus Christ. I'm sorry."

No one said anything. Suddenly the stillness was broken by the sound
of a hand slapping the table—*bam!*

"That son of a bitch," Tex yelled, "—that miserable fucking son of a
bitch!"

The rest were silent. Mac was still standing by the hall. He was squeezing the stocky shotgun in his big hands, as if he was wringing it out like
an old rag, the muscles in his neck standing out. Doc stared at his hands,
folded in front of him. Ricky with his eyes closed, barely breathing, Tex

staring straight ahead, with a look of cold hatred. The men were all silent, but the room felt as if it could ignite, explode at any minute.

Daniel stood up to speak, perfectly composed. His eyes were moist. Nobody looked at him, even as they listened intently.

"Okay. This is what we were afraid of." He took a deep breath, then went on. "The clock ran out. Son of a bitch. Tommy, do you have any idea where Joshua and Taz are right now?"

"I don't know where they are, Daniel," Tommy said, "All I know is that they're out hunting Skorpios."

"I assume they know about Irini," Daniel said.

"Yes, they do." Tommy paused for a moment, looking around the room as everyone thought about what he just said. "They had information—or they seemed sure they were going to get it soon—about where Skorpios is going to be tomorrow night. I heard that from Andreas. But I don't even know where he is now. Except that he's out with the two of them, Joshua and Taz."

"There it is, boys," Daniel said. "Okay, listen up. This is what we're going to do. We need to find Joshua and Taz before they make their move. We'll split up and look for them in the city, inside three zones. Doc, you and Mac will be in the north. Start in Kato Patissia and move east. I want you to start with the places we know are associated with Skorpios. I want those places staked out. Check in with our locals up there, talk to them. And keep your eyes open. If you hear or see anything—I mean *anything*— call it in stat! Do not engage—" he looked around the table, "I repeat, do not engage, unless you think they're in trouble. Ricky and Radio, I want you to do the same in the south. Start in Vironas and make your sweep to the west. Check the locations we know about. Get in touch with our network there. See if they've seen or heard anything. The two teams will move in opposite directions so we'll cover both sides of the dial. I'll be in the center—Tex, you come with me. We'll start it this way, and if we come up empty we'll expand the search area. Let's hope we find something."

Daniel stopped, looking each man in the face one more time.

"Look, I just want to thank you all for what you're doing. I really don't know what else to say. I'm grateful that you're all here right now. I hope you know it. And I expect that you know I'd do the same thing for each one of you. No question." Daniel cleared his throat. "Okay! Stay sharp out there. Watch each other's back. And call it in the minute you've got something. Let's go."

The men got up from the table. They collected any gear they brought with them and, after each man shook hands with Daniel, one by one, the team left the room. Daniel watched them go. The collective look of this group of men was grim, resolved. On the outside they were calm, yet Daniel could sense the rage they were feeling inside them. They were controlling it because they were professionals and they had work to do. So they showed no sign of anger or frustration. And despite the danger, the lack of sleep, the cruelty and near invisibility of their enemy, they showed no hint of self-pity.

The patience, the unwavering commitment and loyalty, the quiet heroism of these men made Daniel think of Joshua. Joshua had been just like them. For as long as Daniel had known him. When the two of them met in basic training, at the very beginning of their careers, Daniel knew he had met someone extraordinary, not only a friend and comrade, but an exemplar. Joshua became a kind of mentor to Daniel, even though Joshua was barely more than a year or two older. Joshua had it all. He possessed all the qualities that Daniel wanted to find in himself—intellect, instinct, courage, toughness, devotion to the service and to the country. And fighting skills. Daniel had been as cocky as the rest when they all entered the training. But Joshua seemed to operate on a different plane than him or anyone else. Daniel realized how Joshua pushed him if only because he needed to escape feeling intimidated by Joshua. Joshua filled Daniel with a fierce desire not to be beaten by this formidable mate. With all that was revealed to him by Joshua's outward example and through his own inner compulsion, Daniel would always feel that it was Joshua who had made him into a warrior.

When Joshua began to change, it broke Daniel's heart. It also filled him with terror. Why had he denied the signs? They had to perform under extreme conditions many times. The service they were called to required it and they knew this was the case. So what if they were waging war in the shadows? When was it ever any different? High noon arrives but once a day. Does anyone expect much more clarity than that, in making war? Dubious conflicts! What conflict isn't dubious, come right down to it? Sure, for those immersed in the fighting, maybe it was possible to become confused. What was merely an ugly act, one you swallow afterwards with a shot or two of regret, and what was a truly savage one. Joshua not only lost the capacity to distinguish the one from the other. He began to cultivate strange beliefs about what they were doing—or what they should be doing—and why they should be doing it. Joshua's rants became more frequent and more intense, and Daniel knew he couldn't pass it off as battle fatigue or stress or disillusionment with the service or with the world itself. Daniel began to see that his beautiful comrade was changing. What exactly had happened to Joshua that impelled him toward his new and violent obsessions, Daniel found it hard to understand. Or in the end he didn't want to know.

Daniel realized it had been the wrong move to ask Joshua to help him this time. He hadn't seen him in a while. Daniel hoped Joshua would have come back to his old self. But he saw at once that the cracks in the façade were not mending but were only growing wider and deeper. To make matters worse, Joshua came to this fight with a companion that Daniel could only describe as a true believer. He was a perfectly likable guy and an excellent soldier—a young man by the name of Patrick Close. He had picked up the nickname of "Taz" because of the ferocity he showed in battle. Like a Tasmanian devil, the men joked. But Daniel could see that this was yet another sign of the new Joshua. There could be no more fitting protégé, he thought sadly, than this young fighter who had already dismissed the idea of limits and seemed prepared to go however far down the road his brilliant and savage mentor was pointing, as far as Joshua might wish.

Daniel had given Tex a rendezvous point and told him to go ahead. As Daniel left the building, he thought about the other thing that was bothering him—what was in fact bothering him the most. Ariani. How would he tell her? How could he break the news to her that her sister was dead? That she had in fact been murdered in cold blood by the very men that Daniel had sworn he would save them from? How could he tell her to her face that he had failed her in the one thing she had wanted from him?

He was afraid how she would react. *That's putting it mildly*, he thought. He wondered how he could get her to stay put, even after he had told her. She would want to do something—she would want revenge. How was he going to get her to wait for him to work things out, especially after his signal failure to save her sister? Top it all off, he couldn't stay more than an hour with her. He had too much to do. Jesus! A sleepless night and a sleepless day ahead, heavy losses already, and a fight brewing that he had a very bad feeling about and that he needed to avoid in any case. *Nothing he wasn't used to, in any of that.* He smiled, grimly. *Thanks to the training.* He just prayed Ariani would listen to him, and that she would agree to stay home. Let him get the situation back in order and let him get her out of here! That would be worth a sleepless night or two, he thought, as he headed up the street.

8.

KNIGHTLY GOT THE WAKE UP CALL AT 6:30 A.M. He splashed some water on his face, got dressed and headed downstairs. The breakfast room didn't open until 7:30, but he knew the lady who set up every morning, so she looked the other way as he grabbed a roll, tore it open and stuffed it with a couple slices of cheese and ham. He wolfed that down and then poured some juice—orange or apricot, or perhaps both—and drained it. Then he poured some coffee into a cup and ran out of the hotel. The coffee sloshed in his face every time he tried to drink, so he finally gave up and threw it away. He was half awake. Entering the Plaka on Byron Street, he made his way to Kydathineon, then to Nikis, crossed Ermou, and before he knew it he was on Stadiou.

The shops on Stadiou were closed and shuttered. He wondered how many were closed because it was early and how many had closed for good. He continued up Stadiou until he came to the National Historical Museum. The entrance to the museum was not on the street. There was a pleasant green space in front of the building, shaped like a triangle, with two retaining walls converging at the set of stairs leading up to the museum. At the very front of this *plateia*, the open side of the triangle, was the equestrian statue of Kolokotronis, one of the heroes of the War of Independence. The Old Man of the Morea.

The handwriting is on the wall, old man.

The statue was famous. Knightly had remembered joking about it with Daniel, because the statue, though august and well-known, was regularly covered with grafitti around its base. The two retaining walls of the *plateia* that tapered toward the museum's door-way were clean, relatively speaking, of grafitti. But the base of Kolokotronis's statue was adorned, as usual, with messages of the profoundest import. Knightly had slowed his pace deliberately: he wanted to read whatever might be there without being too obvious about it.

As he strolled by the statue, he saw one grafitto that he swore he remembered from a year or so ago. It read simply, in English,

FUCK HEROES

Just below it he saw another one that he thought he had seen before:

voítha yéro!

"Help, old man!" This one he found touching. In any case, it offered a counterpoint to the line above it. Indeed, in these two lines one could witness the exchangeable contretemps of Greek politics—a misstep to the left, then one to the right—of the last sixty or seventy years or more.

These two lines had been written a while ago, to be sure, and by different hands, so far as he could tell, though both were done in the same dismal black paint. But what caught Knightly's eye was a line written just below the other two. It was done in a white paint that looked almost fresh:

make a wish

Make a wish. That was all it said. Knightly thought about it. What could that mean? Was it even a message—was it meant *for him*? He began to wonder whether he might even be wrong about the original message, the one Sharon had passed him on the back of his check. He walked more slowly down Stadiou, as he pondered what the fresh line might mean, if it were anything other than just another idiotic flourish of vandal egoism or urban ennui. And what if it were meant for him and pointed to a possible meeting—how would he know what time to show up at the assigned place? It was starting to feel ridiculous again. He stopped and looked at the newspapers that were lying around a kiosk at the end of the block. Then he turned nonchalantly and strolled back down the street, in the direction of the museum and the Plateia Kolokotroni.

As he passed by the statue again and glanced at the base, his blood froze. Beneath that third line and also written in white was a single, simple sign:

X

Ten. The roman numeral. Ten o'clock. That was the time of the meeting, when he was supposed to be wherever he was supposed to be to meet Daniel. Ten o'clock. That was the time, fine. But *where*? Where was he supposed to go? That must be contained in the clue, he assumed—*make a wish*.

Knightly walked away from the square, down the street. As he walked, he racked his brain, trying to solve the riddle. What was Daniel trying to say? What location could that phrase possibly indicate? He turned on to Ermou and walked slowly, mulling over the three simple words. When he reached Aiolou, he turned right. The street was another pedestrian zone, another oasis in a city that had its breathing spaces but tended to hide them with care. As he walked up the first stretch of Aiolou that passes the church of Ayia Irini, he began to relax. He had found the message that was left for him, he felt sure. And it was barely 7:15. He had plenty of time. Why not help the deductive powers along? He looked up and conceived a bold plan. Breakfast had been a hurried, botched affair. Directly ahead of him was Krinos café. Home of the best *loukoumádes* in the city. Perhaps the best in all of Greece. And the coffee was not bad, either. At least, the *café Gallico*. There was a plan! A plate of *loukoumádes* and a cup of French coffee.

He went in, ordered, and took the tray to an empty table. It was only on the second or third bite that it occurred to Knightly what Daniel meant by this second cryptic message, the terse graffito in white,

make a wish

Γιάντες! *"Yiándes."* The name of a celebrated work of the Greek painter, Nikólaos Gyzis, a famous master of the nineteenth-century. Though the title of the painting, "Yiándes," was usually translated as "Wishbone," Knightly had always believed that was a poor translation, or misunderstanding, of its meaning, probably not what the artist had intended at all. The word was in fact Turkish and meant "wish," "desire." Indeed, Gyzis had done the painting after a trip through Asia Minor where Greeks and Turks were of course still living side by side. The painting itself is of a young woman, who tilts her head back slightly and looks aslant, toward the side of the frame, so that the viewer looks at her nearly in three quarter view. Her expression is mysterious—not as famous as that of the Mona Lisa, of course, but equally enigmatic. She is smiling slightly, or at least her lips are parted, and yet her eyes seem to be misting over, even as she gazes out into the distance, outside the frame of the painting that contains her. Is she remembering someone or something painfully lost to her? Or is she gazing toward the future, her eyes directed at an object of desire, present or only imagined, that she hopes to have a chance to win?

It is, Knightly always felt, a creation of aching beauty. He had discussed this masterpiece of Gyzis with Daniel, he was sure. And Daniel had remembered it and was now using it to direct him to a meeting. But—the picture was hanging in the National Gallery. Was that where Daniel wanted them to meet, in such a public place? He must know what he's doing, Knightly thought. He ate the last *loukouma*, finished his coffee, and left the café. Turning down Sofokleous, he headed toward Psirri, to wander the streets there for a while. He had plenty of time before he was supposed to be at the National Gallery. And he wanted to have a chance to think the whole thing over again. So he headed toward the old neighborhood and its warren of slanting and twisted streets.

Psirri had been the place to be, one of the fashionable quarters of Athens, maybe ten or fifteen years ago. Now it was upstaged by other neighborhoods. But Knightly preferred it still. It was funky enough, in his mind, but it was real. It had good places to eat, great live theater, where some of the best shows in the city would be playing, great *tsipouradika*, wine shops, and brew pubs. It was quieter these days, but so what? That contrasted in a favorable way with, say, the mindless clubbing of some parts of Gazi or the fake radical chic of Exarchia. Places that were now cool. *Forget them,* Knightly thought. And he turned off Athinas street on to another narrow one leading to the heart of Psirri.

It was a glancing blow that struck him but luckily not with all its intended force.

Perhaps because Knightly had just turned, the man with the blackjack had missed his angle and the blow was delivered clumsily. Knightly felt it bounce off his skull and then glimpsed a dark shape on his left as his attacker, off-balance now, slid past his left shoulder. Knightly's reaction was swift. He had played football in high school and it must have been muscle-memory from the endless tackling drills that fired up at this moment. Knightly lunged at the form of the man who had attacked him and, with legs pumping, drove into him with his shoulder and smacked him hard into a brick wall on the side of the alley.

As the attacker slammed into the wall, Knightly bounced off him. It was then that he saw a bare shelf sitting on a pair of brackets that stuck out of the wall. He and his assailant happened to be outside a hardware store. Through the dusty window Knightly saw tool-handles and hoses. Knightly yanked the shelf free of the brackets—it came off easily. The board was only about three feet long. Perfect length for the short stroke that he dealt to the face of the attacker. *Whap!*

Knightly and his father had been very different people. Knightly had showed early on his aptitude for books and the kind of learning gotten from books, while his father was an intelligent man but with a purely practical bent. He had been a carpenter and eventually a building-contractor. Knightly always admired the way his father could take a nail and drive it through a couple of two-by-fours, cleanly, with one stroke. Not that his father was a big man or heavily muscled. But he was solid. One stroke. *Whap!*

That is how Knightly hit the man who had tried to attack him. Knightly looked at him and saw that the man's nose was flattened against his face. Knightly hit him again with the board, without any wind-up or back-swing, just the same quick punching stroke. *Whap!* This time the blow hit the man on the side of his head, just above his left eye. Knightly hit him once more, catching him fully on the side of his face. On that last one Knightly had felt the energy flowing all the way from the back of his legs, firing up through his hips, which he twisted sharply in order to amplify the force that finally erupted from his back and chest through his shoulders and his arms to transmit a payload of abrupt furious violence that even surprised Knightly as he applied one last vicious lick.

When he thought about it later, he realized that what he had felt at that moment was not jubilation that he was saving himself, or any sort of vindication or relief that he had defended himself against a surprise attack—it was hatred. Pure hatred. Like the frothy head on a glass of beer. Like a foaming wave-tip welling up from an ocean of rage. Hatred that was the purest distillation of an anger that had been forming somewhere in some remote depths within himself or the cosmos that he had never known or intimated before. Knightly had been happy—overjoyed—to win the fight. But that feeling of hatred haunted him afterward. He had looked at the man he hit and he knew as he was doing it that he hated him and that he wanted to do just what he was doing as he did it.

As the man who had attacked him slumped down and fell to the ground, Knightly caught sight of another man coming at him down the alley. Another attacker. This one had a knife. A serious knife, Knightly thought, with a blade that looked to be at least six or seven inches. The board Knightly had used as a weapon had cracked on that third stroke. It was usable, but it had started to split. Knightly squared off, facing the new assailant, holding the board in front of him. The man didn't hesitate. With a savage grunt he lunged at Knightly. As he was stepping forward, swinging the arm with the long bright blade toward Knightly, just as suddenly the man stopped in his tracks. He was almost knocked backward, in fact. His eyes rolled up toward the sky as if in an attempt to focus on the spike-shaped object that suddenly appeared in the center of his forehead. The man collapsed and fell down heavily in the alley.

Knightly leaned over and he recognized what the object was. He had seen them in sporting-goods stores, with the archery equipment. He had never shot a cross-bow before, but he knew what the bolt of a cross-bow looked like. It looked exactly like what was sticking out of the forehead of the poor bastard that had just tried to stick him and flay him with that seven-inch blade.

The battle was over. As the surge of adrenaline that had carried him this far began to ebb away, Knightly returned to his senses. He surveyed the carnage, the bodies of the two men who had attacked him—or tried to attack him—lying at his feet. What am I supposed to do now, he thought? *Get the hell out of here.* He started to walk as quickly as he could down the alley, away from where he had turned into it and away from the two inert bodies that lay behind him. When he turned the corner and had put some distance between himself and the scene of the fight, he noticed that he was shaking. Natural reaction, he said to himself. And he tried to calm himself down, taking deep breaths with every step he took down the street.

Then a strange feeling came over him, a feeling of unreality. He found himself asking, did that really happen? *I mean, was I just attacked by two thugs in an alley I've walked down many times before in perfect peace?* He was seized by a desire to verify what he was already doubting had even taken place. *No way!* Wasn't that the old saw, about returning to the scene of the crime? He knew it was the worst possible idea, to go back and very likely be caught gawking at the mess he had just played a major part in making. But he couldn't help himself. He had to see the place again, to be sure that what he thought just happened had really occurred. He turned and went back toward the alley by the same way he had just come.

It was empty. The alley was completely empty. No bodies. No bloody carnage. Nothing to see. Had he in fact been dreaming, walking around in some bizarre waking nightmare? He was starting to doubt his own senses when he looked over at the entrance to the hardware shop, with its dusty window. The shelf had been restored to its place, sitting squarely on the brackets. Knightly lifted it off them again and looked at the board. It was cracked. Just beginning to split. He set it back down on the brackets. Turning once more to look over the scene, he walked away down the alley again. He had been attacked, then, it was true. And he had fended off the attack. With some help, however, from forces unseen. Powerful forces, by the looks of it. And these magical powers—blithe spirits—had kindly cleaned up the mess that he had abandoned when he bolted down the alley the first time. Though he could not explain exactly how or why it happened, Knightly felt that he understood essentially what had just gone on. And that worried him deeply.

9.

Knightly walked straight down Athinas Street and then left on Ermou, heading in the direction of Constitution Square. He wanted to stay on the major streets, where there were more people, though it was still early. He walked through the square of Syntagma and turned on to Vasilissis Sofias. He had stopped shaking, and that felt good. He lengthened his stride as he walked along the great avenue. He could hardly believe what had just happened—any of it. It had happened quickly, for one thing. The whole episode was probably over in less than a minute. The attackers had come one after the other and he had reacted so fast he surprised himself. But he hadn't acted alone, especially in the clean-up. Who had helped him? There could only be one answer. He was on his way to meet Daniel at this very moment and yet the fact was that Daniel had already made his presence felt. Lucky thing, Knightly thought.

It was too early for him to go to the Gallery. Knightly crossed Sofias when he got to Rizari. By taking Rizari Street, he was backtracking, in effect, and he reached Spirou Merkouri in a few minutes. He went a couple of blocks, bought a bottle of water from a *periptero* next to the Alsos Pangratiou, and entered the park. Knightly had been alert ever since he left Syntagma, trying to make sure no one was following him. He didn't want to bring anyone with him to the meeting with Daniel. And he certainly didn't want another encounter like the one he had in the alley back in Psirri, if he could help it. He found a bench in a spot where he would be inconspicuous but from which he could see in three directions. He sat down and took a drink of water. He checked his watch. It was 8:45.

He sat for fifteen minutes, then got up and left the park. As he walked down Spirou Merkouri, he allowed himself to relax and enjoy one of the city's loveliest streets, charming for all its lack of pretense. He had barely walked ten minutes when he arrived at the small *plateia* in front of the National Gallery. He looked around. There was hardly anyone on the streets. Glancing up and down Vassileos Konstandinou, he didn't see anyone who looked remotely suspicious, so he went into the museum, bought a ticket and walked down the hall to the lower floor of the gallery, turning right as he entered the first wing. He walked slowly as he passed the paintings from the early part of the nineteenth-century, many of them on historical subjects, stopping occasionally to study one or other of them closely. His interest picked up when he came to the paintings of Lytras. Nikiphóros Lytras, who was a contemporary of Gyzis, was another master painter whom Knightly liked and one who had played a part in the movement toward a naturalistic, albeit sentimental, depiction of common people. Sentimental, Knightly thought, sure. But would he consider trading *The Waiting* or *The Kiss* for some provocative piece of the avant garde—an oblong of burlap stretched out and tacked to the wall, say—all in the name of artistic innovation or the high concept? *I don't think so. Poor figural bastard!*

He had reached the area where Gyzis's paintings are displayed. And there she was. Between two of Gyzis's other paintings, he saw the portrait of a simple girl—no tiara or fancy hat, no ruffles or rich costume, no pride or overly self-conscious presence—with a simple yet curious and compelling expression on her face. *Yiándes.* Whatever the precise emotion playing upon that remarkable visage, the girl in Gyzis's painting looked as beautiful and expressive and undecidable as ever.

The painting was startling, even aside from the captivating face. It seemed incomplete, almost a study rather than a painting that had been fully executed. The girl is wearing a plain red smock and the background of the painting is red. Her shoulders are outlined with a faint black line and her face is surrounded by a black veil wrapped loosely around her neck and draped over her shoulders. From beneath the veil, tresses of her dark hair trail lightly over her shoulders and chest. Red background and black scarf reduce the focus to the perfect oval of her face, training all of one's attention upon that face, drawing the viewer's gaze irresistibly there, to light upon the face and to contemplate the meaning of its expression. The girl's eyes are moist, and she raises her eyebrows slightly, as if she had begun to arch them and stopped. A strong emotion is caught by a moment's reflection. But what emotion? Whatever she was feeling—aroused by a memory, by a word someone has said to her, by a game, or a challenge—the feeling has been arrested by thought. There on her face is visible the first and last traces of the immediacy of her response. Some secret of her heart was called forth and very nearly revealed. Its manifestation is already almost vanished but one is witnessing it there in the artist's representation just before it will have gone away forever.

The beauty of the face is striking but it is also the honesty of the face of that girl and the fleeting baring of her soul in that expression that is startling as well. A distant and a forlorn hope, recalled after some time? Or is it the recollection of something that happened recently, the memory fresh, and so perhaps more painful? Yet some see joy in her expression—Knightly himself found that difficult to see. Given the time it was painted and the likely circumstances of the girl, the way the world was then and the way it is now, Knightly could not help seeing there the sharing of personal loss rather than hope or joy. And yet, if it was grief, the girl seems on the verge of overcoming it. The radiance of the face shines out of that background, as far as Knightly could see, reflecting the spirit strangely undiminished of one whose life was formed by hardship and suffering and loss. If there is a joy in transcending all of that, then perhaps, yes, there is joy in the expression of this girl as well. Desire to have all of one's own back again and the joy of holding all that is lost in one's memory, at least. Γιάντες. "The Wish."

Knightly forced himself to move on. The gallery had many more of Gyzis's works, some other paintings that reflected the trip to Asia Minor with Lytras in 1873, a few portraits, and finally the later works that evinced a mystical or allegorical turn. There was an impressive variety, in any case, from the astonishingly supernal *Behold the Bridegroom Cometh* to the seductive and disturbing *The Spider*.

When Knightly came back around to the side of the hall where he had started with "Yiándes," he stopped abruptly. He saw someone standing in front of the painting whom he recognized immediately. He knew it was Daniel, despite the fact that Daniel was in disguise: a black beret, goatee, and steel-rimmed glasses. The beret struck him as a little funny, but Knightly realized that was only because of the circles he himself sometimes had to move in. Daniel was wearing a light leather jacket and a black tee. It was a casual look that concealed, though barely, the outline of a powerful frame.

When Daniel caught sight of Knightly out of the corner of his eye, what he saw was a man nearing fifty, fit and trim, if a little well-fed, built like a light heavyweight boxer in fact, who moved easily, even gracefully, as he came around the corner, slowing down when, as Daniel realized, he had noticed him. He saw the same hairline—Knightly had taken to keeping his hair cut very close, once it started to recede, even when Daniel was a student. When he saw Knightly, Daniel saw his old professor again, looking slightly older perhaps, but virtually unchanged in respect to the essentials, after all this time.

Knightly tried not to look at the figure who was standing in front of "Yiándes." Knightly knew that Daniel was merely waiting, taking up his station there, so to speak. It was a move required to effect the rendezvous. Yet Knightly couldn't help wondering, was it only his imagination or was Daniel in fact looking at the painting intently, studying it? In that moment, Knightly could see once again the young man who had been his student. Knightly was moved. After all Daniel must have been through, all that he must have seen and done—and in spite of whatever troubles might be brewing at this very moment—he is still open to the delicate beauty of that painting, Knightly thought, and susceptible to the creation of an artist like Gyzis.

Knightly pretended to look at one of the paintings in front of him. Better to let Daniel make a move, he said to himself. There was no one else in the entire wing. Only a middle-aged woman who was on the museum staff and who was sitting all the way down the hall, by the entrance to the wing. She paid no attention to them or to anyone else, talking on her cellphone as obsessively as she was when Knightly had entered. Knightly saw that Daniel was being circumspect, even so, and he tried not to look up when he noticed Daniel was moving toward him. As he passed by, Daniel did not stop or acknowledge him in any way, but Knightly heard him speak in a tone that was low, yet distinct and audible:

Outside your hotel, tonight at nine, look for the taxi.

Daniel continued on, slowly examining the paintings in the rest of the wing. Knightly left the hall, but decided to go upstairs to the second floor. To leave the gallery after such a short time might seem suspicious. He tried to look as if he was paying serious attention as he passed the paintings of

Parthénis, Ghikas, Móralis—all works that he loved. He attempted to act cool, but he found it difficult to concentrate. He had gotten the message he had come for. Now he would have to wait until the evening. He had spent roughly half an hour on the second floor when he decided he had decoyed long enough. He went downstairs, glancing right and left as he entered the hallway to go out. As far as he could see, though he did not want to call attention to himself by looking too hard, Daniel had already left. There was no sign of him. Knightly left the gallery himself and began to take the long walk back to the hotel.

———

Knightly came downstairs at nine o'clock sharp. As he left the hotel, he saw there was a cab waiting up the block that started to move as soon as he set foot on the sidewalk. The taxi pulled up and Knightly got in the back seat. The driver was a young Greek, probably in his late twenties.

He looked at Knightly in the mirror and asked, "Where are we going?"

"I was hoping you would tell me," Knightly replied.

"Right. Let's go see the man."

"Perfect, thanks—"

"My name's Spiros."

"Okay. Thanks, Spiro."

That is all they said. Knightly was silent as Spiros drove north, around the Acropolis and out of the center of the city. Knightly tried to pay attention at first. It seemed that they passed by Omonia, then headed out on Acharnon. Spiros began using side streets and Knightly started to lose track of where they were. Finally, Spiros turned on to a narrow street and pulled over to the curb. He turned off the lights and waited. Five minutes, ten minutes. There was no traffic on the street and no one passed by on the sidewalk, except for a couple of teenagers, a boy and a girl, who were walking on the other side of the street and oblivious to their presence. When the kids had disappeared, Spiros took another look up and down and then pulled out on the street again, without turning on the lights. They went two blocks, turned right, went another two blocks, then pulled over again. After five minutes, Spiros spoke to Knightly.

"Let's go, Professor. I'll take you to the meeting place."

He got out of the car and Knightly did the same. Spiros led him to a building that stood by itself on the block. Knightly was taken aback when he got a good look at it. It was an apartment building, apparently, but it looked like a bombed-out wreck. There were no windows, just gaping holes, most of them bare of coverings or trim. Only one or two of the windows betrayed any sign of habitation. In one, a blanket was hung out and draped over the window-ledge. It had wide stripes of what had once been bright colors, red, yellow and ochre. Along the ledge, flowerpots were set out in a profusion that jarred strangely with the burnt-out look of the rest of the building. Squatters had made a home here, maybe coming from some place where people found a certain delight in vivid colors.

Spiros took Knightly through the front door—or where the door would have been—and they walked down a hallway to the back of the building. The floor was dirty and littered with broken glass. Spiros turned and Knightly followed him. Spiros stopped at a door at the end of the back-hall. He knocked softly. Knightly heard footsteps as someone came to the door and opened it.

It was Daniel.

"I brought you some company, Daniel."

"I take it you mean just Will, nobody else?"

"Don't worry, we came alone."

"Thanks, Spiro."

Spiros smiled and walked past Knightly, back down the hallway and out of the building.

Daniel looked at Knightly. Knightly stretched out his hand and Daniel grasped it tightly. The two men looked at each other and then burst out in laughter.

"For Christ's sake, Daniel, what am I doing!" Knightly pulled Daniel toward him and the two men embraced.

Daniel gave Knightly a pat on the back and chuckled as he pulled him into the room, shutting the door behind them.

"Thanks for coming, Will."

"Don't mention it—it's good to see you!"

"Same here. By the way, you did a good job with the clues."

Knightly flashed a grin. "Sure, thanks. Was that some kind of test—how did I do?"

"You'll get your grade at the end of the course."

"Oh, great. I probably don't want to know."

Daniel smiled briefly as they sat down on the only furniture in the room—a couple of old wooden folding-chairs facing each other in front of a large boarded-up window. A single bulb burned overhead and cast a harsh yellow light over the empty room.

Daniel had a black bag next to him and he took a bottle from it.

"Gentleman Jack!" Knightly sighed. "You are the consummate host."

Daniel poured a couple of glasses and handed one to Knightly.

"Cheers, Will. It's really great to see you again. I'm sorry it had to come about in such a funny way but, anyhow, let's drink to it."

"Cheers, Daniel."

They drained their glasses. Knightly waited for the fire in his chest to subside. He held his glass in front of him, examining it. Then he looked up at Daniel.

"So, Daniel, what the *hell* are you doing in *Greece*?"

Daniel looked back at him.

"Taking a vacation, what the fuck does it look like?" Daniel waved his hand at the surroundings and continued.

"It's going to sound ridiculous, but as a matter of fact I'm here in Greece because of a girl."

"I'll be damned—" Knightly muttered and settled back in his chair, listening keenly as Daniel went on.

"Will, I'm going to be honest with you. I shouldn't tell you anything—for your own sake. But, since I am going to ask you to clear out of here when I'm finished telling you what's going on—"

Knightly stirred, as if about to speak, then he just shrugged and nodded.

"—I'll explain as much as I can. You've got a right to know. Just be careful with whatever I say to you."

Knightly nodded again. "Of course, Daniel."

"I wasn't kidding about the vacation. I was in Greece just to take it easy. I had just come off a mission—it was a tough one…."

Daniel paused. Knightly didn't say anything.

"Anyway, I was here with a couple of guys from the unit. I wanted us to have a good time. I looked up Sharon—you met her. I've known her forever. Since I came to Greece that first time. I asked her if she wanted to hang out with us, maybe she had some friends, and so on. She introduced me to a girl named Ariani. Long story short, Will, this girl—Ariani—she's not just any girl. It turns out she has quite a story. She's from Moldova. The only reason she's in Greece is because she'd been trafficked."

Knightly let out a groan. "Oh my God—what?!"

"She and her sister, too. They were sold into prostitution, conned by a woman from their own country, if you can believe it. She told them they were going to be getting good jobs in Germany. Wherever! The truth was they were being set up. They were sold into the sex trade. Sold like slaves."

"I know this kind of thing exists," Knightly said, "but I've never encountered it, I mean, not personally."

"I've seen it all over the world, I'm afraid. But I had never gotten involved myself. Well, that changed when I met Ariani. She was trying to get herself out of it. The problem is that the guy who controls her—or *used to* control her—is a big deal. At least as far as these things go. And he has—" here Daniel corrected himself "—he had her sister. He had started to suspect that Ariani was getting ideas. For a while, at the beginning, that is, he had marketed and sold them as a pair. It was kinky, and it was profitable. But when he thought Ariani was showing too much spirit, he split them up. Ariani barely saw Irini after that. When she did, there were too many of Skorpios's men around—"

Knightly looked at Daniel quizzically.

"Skorpios is this guy's name. He's the boss. He owns a part of the action in the city. He's smart, though. He works through other people. He invests in their enterprises. Seems he worked his way up from very little. Now he's in a position to 'help' other people out. And they take the risks. He stays invisible. Anyway, after Skorpios split them up, the problem for Ariani was how to get her sister out. And that's where I come in. I've been trying to help her find Irini. I convinced Ariani to get out of the game—she was trying to play along with Skorpios, so that she could keep tabs on Irini. But it wasn't working. So I set her up in a safe place. And I've been trying to track Irini down. There's no way Ariani would leave without her sister—"

Daniel stopped talking. He pushed back in his chair and sighed heavily.

"You want another drink, Will?"

"Please."

"I'll join you."

They drank in silence. Daniel put his glass down on the floor. He leaned forward, looking at his hands. Then he spoke.

"It didn't work out as I planned. Skorpios decided to make a move. I don't exactly know why. Burning a bridge? Acting out of spite? Irini is dead. Skorpios killed her. That is, he had her killed."

Knightly rocked in his chair, slapping his thighs.

"Damn it! No!"

"Yes, he did. He had her killed, murdered in cold blood. And there's nothing I can do about it now, Will. I wish I had found her before this happened. But I didn't do it. I've just got to live with that. Ariani is devastated. She's having a hard time dealing with it, to put it mildly. I don't know how she's going to cope. I think I've got to get her to go home, back to her country, try to forget about this somehow. But she's in shock right now. And on top of all of that I have another problem. A very big problem."

"Jesus, what else could there be?" Knightly asked.

"When I promised to help Ariani and get her sister out of Skorpios's network, I got a team together. As I said, I had a couple of men with me already. There were a few other people I've worked with who weren't too far away. I got in touch with them and they came. That was the nucleus of the group. I have some contacts here in Greece and I used them to throw up a network as quickly as I could. Within a day or two I had eyes and ears all over the city."

"Like Sharon?" Knightly said.

"I'd rather not talk details, Will, even with you. But, yes, Sharon is great. And she has a lot of friends. I mean, friends who are highly motivated. They were ripe for this kind of fight."

"But this Skorpios character is elusive?" Knightly asked.

"To say the least. But that wasn't the problem."

Daniel leaned forward, resting his elbows on his knees, his hands clasped together.

"I asked a very good friend to help me out with this job. We go way back—all the way back to basic training. And I've worked with him quite a few times. There's nobody better. If you thought that I came to this work well prepared and with some talent for it, you haven't met this guy. His name is Joshua."

Daniel paused, leaning back now. He let out a deep breath.

"Joshua is the most gifted individual I've ever met. When he was in school, he studied French and Arabic, as I heard it, but it could just as easily have been computer science and physics. He took two years of Chinese as well. In fact, he knows at least four 'strategic' languages. He's the kind of person who takes three weeks and he's functional, then two months in country and he's fluent not only in the target language but the local dialect. He's just as intimidating, physically speaking. We've all done martial arts training. But he's got a unique gift. He learns a technique and you watch him move and you swear that he was one of the guys who invented it. It's uncanny. And his powers of endurance are frightening. I've never seen anything near it. He can go for days and then sleep for just an hour or two and wake up fresh as the mountain air!"

"So what's the problem?" Knightly said. "This guy sounds like Superman."

"Unfortunately, he's losing his mind." Daniel said.

Knightly looked at Daniel. The words had sounded almost flip, but in fact Knightly could hear that the words came from a wound.

"It started before this," Daniel said. "I had seen signs that he was losing it, but I was hoping it would go away. I thought that working together on something like this would be the best way to help him start over, as a matter of fact."

"What do you mean when you say 'losing it,' Daniel?" Knightly asked.

"At first it was just talk. He would get upset over things that were annoying or disturbing, okay, but they were the kind of things you'd normally shrug off. Well, he was losing the ability to let things go. At least, I can see it now. I'll give you an example. It was the tipping-point, in fact, the last time we were in the field. We had some down-time and Joshua was checking the news. He came across a story—it was coverage of a congressional hearing. A certain representative was questioning a certain security expert from the State Department. In the interest of unbiased reporting I won't name the congressman, or the state he represents."

Knightly winced, "Let's see if I can guess."

"The issue was a recent attack on one of our facilities. The situation was chaotic. There was a flare-up in the region over something that had been reported in the media—another insult to the prophet—and about the same time a group of extremists launched an assault on the U. S. compound there, blasted it with heavy machine guns and RPG's. It was not a trivial incident. We lost people."

"I think I know which incident you're talking about," Knightly said.

"It was horrible, in fact. Truth is, the whole mess had a long history—not to mention that the Company was also involved. Anyway, the congressman was determined to milk it. He started badgering the security guy. It was an election year, right? He wanted a scandal. He wanted the guy to say the attackers were terrorists. He called them Al Quaeda. When the guy from State tried to correct him, the congressman got pissed. '*Let's not split words*,' he said. That's an interesting expression, no?"

"Split hairs or mince words. That's how a native speaker of English might put it."

Daniel grimaced. "Right. Or someone interested in a precise analysis. Only what the congressman was really saying was 'Don't ruin my fucking sound-bite, you pimple-faced little geek.' Joshua came over and as he was telling me about it I could see he was getting worked up. He got so angry he couldn't talk about it anymore. He just stormed off, cursing to himself. *This is bullshit* and *how are we supposed to listen to this crap and just take it?* Words to that effect. *Those clowns underfund our people and then they put on*

*a big show when things get fucked. Why can't you all quit the circus and just
do your goddamned jobs and give us what we need to do our goddamned jobs!*

"There was a company of Marines detailed with us. Joshua went into
their area. He went over to a small group of them and started talking to
them about this story. He pretended he was on the congressman's side. He
acted as though he thought the State guy was a dick. The marines thought
he was cool, just shooting the shit. Then one of the poor jarheads sounded
off about the State Department—don't know their ass from their elbow,
the current administration, blah blah blah. This set Joshua off. He was
looking for this. He told the guy to stand up. 'What the fuck?' the marine
said. 'I'm going to kill you,' Joshua said. The guy stood up and Joshua hit
him in the throat. Two of the guy's buddies tried to intervene, I mean, they
tried to stomp Joshua. He took them out. But it gets worse. He took the
first marine, dragged him into the latrine, found a bowl that wasn't flushed,
and dunked the poor bastard's head in it. Swished him around. Then he
just left him on the floor in the stall, with a note pinned on his chest: SHIT
FOR BRAINS."

Knightly gasped. "Jesus Mary and Joseph! You asked this guy to come
help you, Daniel?"

"The incident was a disaster. That poor kid was a mess. And the marines were furious. It was ironic—they were there to do security for us
and they wanted to kill us! We almost had a civil war. It took some major
peacemaking to settle things down."

"What happened to Joshua? Did he face any music?"

"They got him out of there. There was some ass-kicking, to be sure, but
a couple of guys up the line took the heat. They did it for Joshua. Nobody's
indispensable, right? But some are less dispensable than others. I'm telling
you, Will, Joshua has extraordinary gifts. And he has done some things,
some pretty remarkable things—I mean on the right side of the ledger. He

had a lot of credit in the bank. So they whisked him away and basically whitewashed the incident."

"Was he contrite at all? How did he react?"

"That's why I wanted to see him again. I never really talked to him about it. At the time, he didn't have much to say. Then he was gone before we had a chance to talk it out. I convinced myself it was an aberration, that he'd be okay."

"Were there other incidents?"

"Not really. Though he had been talking that way for a while. He would get outraged at this or that, trivial things, but after the tirades he would settle down and things would go back to normal. When he came to Greece this time, and we started working out the plan to nail Skorpios, it didn't take long to see that he wasn't right. First of all, he started to roll some of the hoods who were working for Skorpios. Jump them, give them a beating and steal their cash. He argued that it served multiple purposes. You rip them off, it finances the operation. Also, it puts the fear of God into the enemy. Finally, you hit them selectively. So Skorpios starts to wonder, they hit Mr. X and Y, why didn't they touch Z? Can I trust him? Sows the seeds of distrust and division, so Joshua said. Only the attacks were not exactly surgical. They were brutal. That was only the beginning. You know the politics of Greece, Will."

"Oh, my God," Knightly rolled his eyes, "you mean to say that Joshua began to take a serious interest in Greek politics? Not a good idea for anyone who's overly sensitive to grotesque posturing and fakery."

"He started to follow the demonstrations. I mean, literally. Right or left, it didn't matter. He developed a special tactic. He would go by himself, or with two or three 'troops' in support—there are a couple of men in the *diktyo*, by the way, who are fanatically loyal to him. They would join the demonstration by a side-street, parallel to the main route of the march, and they would 'eat their way in,' so to speak. *Rogue cells* is what Joshua called the tactic. They would eat into the crowd like a cancer. Not to kill but to wound and cripple. With a lead pipe in one hand and a combat knife in the other. Joshua said the variety and severity of the wounds were a good thing. It was necessary for the anarchists and fascists equally to be forced to accept some consequences for their actions, he would say. Not being able to walk for a couple of weeks was a good start. When he and his team had dealt enough punishment, they simply withdrew along a short line of retreat, back the same way they had entered the mass of protesters. He never had any problem getting out."

"I understand why he'd be angry at those losers," Knightly exclaimed. "But that's just what they are—losers. So why go after the minions? Why didn't Joshua take his fight to the top?"

"The people behind the hoodies and the blackshirts, you mean?"

"Exactly. Either the people who support them or else the thrones, dominations and princedoms who drive the crazies into the streets in the first place. Why not go after them? Otherwise, he's doing the very thing the anarchists and the nazi goons are doing—taking out their frustrations on other small fry who are not much different from themselves. The anarchists will smash store windows or torch a bank, but you don't see them marching to the prime minister's house."

"Joshua recognized that. Believe me, he's thinking big. But he'd say he was starting at the base—'you have to start at the bottom to work your way to the top.' I think he's convinced himself he's got infinite time to do whatever it is he has in mind."

"My God," Knightly said.

"Anyway, when I got wind of the first attack, I laid into him. I was seething. What I should have told him was that he had become a megalomaniac and that he was now as self-righteous as any of the morons that he was unable to tolerate anymore. And a hell of a lot more dangerous— to others and to himself. Instead I just told him he was endangering the mission and, besides, he was putting at risk the men who had come to do the job—at the very least, he was risking their careers. I said that he had lost the path. He wasn't serving anything or anyone. He was just in the fight for himself. *Remember what this fight is supposed to be about*, I told him, *or fuck off!*

"He looked at me, Will, as if he was astonished. He told me that I was the one who had lost sight of 'the big picture.' There were forces in play that I couldn't see. *I have always been patient with you, Daniel. I've always tried to help you to overcome your limitations. But I can't let you ruin this mission because you are too weak to carry it out.* He said that to me. With his hand on my shoulder. Like an older brother. Then he left. I haven't spoken with him since—only through some of the men—and now he's gone dark and I can't get in touch with him. He's after Skorpios. And he's doing it solo, or with the couple of men who are ready to follow him into the backdraft of a neutron bomb-blast."

Daniel fell silent. Knightly waited before he spoke.

"Why, Daniel? Why did this happen? I've heard about post-traumatic stress, but this seems so extreme. Do you understand what's happened to him?"

"I don't know, honestly. I've seen cases of PTSD, sure. But you're right, this goes beyond even the bad scenarios. Though it's not totally unrelated to combat stress either. It's complicated—a combination of factors, I think. Joshua has seen some horrible things. But so have we all. The last mission was very tough, I told you. We lost two men. The enemy lost a lot more. And the people we were there to help lost some people. Officially speaking, the mission was a success. We achieved what we were sent in for. But you come back and you think about what happened and sometimes it's hard to square all the corners and get the whole damned thing back into the box, if you see what I'm saying."

Knightly nodded.

"Joshua took all the losses to heart. He always acted as if he was above it all, but I believe he acted that way precisely because it hurt him too much to admit to himself or to anyone else. Don't get me wrong, there's a lot of satisfaction in what we do. We're serving our country, after all. But not every mission makes sense. Most times, you don't see the whole picture, where your task fits in. What's worse is when you do see, and you just disagree with the drift, period, and yet 'orders are orders.' It can be very difficult when you think you see pretty clearly what ought to be done, but you come to realize that the powers that be will never see it the same way. So there's a need for compromise. You need to speak as forthrightly as you can, when the time is right, but then you have to do what you're told once you've had your chance to speak and the issue has been decided, however it's decided.

"Joshua lost his grip on the art of compromise, you might say. He came to believe that he could see solutions and no one else could. He got to a point where he couldn't reconcile his sense of himself and his abilities with the way things were going in reality. So he started to take liberties."

"He took arms against a sea of troubles," Knightly said.

"At some point he took it upon himself to take everything and make it right and it has driven him crazy," Daniel said. "I really think it's about taking liberties. At first, you might say Joshua was taking on a burden, trying to fix all the world's problems. But then he began to indulge himself. He gave himself too much freedom. Do you remember where Plato talks about the 'democratic man,' when he suffers from an excess of freedom—it's in *The Republic*, isn't it?"

"Right," Knightly said, "you've got a good memory—it's in Book Eight."

"He talks about how the skin of the citizens becomes so tender—so sensitive—that they can't tolerate even the slightest imposition, or they believe they're being subjected to a master. That sounds to me like Joshua's problem. He got to a point where he couldn't tolerate any vexation or slight from anyone or any failing or injustice anywhere, no matter what the magnitude, until finally he assigned himself a kind of overlordship that both required and empowered him to rectify all the imbalance in the world's accounts. And to carry out the crusade ruthlessly. He's bent on working his way through the whole sum of evil in the world until he has eliminated it and reformed the earth itself, all by himself, because that is what he believes is needed."

Knightly looked at Daniel.

"So you believe Joshua has devolved into a stunning instance of the tyrannical soul?"

Daniel didn't answer right away.

"There's another way to see it, Will. The world is full of evil. Did you know that?"

Knightly smirked at this, but Daniel just shook his head.

"As thick and as banal as black tar. As rank and never-ceasing as the tides of waste that stream beneath any big city—most people don't even perceive it or ever need to deal with it. When you find yourself fighting against it and you wade into it, there's the danger that you're going to get so covered with the slime and the rot that before you know it no one recognizes you anymore and you don't even know yourself. Sometimes you wonder if you've simply drowned. Or joined the evil."

"But what about you, Daniel? It hasn't affected you that way, has it?"

"But for the grace of—" Daniel whispered. "The whole thing has gone to hell, Will. Irini is dead. And Joshua has gone off the deep end. Do you know that he'd become obsessed with her? He never actually met her. Yet he felt it was his destiny to save her—his own words, more or less. Now he's out there, hunting for Skorpios. We're going to have a big problem with the Greeks if Joshua pulls another stunt. When we started the operation here, I was able to keep everything under the radar. Now we are right up against the line. I'm going to be hearing from my CO, or our embassy, if he makes one more splash. I don't want any of that. I have to find Joshua before he finds Skorpios."

Daniel looked at Knightly.

"So, Will, what brought *you* to Greece?"

"I come here a lot, Daniel, you know. This time it's a little different. I'm divorced now."

"Really? I'm sorry, Will. When did this happen?"

"About a year and a half now."

"Are you okay?"

"I'm fine."

"How are your kids—Peter and Hannah?"

"They're growing up, Daniel. They're almost finished with college."

"I remember them. They're great kids. You should be really proud of them."

"They're doing great, Daniel, thanks. And, yes, I'm incredibly proud of them. As for me, I'm visiting a woman I met here a long time ago."

"Ah! I never heard about her, did I?" Daniel said.

"No, I doubt I ever said anything about her. I thought it was a dead letter, so to speak. In any case, I looked her up when I got here. So far, so good. We're going to spend some time together. She lives in a little village—it's called Kremni, just east of Tripoli. By the way, Daniel, what were you doing in Tripoli?"

"I was tracking down a lead. I was supposed to make contact with someone in Skorpios's network. You know that he's got a healthy portfolio down there in Tripoli. Here it's mainly prostitution and drugs, down there it's drugs and prostitution. Anyway, the guy I was looking for never showed. But you did! I was on my way out when you spotted me."

"Sorry about that," Knightly muttered.

"No harm done—nothing irreparable, anyway," Daniel quipped.

"I probably shouldn't even go there, but—what the hell. How have I done? I mean, if you had to give me a grade. That's a nice way to turn the tables, after all these years. What grade would you give me?"

"Do you really want to know?" Daniel asked.

"No. I mean—yes. Go ahead, shoot!"

"For the Tripoli escapade. Let's just say it wasn't the most auspicious start. I'd have to give you a D—and that's being generous."

"I guess my approach was lacking in stealth."

"An honest self-appraisal."

"What about in Athens? I picked up on your clues, didn't I? Bloody abstruse as they were!"

Daniel laughed. "You did a good job with those. Okay, you get a B for handling the code and carrying out the rendezvous with some discretion."

"Well, I didn't know I was supposed to come in a disguise."

"I thought you *were* in disguise. You did an outstanding job of looking like an academic."

"Okay, okay, *touché*. But wait a minute—what about the alley? That went down pretty well, didn't it?"

"I have to give you some credit there. Your reaction-time was good, as I heard it. Though you came right back to the spot, didn't you, like a freaking boomerang, after you'd cleared out of there?"

"Yes, well. By the way, who were those guys? Do you have any idea?"

"They were from the same bunch that was giving you trouble in Tripoli. They were watching me that day—that was our idea, we were trying to flush them out—the day you saw me..."

"When I went running after you and wrecked it."

"Don't beat yourself up, Will," Daniel joked, "They must have associated you with me. They lost interest in you pretty quickly, but I suspect that when you came back to Athens so soon, you put yourself right back on their radar."

"Okay, I see your point. Even so, I hope I'm passing the course."

"You're doing fine, Will. But don't let it go to your head. We have an agreement, after all, don't we?"

Knightly nodded.

"Daniel, seriously…this woman you mentioned, Ariani. I get the idea that you have feelings for her. Is that right?"

Daniel looked away for a moment. Then he looked back at Knightly.

"I love her. I know that sounds crazy, Will. I haven't known her for that long. Not long at all. But—it's a strange thing. I don't know if I can even explain it. The feelings we have for each other. They're very strong. I've never felt this way about anyone."

"You were dating someone when you were in school, weren't you? I remember her."

"Yes, I was. That lasted for a few years. When I got more and more involved in what I'm doing now, though, we sat down and had a serious talk. The way she cried, you'd have thought I was the one that wanted to break it off. But it was her decision. There hasn't been anybody after that, really. I mean, that I've gotten close to. Until Ariani."

"I hope she's going to be okay. The situation has got to be unbelievably hard on her."

"You know, I think that's why we're so close. Why the feelings we have for each other are so powerful. What she's been through, it makes her able to begin to understand what I've been through. Not the same things exactly. But the intensity, the kinds of things I've had to see—and do. And given what I've experienced I guess I'm in a better position than most to empathize, to understand her and help her talk about what's happened to her. And to her sister."

"Daniel, the police know about you. There's a cop who's approached me a couple of times."

"I know, Will. That's why I don't have a lot of time to wrap this up. The news about most of what is going on here is not official. Hopefully it never will be. But we're pushing it. The sooner this situation is resolved and I get the team out, the better."

"What should I say to this fellow, if he keeps coming around?"

"Don't worry about it, Will. Just clear out. Get out of town, so you won't be around if things get ugly in the next day or two. I don't want to have to worry about you. Go back to Kremni, where that woman of yours is. What was her name?"

"I know it's just a figure of speech, but she's not my woman, Danny. Would that she were! Her name's Elli. Eleftheria, that is."

"Eleftheria—*Freedom*. That's a beautiful name."

Knightly gave a nod. "She *is* beautiful, Daniel, through and through. I wish you could meet her."

Then he reached out his hand, resting it lightly on Daniel's knee.

"I know the timing is terrible, Daniel, but I have to ask. Did you make the right choice?"

Daniel looked at his old teacher.

"No doubt about it. None. No matter what else I've said. This *is* a bad time to ask—at least, under the circumstances, it's hard for me to give you a thoughtful answer. But that has nothing to do with the path I took. It's just a bad time."

"Understood. You would have made a fine scholar, you know. A fine anything, no doubt. But I get the sense that you did take the right path. I just hope it's not too full of these 'bad times,' that's all."

Daniel's phone made a sound. He glanced at it, then looked up at Knightly.

"It's time for us to go, Professor."

The two men got up from their chairs.

"When I open the door, just turn right and go down the hall. You'll see a door—you can get out there. Spiros will be waiting for you. He'll get you back to the hotel."

Knightly grasped Daniel's arm. "Be careful, my boy."

Daniel smiled, "I will, sir. You, too. It was really good to see you again. Thank you for talking. It helped me, it really did. Just like in the old days."

"I hope so," Knightly said. "I know you've got things to do. I'm glad we got a chance to talk. Let's do it again—but let's not wait so long next time!"

"*Hereafter, in a better world than this,*" Daniel said, as he opened the door.

Knightly added, "*I shall desire more love and knowledge of you.*"

And he left the room. Knightly turned and walked to the end of the hallway. He found Spiros waiting for him outside the building and they left together.

10.

COME NEAR, PUT YOUR FEET UPON THE NECKS OF these kings…for thus shall the **Lord** *do to all your enemies against whom ye fight.*

Joshua 10:24-25

There were three men standing in front of the night-club *Jericho* that evening. It was getting late and the air was hot out on the street, a languid night without so much as a hint of a breeze. The three men were talking and laughing, just passing the time. One was the club's bouncer. It was his job to keep things mellow. The other two were cops. They were there to protect the place. They earned a little extra cash that way. And they were able to obtain certain favors on occasion in exchange for their trouble. The women who worked in the club were part of the deal.

What they saw coming down the street a little after midnight caught their attention because it was so weird. It was some idiot with two bimbos. But this idiot stuck out from the usual ones because he was wearing an out-fit that was truly outrageous. A bright yellow tuxedo, with lapels outlined in gold sequins, a white shirt with ruffles, a cummerbund and a bow-tie, both made of what looked like black silk. The clown wearing this outland-ish outfit was also wearing a clown hat—a big white fedora with a black band. And white gloves. The guy strolled up to the three men standing in front of the *Jericho* and he just stopped there and looked at them, as the two bimbos stood, one on either side of him, each one squeezing his arm and pressing against him, ogling at the three men and giggling.

"This is the place I was telling you about, ladies," the strange man said. Then he turned to the bouncer. "Would it be okay if we went inside for a drink? It's not too late?"

The three were silent. They didn't know what to do except laugh at the bizarre character in the yellow suit who had shown up to a strip-club and whore-house with two girls he'd already paid for. *Whatever turns you on.*

The bouncer just looked at him with an expression that seemed to say, "If you've got money, sure, you can come inside and buy all the drinks you want, asshole."

One of the cops simply smiled at the stranger, probably fantasizing about what this guy would be doing with the two whores in just an hour or two. The other cop had a different look, eyeing the strange man suspi-ciously, as they all stood there in front of the club.

"You know what? Wait a minute!" cried the man in yellow suddenly, turning to the girls with an exaggerated look of distress. "I think I've had enough of you two, as a matter of fact. Go home now! *Shoo!*"

He was laughing as he pushed them away. He had come up with a fistful of bills and he was jamming them into the hands of one of the girls and he stuffed a couple of bills down the front of the other girl's dress. Big notes, one-hundred notes, a few for each girl, the men at the door could see—they were nice and new and crisp.

"I think I have something to give you gentlemen, too," said the man. He was an odd one, no doubt about that, but he was amiable enough, smil-ing and laughing, just like the two girls as they shoved off, holding each other up and walking away down the street with their arms around each other. *Probably all high on some shit or other.*

The stranger put a hand into his pocket, fishing around for some more of those big bills. What he pulled out instead was a small gun, really small, a .22—it looked more like a toy-gun or a novelty, like a cigarette lighter.

It was a gun that Joshua had bought in Thessaloniki from a pawn shop, a few blocks from the train station, a run-down section of town. He had taken it home and cleaned it, treated it with loving care. He called it the "Bargain Hunter," because he had bought it for a bargain, barely twenty US dollars, and because he was going to hunt with it. It would prove to be a very good hunter. The gun had no stopping power. But it could kill when used with accuracy and at close range. It killed when you put one shot in each one of the victim's eyes. Killed him just as sure as it would if you used a gun of twice the caliber. And the Bargain Hunter didn't make much noise. It was a modest creature, as far as that went. Just a *pop!* and not much louder than if someone were kick-starting a motorbike or slamming a door.

Pop! Pop! he drilled the first cop directly through his eyes, first one, then two, with a smooth motion and without any hitch *Pop! Pop!* and then the bouncer, one shot in each eye, again, *Pop! Pop!* the third cop, too, the one who'd given him the suspicious look, one shot in each eye. All three went down, almost at the same time.

As he walked past, Joshua gave them a sidelong glance. They were dead. One of the cops and the bouncer looked just as fat and happy as they had a minute ago, when they were still breathing. The other cop, bloody-eyed now, had a leaner look. He'd been the anxious one. "No worries now," Joshua muttered. They would have stayed for another couple hours, until closing time. Then they would have gone home to wives, daughters, girl-friends. And what then? Would they have treated those women with a certain respect? *Then why not these*, he thought, *the least of my sisters*, meaning the women who worked in the bar, that is, who waited to be picked up by some guy off the street, after a couple of drinks and some small talk. Joshua paused, whispering at the three dead men: *Why did you treat the girls that work here like shit, eh? Did you treat your mother that way? Or your wife? Or did you treat them all like shit? All the women you knew? Who the fuck cares! Now you're dead. If only we could leave you like this for a little while, you'd turn into ripe stinking fecal sacks, like you were inside all along, all of your fucking miserable lives!*

"You were all three garbage and of no use to the rest of us," he said to them aloud, "you were dirty pigs—fucking dirty swine. Now you'll pollute the earth no more."

Joshua pushed open the door and as he entered the hallway leading into the club he ejected the clip from the .22 and rammed another one into place. He reached the door at the end of the hall in three strides. A red neon sign glowed above the door,

JERICHO

it said, written in English and in a kind of fancy script.

"*Jericho*," Joshua said to himself, shaking his head. "This must be some kind of joke."

He kicked open the door and walked into the bar. That got the attention of the bartender, whose eyes darted toward the sudden noise. He saw the outlandish figure in the canary yellow suit and floppy white fedora holding a pistol that looked dwarfish in his big gloved hand. Joshua saw the bartender reach under the bar and come up with a sawed-off shotgun. Already in the center of the room, Joshua took one step toward the bartender and calmly drilled him in each eye—*Pop! Pop!*—with the tiny pistol. The man slid behind the bar, hitting his chin on the dark wood as he went down. Another man in a red leather jacket was sitting at the end of the bar, stunned. Recovering himself, he was just slipping a hand inside his

jacket when Joshua strode up to him and put two taps in his forehead—
Pop! Pop!—as the man's eyes crossed in a look of helpless alarm and he fell
backward off the stool.

"Taking out the trash," thought Joshua grimly. He spun around. There
was the booth. It was his target. And it was empty!

"Son of a bitch!" Joshua roared.

At the same instant, the back door of the place was flung open and Taz
crashed into the bar, holding a Beretta, his eyes scanning the space until
they settled in the half-dark on Joshua's features. Taz stopped, startled by
the agonized expression on Joshua's face.

"He's not fucking here! Goddamit, Taz, did you see him go out the
back?" Joshua screamed.

"No way. Nobody went out that way. There wasn't anybody in the back
at all, except for one cook who's shitting bricks right now."

"Son of a fucking bitch." Joshua cursed. He lowered his gun. "He's
slipped through the net again! What the fuck?! There's no way he knew we
were coming. Why'd he change his mind? That dirty son of a bitch. He's
got the fucking ESP, that ugly motherfucking son of a bitch."

Joshua let out this raw stream of expletives in a surprisingly calm tone
of voice. And yet he was trembling with fury. Taz let his arm drop as well,
lowering his weapon. They stood in the middle of the bar, empty now,
save for the two corpses of a couple of former employees, and two or three
patrons, still very much alive, each of whom sat with a young woman, all
of them huddled against the wall, paralyzed with terror, as they waited and
watched the bizarre man who had done the shooting and his newly arrived
accomplice.

Joshua gave them barely a glance. "Fuck you whoring sons of bitches,"
he said in a weary voice. He waved the Bargain Hunter vaguely in their
direction but without interest in continuing the conversation, then nodded
to Taz as if to say *let's go*. They left the bar by the back door, avoiding the

dead bodies that lay in front of the club as well as any crowd or witnesses that might already be collecting there and seeing those bodies and wondering about these men who were freshly slain and how it had happened.

———∿∿∿∿———

Kazantzakis stood leaning against the doorjamb, his handkerchief pressed against his mouth.

Why did the sight bother him? He'd seen bodies before, more than enough, and more than enough murder-scenes in the course of his career. Some he had investigated were grisly, but some were almost sedate, where the murder seemed a matter of quiet disposal. Why had he found this one disturbing? Was it true, then—was he going soft? Or was it the cruelty of this scene, the sadistic touches, that had managed to leap over his defenses, not only offending but sickening him?

He went back in.

His assistant looked at him. "Thirty-nine."

Kazantzakis said nothing. Thirty-nine burn marks on the body of the deceased, made by the glowing tip of a cigarette. Thirty-nine—a number with some resonance. He'd heard it before. But was there a point? Or was it a meaningless symbol, except as a token of the killer's mental disease? There were also cuts all over the body of the deceased. These were numberless—thin cuts, made by a razor or some other very sharp blade. And the most disgusting thing of all was that, at some point during the torture, or after it was all over—a determination he would leave to the medical examiner—the perpetrator had sliced off the victim's genitals and stuffed them into the victim's mouth. In reference to this, the murderer had pinned a note to the flesh of the dead man's chest with the advertisement: BEST I EVER TASTED!

A double entendre, Kazantzakis supposed. But why—why the mockery? Aimed at whom, precisely? At the dead enemy? Or at his friends, intended for the moment when they found him? Or was it directed at himself and at the police? Was it meant not to amuse, but only in fact to belittle us and point to our powerlessness to stop the madness that this killer unleashes at his will?

Homer has his heroes vaunt, Kazantzakis recalled, after they kill their enemies. They do it to magnify the victory over the enemy and stake the first claim to glory. But they also boast and crow over the fallen opponent out of an excess of battle fury, the surge of anger and madness and adrenaline, not to mention the exhilaration of surviving the encounter with an enemy who would have just as gladly killed them.

But this mockery seemed to be an indication of something more. A sign or a cry of a greater fury. Perhaps that, Kazantzakis thought, is where it had come from, the sickening feeling in his gut.

He looked at the body. He knew who this was. The man who had inhabited this body, now mutilated, when the two had a name. Dimitrakis Papagalos. He was called "Takis" on the street. He had a couple of clubs. He was a known associate of Skorpios, and lately he had become nearly as elusive as Skorpios himself. But not elusive enough, apparently.

It wasn't hard to connect the dots. There had been a shooting in a club just after midnight, only a couple of hours ago. It was one of the clubs of the sort that Skorpios liked to frequent, as rumor had it. The man-beast that had done this to "Takis" had wanted information. He was looking for Skorpios. One monster pursuing another. Were they in fact two of the same kind? Or was that the wrong idea?

Is *that* what's really bothering me, Kazantzakis said to himself. That at some level I'm rejoicing at what I see here? To think that someone—angel or animal—is hunting down the monster that we are hunting, too, but that we seem never able to catch? Is what I'm experiencing the taste of a temptation to stand aside and let it happen, let the beast-man hunt Skorpios down and deal with him in the savage way that may in fact be what Skorpios deserves, given what he's done to so many others?

No. There's no real temptation there. The law is the law. And the law must be served. By a man like me, anyway. Barbarism has no place. Not the barbarism of Skorpios or the barbaric acts that this perverted warrior is performing all over the city in pursuit of his great villain. But is it only Skorpios he's after? Would it end if Skorpios fell to him at last?

He wondered how much longer this would go on. He was getting no closer to Skorpios. In fact, Kazantzakis feared that the hunter would drive Skorpios underground for a time, and the carnage would last even longer while the hunt went on. And he would remain helpless, following the bloody trail that was leading him round and round, leading him—the policeman, the representative of the Law—to neither of the men whom he had to find and arrest in order to fulfill that law. He looked once more at the wretched "Takis." A stop had been put to his career outside of the law, but it had not been done by means of the law. Takis's death merely served as a pointer to the violence that would yield eventually and inevitably to the law's power. There could be no other way. Not for Kazantzakis, at least. He would see to it that the law was served, if the task took him to his last breath.

—⁓—

The car had driven by the night-club *Jericho*, barely slowing down. Skorpios had seen what there was to see—a bloody mess—through one of the tinted windows in the back of the car. *Drive on*, he had croaked, *get me out of here!* And the car had accelerated and left the scene behind in a thin cloud of exhaust. Who the hell was it? he wondered. Who is this that's going after me? *They must have gotten to Takis.* He shuddered. *But how?*

He had no idea how. Or who was trying to close in on him in this way. He was only glad that he had had the premonition. That little itch that said, *Don't go there tonight. Change your plan.* Survival. It was always a matter of survival. Trust your instincts. Listen to them. That's a good thing, it's always a good thing. He would go home, go somewhere, get some sleep. No point worrying about this now. Tomorrow he would wake up early and he would get up and he would figure out who it was that was messing with him and that had gotten to Takis and invaded the *Jericho* and he would deal with them in a way that would leave no doubt about who was going to survive this war. He would find out. And he would stop them, whoever it was. They would learn how foolish and how dangerous it was to mess with him. And that would serve a purpose, after all. Better that everyone be given a reminder of how dangerous and useless it was to challenge him. And to witness the pain he would deal out to any fool who tried.

PART THREE

Αετοράχη

the eagle's ridge

1.

THE TRIP WENT QUICKLY—HE WAS LOST IN THOUGHT for most of it. His timing had been good. At first, the road was busy, but after he escaped the city traffic was light. Of course there was the usual craziness. Cars whizzing by in the left lane, passing at breakneck speeds, while in the right lane others seemed to have entered in a secret competition for most bizarre thing on four wheels. His favorite was a truck of remarkable vintage that could not have been doing much over thirty miles an hour, whose owner had loaded on its back an old mattress, along with a rusty bed-frame, an ancient chest-of-drawers, and a pine bench, all of it trussed up with ropes that had seen more years than the sum total of truck, driver, and all the weathered pieces on the back of the truck combined.

The craziness helped. After the onslaught of the past twenty-four hours, Knightly needed a diversion. By finding Daniel or letting Daniel find him, he had done what he set out to do. Now he wanted to be fully there once he returned to Elli in Kremni. But the meeting with Daniel had raised more questions than it answered, as good as it was to see his old student again. He went back over their conversation in his head, until he had exhausted himself with speculating about how it would all play out—everything

Daniel had alluded to. Knightly finally gave in to the sheer animal require-
ments of surviving a drive, even a short one, on the highways of Greece and
put out of his mind all thoughts of the impending battle in the city that he
was leaving behind.

So it was with an even greater relief than usual that Knightly turned
off the national road and took the coast road along the gulf. There were
almost no cars on this stretch of road and the views as one looked out over
the water were as stunning as ever. When he saw the sign pointing toward
Nafplio, he felt the itch to take a detour and visit the town, an outpost of
the imperial Venetians and their gift, unwitting or not, to Greece and to
posterity. *Not now*, he said to himself. It would be a nice outing to take
with Elli, not far from Kremni. Maybe Chrysa could take Giannakis for
the day. Or Giannakis could come along. Knightly wondered what Elli
would want to do.

Myli, Kivéri, Xiropígado. He passed through each place, until he
reached Astros, a truly charming town, and then turned inland, picking up the road to Kremni there. He passed by Kato Doliana, which
he knew had a traditional bakery with splendid breads and *pitas*. It was
tempting to stop, except that he was close to his goal, so he pushed on.
Now that he was headed into the mountains, and the road began to rise,
he began to think of other excursions that he could take with Elli. Why
not take the road to Tripoli, he mused, and just keep going? All the way
to Dimitsana. That would be a wonderful getaway for both of them.
And if Elli thought that it would do Giannakis good to get away as well,
they could all go together.

As he pulled into Kremni, he saw the *plateia* and decided to take the
car all the way to Elli's house. He thought he remembered how to get
there from the square and indeed within minutes he could see the wall
in front of Elli's house and the lemon tree in her yard and the verandah
as well. The street was narrow but he found a place to park where others

coming along the street would be able to squeeze by. Knightly walked to the gate of Elli's yard, opened it and went up to the front door. It was locked. He rang the bell and waited, but he didn't hear anything inside the house. He rang again, then knocked. There was no noise inside at all. He walked around the house, pausing at the verandah in the front and peeking in through the kitchen window on the side of the house. Nothing stirring. No one home.

He hadn't called Elli because he had left Athens more or less suddenly. He had taken Daniel at his word. He saw no reason to hang around the city, so he got up that morning, had a quick breakfast, hopped on the metro to the airport and picked up another car there. Since he would be in Kremni in two or three hours, he decided to surprise Elli. Now it looked as though he was the one who was getting the surprise. He thought of calling her, but then he realized that she might be at Chrysanthi's house, and so he set out in that direction. When he got there, he saw a girl in the yard, picking lemons. Knightly recognized her only because she bore a striking resemblance to her mother.

"*Kaliméra*," Knightly said.

"Καλημέρα," replied the girl, hesitantly.

"I'm sorry, I'm a friend of your aunt's. I'm looking for her. Is your mother home?"

The girl smiled and relaxed a little. "Yes, she's inside. Come on in."

The girl turned, clutching half a dozen fresh lemons, and led Knightly to the door and inside the house.

"Mama," the girl cried.

Chyrsanthi came out of the kitchen and when she saw Knightly she gave a wide smile and greeted him with a hug.

"Will, how are you? It's good to see you."

"It's good to see you, too, Chrysa," Knightly said. "I went to Elli's house, but no one's home. I thought she might be here, but I guess not. Do you know where she is?"

"She's gone to our village. She and Giannakis left early this morning."

Knightly looked puzzled.

"Sit down, Will." She took him into the living room and led him to the couch. She sat down in a chair. "Would you like something to drink? Eva will get you something."

"Is that your daughter's name? She's a lovely girl, Chrysa. And I'm not just handing out compliments today, but she looks like her mom."

Chrysa laughed. "Do you want anything, Will?"

"No, thanks, I'm good," Knightly said. "So why did Elli go to the village. It's Aetoráchi, right? I didn't think you all went there very often—or do you?"

"It's not that far away, but it's far enough," Chrysa said. "So I don't go very often, to be honest. I try not to worry about it, but Elli is different. It bothers her to think of our old house empty, with no one there. She also gets herself upset about our parents. You know, they're buried there, in the cemetery of the village. Obviously, we can't take care of things ourselves. We depend on friends we have there."

"She takes it seriously, I mean, tending their graves?"

"She does, Will. That I understand—I feel the same. You know, that's the way we are. But I'm living here, with my family. You have to be realistic. I tell Elli that she has enough to deal with. She doesn't need to add to it by worrying about our parents' graves. She listens, but she still lets it eat at her. There's nothing I can do about that."

"Was she going to stay there for a while?"

"She was planning on being there for a couple of days. She was expecting you to call, I think."

"That's right. I left Athens a little sooner than I thought. Well, maybe I'll drive up to the village and meet her there."

"I think she'd love to show you around. Do you know how to get there?"

"Let me go get a map."

Knightly went out to the car and returned with a map of the Peloponnese. He sat down on the couch and opened the map, studying it in silence.

"I think I found it," he said. He got up and showed Chrysa where he thought it was.

Chrysa looked at the map for a moment and said, "That's it."

"Aetoráchi—the eagle's ridge," Knightly said. "Is that because you've got to have wings to get to the bloody place?"

"That's another reason I don't get up there very often," Chrysa laughed. "Have you seen the road you have to take to get there?"

"No, but I can imagine. Anyway, it won't be the first time this trip I've risked my life on your mountain roads, Chrysa."

"You're a good sport, Will. I know Elli will appreciate it."

He got up from the couch. "I guess I'll get going. Maybe I can get there for lunch. It was nice seeing you, Chrysa. I'll see you again when we come back down from the mountains, okay?"

Chrysa smiled. "Okay, Will. Sounds good."

Knightly folded the map. He went toward the door and Chrysa followed. When they had reached the gate, Knightly stopped and turned to Chrysa.

"Chrysa," he said, "can I ask you something?"

"Sure, Will, of course. What is it?"

"I had meant to ask you about Giannakis's condition. I see how he doesn't really interact with anyone, even with Elli. Has he been like that for a long time?"

"Yes. He's been like that for five or six years. I know that Elli told you the story. The drugs were hard on him. He had a horrible experience and obviously it took a toll."

"I'm impressed with both of you, how good you are with him."

"Despite what's happened to him, he's really no trouble. It's just that I miss him—you know what I mean? I miss the little boy that he was. I miss our Giannakis."

"I understand, Chrysa. But I guess my other question was about his father. What about him? Why does Elli have to do everything for Giannakis? Is the father still around here? Or did he just disappear?"

Chrysa was silent. She looked at Knightly, as if she were thinking about what to say.

"He wasn't only useless. He was worse than useless."

"Who was it, Chrysa? Does he still live around here? What happened?"

"I'd rather not say, Will," she replied. "Please don't get me wrong, I don't mean to be mysterious. It's just that you and Elli have a lot to catch up on. I know she'll tell you the whole story. I would rather that she told you. I just don't feel right stepping into her place."

"I'm sorry, Chrysa, I didn't mean to put you on the spot."

"No, you didn't, please don't apologize. It's just like I said. Elli will tell you what happened. It's better that she tells you and that she does it when she's ready. Please don't think I'm holding back. I am so glad to see you again, Will. I think it's the best thing that's happened to Elli in a long time. It will be good for her to talk with you."

"It's so good to see her again—I can't tell you. I'll go to Aetoráchi and see if I can find her. Will it be hard to find your house?"

"The village is smaller than this place. Just stop at the *plateia* and ask anyone for the Parthénis house. They'll tell you where it is."

"Okay, I'll say hello to the ancestral manor for you. Take care, Chrysa."

"Good-bye, Will."

Knightly got into the car and drove back to the square. When he got there, he found a place to park. He decided to pick up a bottle of water before he got back on the road. He bought one at the *periptero* and was heading back to his car when he saw a police car coming around the *plateia*. It slowed down and pulled up next to him. The window came down and Knightly saw a young police woman, in full uniform and wearing dark sunglasses. She was looking directly at him.

"Mr. Knightly?" she said.

"Yes, that's me."

"Mr. Knightly, I'm with the police in Tripoli."

Knightly thought about asking to see her badge, but the cruiser and the uniform, not to mention her pleasant yet decidedly authoritative tone made it pointless.

"Inspector Kazantzakis would like to speak with you," she continued, "I've come by to give you a lift. Why don't you hop in."

"I've got a car here," Knightly said, gesturing at the rental.

"I'll give you a ride back here, when you're done," she replied, not unpleasantly, but not quite cheerfully.

Knightly shrugged his shoulders and walked around to the side of the car. When he got in, he held out his hand.

"My name's Will."

"Hello, Will. My name's Athena."

"It's nice to meet you, Athena."

Knightly found his seat-belt and buckled it.

"By the way, I'm not in trouble, am I?"

Athena laughed. "No, Mr. Knightly—I mean, Will. You are not in any trouble. But Inspector Kazantzakis has something he wants to talk to you about. It's important, otherwise we wouldn't be bothering you like this. But you are not in any trouble. I'm sorry if I gave you that impression."

She said it and it was clear that she meant it. She was a decent sort, Knightly thought. He was impressed. He had gotten to know two Greek cops in the space of a week, including this young policewoman, Athena, and he was impressed with both of them. Still, he wondered what in the world Kazantzakis wanted to talk about. He'd find out soon enough, he thought. Important, but no trouble. *We'll see about that*, he said to himself.

2.

THE DRIVE TO TRIPOLI PASSED WITHOUT INCIDENT. ATHENA PROVED to be a delight. She and Knightly discussed various things during the ride. Athena talked about growing up around Tripoli, the decision to join the police force, and the difficulty of juggling the demands of the job and a personal life. Knightly told her why he was in Greece. When he started to describe how he had fallen in love with Greece in the first place, Athena shot him a skeptical look, but the more he spoke, the more she listened with apparent relish while he talked about why he cared so deeply about her country. By the time he had finished they were agreeing heartily that while Greece had many problems where else in the world would anyone with any sense want to live?

When they got to the city, Knightly asked if they could make a quick stop for some food—he hadn't eaten since before he left Athens. She took him into town and he ran into a shop just off the Plateia Petrinou. He came out with two *kalamakia*—skewers of grilled chicken, in this case—wrapped in a pita, and a diet coke. He had offered to get something for Athena but she said "no thank you." When he asked if he could eat in the car, she looked at him with amusement, as if to say, "sure, if you promise not to mess it up." Knightly looked flummoxed.

Athena laughed, "Go ahead! What do you think *we* do?"

So he ate.

They pulled into the small parking lot next to police headquarters. Knightly threw away his trash and they walked toward the building together, Athena waving at the cop who was posted in a kiosk outside and again at another cop who sat at a desk just inside the entrance. They went up two flights of stairs and turned into a hallway. Knightly could see an office at the end of the hall with its door open. There were desks on both sides of the door. One was Athena's, apparently, because she tossed her keys on it. Another cop was seated at the other desk. He was an older man, a little more than middle-aged. He appeared to be going over some papers, though he looked up as they came in. The fellow had a lantern jaw, a large nose and eyes that protruded from underneath thick brows—striking features that however did nothing to dispel the air of dullness surrounding him. He looked back down at his papers without saying a word to either Knightly or Athena.

"Mr. Knightly, this is my colleague. His name is Mitsos."

At the mention of his name, Mitsos raised his eyes again. He looked at Knightly without any particular expression, acknowledging him with a curt greeting.

"*Kalimera.*"

"*Kalimera,*" Knightly replied.

Mitsos went back to his work.

Athena ushered Knightly into the office and he saw Kazantzakis sitting there, speaking to someone on the phone. Kazantzakis smiled briefly at Knightly as Athena gestured for Knightly to sit down. Then she left the office, closing the door. Kazantzakis finished the conversation and set the phone down. Leaning over his desk, he stretched out his hand to Knightly and they greeted one another.

"Thank you for coming in, Professor Knightly. I'm glad to see you."

"It's a pleasure to see you again, Inspector. And I should thank you for sending one of your finest officers to pick me up."

"I thought you'd enjoy talking with Athena."

"I did, as a matter of fact. And I especially appreciated it when she told me I was not in any trouble."

Kazantzakis chuckled softly. "Indeed, I wouldn't correct her. You are not in any trouble, Mr. Knightly. Not with us, at any rate."

Knightly nodded at this, but said nothing.

Kazantzakis was quiet himself, then began to speak.

"I'm glad you've left the city and come back here. The situation in Athens has become complicated. I've learned from certain sources that there is not just one American who is making waves there—you recall our Romanian friend had indicated he was following another American besides yourself that day in Tripoli."

"I remember," Knightly said.

"My sources inform me that an element of one of your American military services has gone amok, that he is in Athens and that members of his unit are trying to track him down. None of this would be any concern of mine, except for the fact that this rogue agent or soldier or whatever he may be is trying to hunt down a figure who goes by the name of Skorpios who happens to be the principal target of the investigation I am conducting. So, quite aside from questions of sovereignty, the activities of this rogue agent are disconcerting, to say the least."

Kazantzakis took a long look at Knightly. He could see that the professor was not surprised by anything he was saying.

"Of course, you probably aren't aware of any of this, Professor," he said, "but if you were, you'd be on the side of those trying to track down this rogue beast, I'm sure."

"Of course, Inspector, that's correct," Knightly said, "I mean, in the hypothetical sense you're talking about."

"The truth is that these things are going on above our heads, Mr. Knightly," Kazantzakis said.

"Above your head, perhaps, Inspector, but certainly far above mine," Knightly added. "But this Skorpios you mentioned…he has a picturesque name, doesn't he?"

"He's earned that name. He earned it by being deadly and by proving elusive, not to say invisible. He started out as a small-time operator, right here in Tripoli, as it happens."

This seemed to catch Knightly's attention, Kazantzakis noted.

"After he acquired sufficient resources," he continued, "he moved to Athens, probably more than twenty years ago by now, and he ceased to operate under his own name. Rather than buy property in a way that would allow it to be traced to himself, he simply loaned out money to others, on various terms, but all of it extremely profitable. And he adopted his nom de guerre—Skorpios, 'the Scorpion.' Hard to see, and very dangerous, once encountered.

"It's hard enough to deal with the average criminal. As it is in your country, I believe, so it is in ours. The law has many safeguards that are designed to protect the innocent and to prevent abuses of authority. Unfortunately, these protections can be exploited in cynical ways, to thwart the law itself. I'll give you an example. Just recently, there was a case in one of the small towns around here, not too far from Kremni, in fact. A local mailman was carrying drugs—I'm not making this up! He had decided to use his delivery route for a secondary purpose. He was put under surveillance and enough evidence was gathered to put him away for a good amount of time.

When he was arrested, however, it was found that he did not have any of the narcotics on his person. His home was searched, turned upside down—nothing. There were hours of surveillance tapes detailing all of the deals he was doing, but this evidence was treated as hearsay. And everyone in town knew what he was up to—more hearsay. Rather than depress you further, let me just tell you that the scoundrel got off scot free."

"I wonder how pleasant his life is at this point," Knightly said, "given that everyone knows what he did."

"He was dismissed when charges were filed," Kazantzakis said, "but that order was challenged and overturned once he was acquitted and he was reinstated in his old job. He's back walking his former beat!"

Knightly scowled. "And yet, if certain citizens were to take matters into their own hands," he said, "let's say some of the parents of the kids who got their drugs from 'the mailman,' then they'd be punished for anything they did to him, correct?"

"The concept of 'self-help' is not looked upon as sympathetically in the modern age as it was in ancient times, as you know, professor. But it's even worse than that. The law is heavily constrained, as I said—and I'm not sure you or I would want to do away with that—but the criminals have thoroughly penetrated the law itself. Let me put it this way. Who knows the way the black market works better than those who are assigned to fight it? Who study it and pursue it, until they either get very good at interrupting it or decide that there's too much easy money to be made for them not to get involved themselves. There are some in the police—I can hardly call them colleagues—who have ended up working with the likes of Skorpios. Warning them of investigations, moving freight for them, whether it's drugs or arms or stolen goods—or even human beings. Providing muscle or looking the other way when the bosses use muscle to intimidate or punish clients who step out of line. Corruption is an enormous problem here.

It's the same elsewhere, even in your country. But here in Greece, where the country is so small, the problem takes on greater proportions."

As Kazantzakis finished his speech, Knightly noticed for the first time that the inspector looked tired.

Kazantzakis shook his head, then looked up at Knightly. Again he saw that the professor did not seem surprised by anything he had told him. When he spoke again, he was watching Knightly carefully.

"There is something else I need to share with you, Professor Knightly. I am not sure whether I should say anything—it's a difficult matter. But I've decided it would be best that I told you what I know. I feel that you should be aware—"

Knightly was suddenly on the edge of his chair.

"What—?" he said abruptly, "what are you talking about?"

"It has to do with your friend, Eleftheria Parthenis," Kazantzakis said.

The inspector watched the blood drain from Knightly's face. Knightly sat motionless as he listened to what Kazantzakis was telling him.

"You see, Mr. Knightly, we believe that Mrs. Parthenis and the man we are calling Skorpios were involved at one time. It was a long time ago, almost twenty-five years at this point. We really owe you a debt of gratitude. We had no idea who Skorpios was—I mean, what his real name was—until Athena looked into Mrs. Parthenis's past."

Knightly stiffened at this, but did not utter a word.

"It's stunningly fortuitous," Kazantzakis continued, "but we only discovered him, so to speak, when you caused us to look in a direction we wouldn't have looked in otherwise. We believe that the man now known only as Skorpios once went by the name of Angelos Mavroudís. He managed a restaurant in Tripoli, where your friend Eleftheria worked as a waitress. They had a child together, a boy, named Giannakis, twenty-four years ago. We don't know the circumstances, but we do know that they were married only three months before the boy was born. And the marriage was ended just two months after that. It must not have been a happy situation."

Kazantzakis saw that Knightly's face was ashen. He suddenly felt tremendous pity for the professor. It was obvious that the story he was telling Knightly was complete news to him and had sent him into shock.

"I'm sorry, Mr. Knightly," Kazantzakis said.

"No, Inspector, no, don't be sorry," Knightly stammered. It was not clear where he was looking, his eyes barely focusing.

"I hope you don't feel I've interfered in your private business by telling you this about Mrs. Parthenis," Kazantzakis said. "You must believe me, I was startled when I found out about the connection to this Skorpios. I considered talking to her about it, but I decided against it. It doesn't seem right to call her in or bother her, since it's been such a long time. Still, this matter troubles me."

"I can't believe she has anything to do with that man anymore," Knightly sputtered, trying to shake off the sudden paralysis.

"I'm sure you're right," Kazantzakis replied. "I don't think there's any contact between them now and there probably hasn't been for a long time. Even so, I thought it would be best for you to know."

Kazantzakis was about to say more, but when he looked at Knightly the professor looked so ghastly that he stopped himself.

"Can I get you a glass of water, Professor Knightly?" Kazantzakis asked.

"No, thank you, Inspector," Knightly answered. "This has come as a shock, as you can imagine. I don't know what to say."

Knightly stared intently at Kazantzakis.

"I have a feeling that something terrible must have happened," he said, "between Elli and this—this Mavroudís. I don't know—I want to talk to her about it, but how? If it was an ugly situation, it won't be easy for her to talk about—it will be torture!"

"I was thinking the same thing," Kazantzakis said. "That's why I wanted you to know. Now that you know, you can decide how best to approach it."

"Inspector, you're telling me that they worked at the same place?"

"That's correct."

"And that this man was Elli's boss?"

"Apparently. According to tax records—not always perfectly forthcoming, but with respect to this detail, it seems, they're accurate—he worked there as manager."

"And something must have happened—they had a child together?"

"The hospital record of the birth of Eleftheria's son lists the father as one Angelos Mavroudís. There is also a record of a marriage with the church. It's the same name, along with Mrs. Parthenis's, of course. She became, though for only a brief time, Mrs. Eleftheria Mavroudís. Around this same time, Mr. Mavroudís's name appears on the title of a property in Tripoli. He bought it with cash and some credit but paid off the loan in just under three years. He then sold the property—it was a club—to two men who later were arrested on various charges, including racketeering. Drugs and prostitution, mainly. After that, Angelos Mavroudís disappears from the face of the earth."

"Wait, Inspector. You're certain that this is your man? How can you be sure? Do you really think that this Mavroudís character is Skorpios?"

"Mavroudís was charged himself. But nothing came of it. He was never even brought to trial. Then he disappears. No mention of the name again anywhere. Yes, Mr. Knightly, the idea that this Mavroudís and our man Skorpios are one and the same, it's an hypothesis. But it seems to be a good one. We know that Skorpios started in Tripoli. The people we've talked to are clear on that point. And I suspect that the moment when Mavroudís disappears from the record is the time when Skorpios left Tripoli for wider pastures. He went to Athens and he thrived in the city. It turned out to be a highly successful move."

Kazantzakis looked at Knightly, who seemed to have recovered a little. "I'm sorry, Mr. Knightly, really—"

"No, please, Inspector," Knightly insisted, "You did the right thing. I think that I would have been more upset with you if I had found out you knew all of this and you hadn't told me. It's better to know what one is dealing with."

"I'm sure Mrs. Parthenis would have told you in time. But, as you said, it would be extremely difficult for her. Now you can help her talk about it, if that's what you want to do."

"I do, Inspector, I do. I can't believe what she's been through. This, too—on top of everything else."

"Would you like to have Athena drive you back to Kremni, Mr. Knightly?"

"Yes, please, Inspector. Whatever I'm going to do, I'd like to get started with it."

Knightly looked at Kazantzakis and held out his hand. The inspector grasped it and the two men shook hands.

"Well, Inspector, I don't suppose you have a *mantinadha* for me this time, do you? I would be amazed if you have one ready at all, all the more so if you have one that's suited for *this* occasion."

"Professor, you do realize that what you have just said would be taken, in my native Crete, as a direct challenge—nay, even as a serious affront. You may as well have drawn your dagger and confronted me with that!"

Knightly smiled.

"I do have one, of course," Kazantzakis said, "—or I'll make one up as quickly as I can think of it. Okay, how about this:

In war we struggle for honor, to win or lose on the field,
While in love it's survival first and the hope we need to heal."

Knightly gazed at Kazantzakis with a certain wonder.

"I am putting the dagger back in its sheath, my friend. I wouldn't dare to challenge you. That is a lovely couplet, and fitting, too—and you did it on the spot!"

"Years of practice, dear Professor. Years of hearing these poems and years of making them up myself. And perhaps some advantage in respect to the genetic material."

As Kazantzakis and Knightly came out of the office, Athena got up from her desk.

"Shall I give Mr. Knightly a ride back to Kremni?"

"Yes, Athena. We must let him go. He has matters to attend to."

Knightly turned to Kazantzakis once more.

"Thank you, Inspector. I am grateful to you for our talk."

"Don't mention it, Professor. Good luck, and even while you are out there in the countryside, or up in the mountains, tread cautiously."

"I will heed the advice," Knightly said.

Athena had her keys in her hand. She smiled at Knightly, who followed her down the hall and out of the police building as they stepped into the brilliant light of day once again.

3.

KNIGHTLY WAS SILENT AS THEY LEFT TRIPOLI AND HEADED toward Kremni. Athena waited until he said something and then slowly they began to talk about the situation in Tripoli and the surrounding towns and about the investigation, even if in general terms. She told him how the city absorbed a good deal of the drug trade but how it extended to the local towns as well. The market for substances of all kinds was flourishing. Knightly asked what kids were using these days, and whether marijuana was popular. We used to call it *weed*, he said, back in the day. Sure, she answered, the kids around here smoke a lot of *grass*—*hórto*, she said, using the slang—but they're into harder stuff, too. Knightly asked whether it felt like an impossible task, to stop the trafficking, like trying to keep the waves from reaching the shore. Athena frowned. *It's a full-time job, for sure.*

When they reached Kremni, Athena asked Knightly if he'd like her to take him to Elli's house, where he had left his car. He said it would be better to drop him off at the square. *What will the neighbors think if they see me pull up in a police cruiser from Tripoli!* Athena laughed and said she would leave him at the *plateia*. As he got out, he thanked Athena for the ride. She smiled at him. She was happy to do it, she had enjoyed talking with him.

Good luck, Mr. Knightly, she said. *Thank you, Athena.* He closed the door. The cruiser sped away and disappeared down the street.

Knightly set off at a brisk pace. He saw the same shops as before and passed all the now familiar landmarks. About half-way, he came to the house of the old lady. She was sitting in her courtyard, just in front of her house, watching the street. He managed to escape with a simple *kalimera* as he smiled at her and kept up a quick pace. Maybe she recognized me, maybe she didn't, he thought. He would put money on her powers of recollection, however, and either way she'd have a story to tell when the women of the neighborhood dropped by later in the evening.

It was already past five o'clock when he got into the car. He headed back to the square and pulled over to look at the map—how far before he turned off to go to Aetoráchi? It came up soon enough and the road to Aetoráchi was actually marked with a sign. The road climbed steadily from that point on, with every turn of the switch-back road putting Knightly on another loop from which he could take in the impressive views of the slopes that swept down the sides of these local hills, covered in clusters of pine, in the ubiquitous rock and scrub redolent of wild oregano and thyme.

He took his time and arrived at the village about forty-five minutes later. He pulled up in front of the single taverna that stood at the head of the *plateia* of Aetoráchi—there weren't a lot of options, he noted—and got out of the car. He decided to go into the place and ask for directions to Elli's family-home. He stepped into the taverna. It was just six o'clock and no one was there, except for an older woman who was working in the kitchen that was open to the rest of the taverna and was fitted with the usual grill-surfaces and a heavy skewer on which chickens were already turning and sweating over hot coals.

Knightly asked the woman about Elli's house and she smiled graciously and walked to the door with him to point him in the right direction. Knightly thanked her and as he left he told her that the food smelled delicious and he would come back soon for a meal. She smiled again and said, *Very good, sir*, and went back inside to her work. Knightly cast a longing eye back at the fragrant, glistening rotisserie, and then set off in the direction that the woman of the taverna had indicated.

He found Elli's house and knew it immediately because she was sitting on the front porch. It almost looked as if she was waiting for him.

"Aren't you surprised to see me?" he said.

"Not really, Will. Chrysa's already been here!" she said.

"What?" he exclaimed.

"She told me she'd seen you and you'd be coming by soon. She took Giannakis for the night." She paused and smiled. "My sister said we ought to have some time alone."

Knightly smiled and shook his head. "Your sister is a sweetheart, that's for sure."

"So, no, I'm not surprised to see you, Will. But I'm very *glad* to see you!"

Elli got up and ran down the steps to give Knightly a hug. He held her for a moment and then kissed her on the cheek. She took his hand and they went inside the house.

"I'm glad to see you, too, Elli. You have no idea!" Knightly said.

As they stepped into the house, Knightly had the feeling that he had stepped back in time. It could have been the sixties, even the fifties. The place looked and felt as if it was still inhabited by the parents, Elli's and Chrya's, yet everything felt clean and fresh at the same time. It was an odd feeling, almost provoking a sense of vertigo. The place felt uncanny, Knightly realized, mainly because the furniture and the knick-knacks and pictures that filled the house all belonged to that bygone era and faithfully preserved the presence of those who had collected these accouterments of everyday life and dwelled among them for so many years.

They sat down on a couch and Knightly looked out the window and then began to study the curtains framing it that were made of a delicate white-lace.

Elli looked at Knightly and said, "Chrysa also told me that you were in Tripoli and that you were talking to the police! Is everything all right, Will? What's going on?"

"Everything's fine, Elli. It's a long story but, look, here's the gist of it. I saw a former student of mine the very first day I was in Tripoli. It turns out he was involved in something that also concerned the police—"

Elli gave a look of alarm but Knightly reassured her.

"He has done nothing wrong. It's complicated. He works for the U.S. government, in fact, in a certain capacity. I don't know the whole story," he said, bending the truth somewhat, "and I don't care to know. The police wanted to talk with me, but it was mostly a formality, as it turned out. Thank goodness!"

"But what was it all about?" Elli asked. "What did it have to do with your student?"

"The policeman I spoke with just now—it's Kazantzakis, the same one I talked to when my room was broken into in Tripoli, remember him? He's a good man. Anyway, he's investigating someone who's a big drug dealer, mostly in Athens, but here in this area, too."

Knightly saw Elli shudder when he said "drug dealer" and he regretted his choice of words.

"This Kazantzakis fellow thought that my old student might have some information about a key figure in the case. Given the kind of work my student does. It became obvious pretty quickly that I had nothing to contribute to the discussion. Anyway, it was this student of mine that I was trying to track down in Athens. That's why I had to disappear so suddenly, Elli. I wanted to try to find him. I missed him in Tripoli—it was a strange encounter—and so I wanted to put my mind at rest and make sure he was okay."

"Did you find him?"

"I did—I got lucky. Anyway, we had a great talk. He's fine. It was really good to see him. It had been a long time."

Elli touched Knightly on the shoulder, smiling at him.

"This seems to be the theme of your visit, Will. Reunions and rendez-vous with old friends."

"I came here to see you, Elli. This other thing—seeing my old student, Daniel—was a complete surprise. But it does remind me how much I have to be grateful for."

Knightly stopped talking. He looked at Elli, taking a moment to drink in the extraordinary beauty of her features. The sun was lower now and the light was coming in directly and washing over every detail in the room in a final outpouring of exuberance. Elli's hair was ablaze, the sunlight turn-ing its coal-dark color to a fiery red and tracing a few fine stray hairs that floated around her head like white-hot filaments. She looked beautiful, serene, well-nigh angelic, Knightly thought. *Is this really the time*, he asked himself, *to bring up what I want to talk with her about?*

"Elli, there's something else."

Elli waited as Knightly thought about what he wanted to say next.

"The man that Kazantzakis is investigating is a big deal, apparently. He goes by an alias nowadays. He's called Skorpios."

Knightly saw Elli's eyes flash.

"Skorpios?" she said.

"Right. Skorpios. 'The Scorpion.' He's dangerous, brutal, in fact, and also very hard to track down. I'm not sure that Kazantzakis has been on the case for years, but he's been looking for this Skorpios for a while and so far he's come up with very little. The man is elusive. He operates in the shadows. But the police do know, or at least they are fairly sure that Skorpios started out here in Tripoli. That's the weird thing. In fact—"

Knightly paused and he looked at Elli. He saw that she was looking at him curiously.

"Elli," he said, "when the police looked into me, as a routine matter, they found out that I was visiting you, so they looked into you, too—again, as a routine matter. This is what the police do, I guess. They keep looking, working from what comes their way, probing, gathering information, sifting, making connections, until they come up with a story that tells them what they want to know."

Knightly saw Elli's eyes go wide.

"Elli, the police think they have found out who Skorpios was before he became Skorpios. They believe he's originally from Tripoli, born and raised there, worked there for a while, got involved in criminal activity, and then moved to Athens and hit the big-time, so to speak. The police think they've found out who he was, back then. They think that at that time he went by the name of Angelos Mavroudís. I don't know how to say this, Elli. They've found records—"

Elli looked horrified. Her lips quivered but otherwise she sat unmoving, like stone. Knightly looked at her and he felt sick but he kept on with what he was saying.

"They have found records that indicate that you and he were involved. That Mavroudís was Giannakis's father, in fact. Is it true? It's not hard to read between the lines, Elli. It looks like the guy was a creep. That he was capable of terrible things. What happened? What happened between you and this guy, Angelos Mavroudís—this Skorpios?"

Elli had started to shake just before Knightly stopped speaking. She had gone pale, staring at the floor, silent. Suddenly she looked up and her eyes were wide again and flashed angrily as she spoke to Knightly.

"I can't believe the police told you that! This inspector—whatever his name is—Kazantzakis—what right did he have to tell you all this! What right do they have to look into my personal business? I don't understand it. And then to go ahead and tell you about it—what was the point?"

She was shaking and her eyes were filling with tears as she looked at Knightly.

"Elli, I'm sorry, I didn't want to tell you about this. But I didn't know how I could just sit here and hold it all back. Please don't blame Kazantzakis. I don't blame you for being upset, but he was just relaying information—"

"Relaying information!" she shrieked, rolling her eyes.

"I think he cares, I really do," Knightly insisted. "I think he realized how hard all of this would have been for you to tell me. And I guess he assumed that you would have wanted to tell me. And that I would want to know about anything that had happened to you that was this important. Am I making sense—?"

The look of anger and disgust on Elli's face had begun to soften. She looked pale again. The corners of her mouth were screwed back in an anguished expression as if she were trying to speak while choking on something. She began to totter and at last she fell against Knightly's shoulder and dissolved into tears, sobbing, shaking, helpless in a way that terrified Knightly and made him feel an unbearable sadness for her.

"Elli, Elli, I'm sorry!" he said.

He couldn't see her face. She had buried it in his chest, but it felt to him as if she were trying to say something, a single word—"*no!*"

They stayed that way. Elli shaking, sobbing, Knightly holding her, both silent, for a long time. At last, Knightly sat up and gently helped Elli straighten herself. He brushed the hair from her eyes and stroked her cheek.

Looking at her, their eyes meeting, he said softly, "Elli, please, tell me. Tell me what happened? What in God's name was it? What happened back then?"

"I wanted to tell you, Will. But it's hard. I suppose I should be grateful to your inspector friend. I didn't know how I was going to do it."

She sighed deeply, a shudder running through her. She began to talk.

"It was just after we met. Just after you left and went back home. I was working at the restaurant. I thought about you constantly. I waited for you to write to me."

Knightly swallowed hard. He recalled what it had been like when he got back home. How he had thought about Elli, too, but how he had let the time go by, how he had procrastinated, before he sat himself down and put pen to paper. Fatal delay, he thought.

"Mavroudís was managing the restaurant. I don't know if he's the Skorpios that the police are looking for or not. I do know that he got involved in shady dealing, but I didn't find that out until later. When I first knew him, he was just Angelos Mavroudís, the manager of the place where I worked. Anyway, he asked me out. It was barely a week after you left. I said no. He kept asking. After a while, I felt foolish. He said it was no big deal. Just a drink. Just friends. And you didn't write. I started to doubt what had happened with you and me. It started to feel slightly unreal, or like I had misunderstood what had gone on. As if I made too much out of it or had made something up in my head that wasn't really what you were feeling yourself. So, finally, I agreed to go out with him. We went out once or twice, for coffee. It was okay. He was pleasant enough. He seemed like a successful man. And he was ambitious. He would talk about what he wanted to accomplish. He was working hard and the restaurant was doing well enough but he had hopes that he could do more. I was impressed by what he said—I was so naïve. There was nothing evil in him as far as I could see at that point.

"One night, it was late, we were closing. Everyone was leaving, one by one. I was cleaning up. Mavroudís was in the office, going over the checks and making sure everything added up. Just like any night. By the time I had finished, we were alone in the place, everyone else had gone home. He was sitting at his desk. I came in to say goodnight and he began to praise me, saying how good I was and how I was so loyal and worked so hard and what would he do without me. He talked about how difficult it was to keep the place going, the expenses, the competition. I was flattered by the praise but even more flattered that he confided in me. Or should I say I was taken in by his act. He apologized and asked if I would mind bringing him something from the kitchen because he had more work to do. I brought him some food and he thanked me and asked if I'd just keep him company while he ate. I was tired but I said yes. We talked. I was exhausted and I didn't feel like eating anything but I had a glass of wine while he ate. Maybe two. I don't remember much after that. I do remember him on top of me—"

Elli said this so calmly, it startled Knightly.

"I barely even remember going home that night. But when I woke up early in the morning, I felt terrible. I was in shock. I was confused, embarrassed, ashamed. And then, the more I thought about what happened, I got angry. I couldn't *believe* what had happened. I couldn't believe that he would do what he did. And I couldn't believe that I had been so stupid, to get myself into that situation."

"Elli," Knightly said, "you were raped. You didn't get yourself into any situation. You didn't do anything. He raped you. It's that simple."

"You and I can say that now," she said, "but at the time—it was difficult, Will. It was very difficult. I knew what he had done. But I didn't know what to do about it."

"Did you go to the police?" Knightly asked.

"I thought about it," she said. "But, no, I didn't. I was afraid. Who would believe me, if it came to that? I was a young girl, a waitress, and he was a man, an older man. At that point, he was successful, hard-working, or at least that's how I saw him. Who would believe me over him, I thought? Policemen would come into the restaurant, and he would pal around with them. I imagined trying to tell one of them what had happened. It was too humiliating."

"I understand," Knightly said.

"I just stayed home for a couple of days. I really didn't know what to do. My family was in the village here, but they may as well have been in Thessaloniki. I felt completely alone. I went back to work, but I avoided him. I wouldn't look at him or speak to him. Finally, he came up to me. He took me aside and told me how horrible he felt about what happened. He said he was ashamed. Talk about an act! He was the very picture of contrition. I didn't buy it. He disgusted me. But he did manage to fool me about his intentions. Every chance he got, he told me he was sorry. He wouldn't blame me if I hated him. What he had done was unforgiveable. He claimed that he had feelings for me. He said he felt things for me he had never felt before. He said he loved me and he was afraid that I was young and pretty and I would never love someone like him. So that when he had a chance to talk with me and 'pour out his heart' and I was so kind to him he got confused. He was drunk and he acted out of instinct, so he said, and that was why he did what he did and he realized he had made a terrible mistake. He told me that he would understand if I never spoke to him again. But he just wanted me to know that he was sorry and ashamed and he wished he could erase what happened but he couldn't. He asked me to forgive him if I could some day.

"I didn't buy it. I hated him. But he was successful, Will, because he managed at least to blunt my anger. So I kept working there. It was uncomfortable, but I kept working. Then I started to feel sick, every morning, same thing, a nauseous feeling that wouldn't go away. I was pregnant. At that point, I really didn't know what to do. I thought about having an abortion, but I couldn't bring myself to do it, even though I hated the thing inside me, whatever it was, at first. Before I could form a plan, before I could even call Chrysa and ask her to come to Tripoli, Mavroudís figured out what was going on. He took me aside again and asked if I was pregnant and I told him that, yes, I was. He looked at me very seriously and said that he had a proposal to make and would I please hear him out. He said he felt responsible and, since he couldn't change what happened, would I consider at least letting him help with the child, assuming I wanted to have it. It was up to me, he said. Very decent of him. But if I wanted to have the baby, he would be willing to marry me. I almost hit him when he said that. But he said that of course it would only be a marriage on paper. It would give the child a name, it would lend some dignity to what was happening, and it would insure that the baby and I would not go hungry. I believed him. I thought he was doing the right thing because he was truly ashamed. Of course, he was just shutting me up. Ironically, he was as afraid that I would make trouble for him as I was of going to the police with my story.

"So we got married. That is, we went through the formalities. And Giannakis was born. He had a name. And I received support from Mavroudís, for a while at least. For a couple of months, he sent me money. I had gone to live with Chrysa at that point. It was incredibly difficult to tell my parents. I avoided it as long as I could. When I told them they had a grandchild, they were confused, to say the least! Chrysa came to my rescue, as usual. She explained to our mother that I had met someone and he had seemed so nice and that we had gotten married but that it turned out that he was abusive. She told Mama that I was too humiliated to tell them. It worked out in the end. Giannakis was a beautiful baby and soon they forgot all about where he came from. Or at least they put a good face on things and never bothered me about it. We said very little about the whole thing to anyone else in the village. Not an easy feat, as you can imagine."

Knightly stared at Elli and said nothing. "Jesus," he said, finally, "I can't believe it, Elli. What you had to deal with! It must have been incredibly difficult to go through with the pregnancy. How in the world did you do it?"

"It was not easy, Will, it's true. I thought very seriously about getting an abortion. I hated the thing—especially at first, when I was sick every day. And it made me think of him, of Mavroudís. But as time went by I started to feel differently. Whatever was growing inside me—I know it's going to sound ridiculous to you, but I started to feel a bond with it. Eventually, of course, I could feel it move, and kick, and the whole thing, you know. I started to talk to it. I began to identify with the baby inside me. It was as innocent as I was of what that man had done. I felt sorry for it. Finally, I felt a tenderness for it. For him. At some point, I don't remember exactly when, he became my little boy. I think I figured out it was going to be a boy—I didn't have an ultrasound or anything like that, I just had an intuition about it. I named him Giannakis before he was born. My father's name was Giannis. So the baby inside me became Giannakis.

"I can understand perfectly why a woman in the same position might get an abortion. There are infinite circumstances, and every woman has to do what she feels is right under the circumstances she has to deal with. I was feeling isolated in Tripoli, I was young, and I was too ashamed and afraid to reach out to anyone, even my own sister, until it was already an accomplished fact. If my circumstances had been different, I might have made a different decision. But I don't regret the decision I made. Giannakis gave me a very great happiness, once he was born. He has been nothing but a blessing to me. I don't regret—I have *never* regretted the fact that he is in my life—not one bit."

Elli was looking at Knightly and he saw that her color had returned. The light was fading in the room but it still lit her face so that it shone with a subdued strength. Knightly was about to say something when she put her fingers to his lips and stopped him.

"You've listened to me talk on and on, Will. Why don't we take a break? I haven't been very hospitable. When was the last time you ate? You must be starving! Come into the kitchen and I'll get you something to eat."

They went into the kitchen and Knightly sat down in a heavy wooden chair while Elli looked in the refrigerator.

"I have things for salad. What else would you like, Will? I have some *moussaka*, it's nothing fancy, I'm afraid…"

"*Moussaka* would be great, Elli *mou*."

She turned on the oven and started to chop vegetables she had taken out for the salad. When she put the *moussaka* in the oven and it began to warm up, the kitchen filled with aromas of cinnamon and nutmeg and a hint of *bakhéri*.

"Let's have some wine," Elli said. "Would you open a bottle, Will?" and she nodded toward a couple of bottles standing on the counter next to the refrigerator.

Knightly picked up one of the bottles and examined it.

"This is making me very happy, Elli. A red from Nemea."

"Go for it," Elli said.

"It smells fantastic in here, by the way."

"I wish I could say I made it, but I didn't—it's from the lady who runs the taverna."

"I met her today, as a matter of fact."

"She's very sweet, and she's a wonderful cook."

"She looked like she knew her way around the place and, yes, she was very friendly."

Knightly opened the wine and found a couple of glasses. He poured a little in each and offered one to Elli.

"To the cook," he said.

She had a loaf of bread next to the cutting board and she tore off a piece of it and offered it to him.

"Try this."

Knightly put it in his mouth.

"It's delicious."

They tasted the wine.

"This is delicious, too. It will go great with the *moussaka*."

"I think it's ready," she said, and turned off the oven.

She put out the salad with some bread and they ate these as they talked. Knightly asked about the house, about what Elli remembered about growing up there, about her mother and father, were they from Aetoráchi or from someplace else. When they finished the salad, Elli got up and took the *moussaka* out of the oven. She uncovered it and cut a piece for Knightly. She put it in front of him and he grunted with satisfaction.

"I wish I could say I made it," she said.

"You and our lady of the taverna would make a great team, Elli," he said, as he took a bite.

She poured the wine and they ate the food and Knightly asked again about how it was when Elli and Chrysa were young and growing up in this tiny village high in the hills of eastern Arcadia. Elli asked if he wanted more and Knightly obliged her, saying, *A little more, Elli, sure,* and she poured a little more wine for each of them, and the stories of the old days continued, with Knightly pressing her to tell him more, of aunts and uncles, of feast days of saints, holidays, name-days, of births and passings, funerals and ritual days of remembrance. Until Knightly had emptied his plate again and Elli asked if he wanted anything else, and Knightly put up his hands as if to say, "I surrender." *Hórtasa—I'm stuffed!*

Elli laughed and said, "Okay, I won't tell my poor old friend that you hated her *moussaka!*"

Elli got up and cleared the dishes.

"Let me wash them, Elli," Knightly said, getting up from his chair.

"No, Will, thank you," she said.

She washed them and gave them a quick rinse. Then she turned to Knightly, who was standing beside her.

"Come here, Will. I want to show you something."

She led him out of the kitchen and through the living room, down a hall that led past a couple of bedrooms. At the end of the hall, she opened a door and they went in. Knightly saw it was a fairly large room. It was neat enough but felt like it had not been entered for a long time.

"I never go in here," Elli said. "But I wanted to show you something."

It looked like the room of a teenager, only of someone who was a teenager ten years ago. There were posters on the wall of soccer players and rock bands, all from the late nineties. Elli led Knightly to a desk which was placed against the wall underneath a large window with wide panes that looked out over the yard on the side of the house. There were a few books on the desk along with some bric-a-brac. Elli reached for something at the far edge of the desk beneath the window. Picking it up carefully, she turned toward Knightly to show it to him. He saw that it was a plastic model of a fighter jet. It looked like an F-15 or F-16, he couldn't tell. The plane was painted a gun-metal grey and affixed with decals that marked it as one of the jets in a squadron of the Hellenic Air Force.

"Do you know about the Icari, Will?" Elli asked.

"That's what they call the young pilots, right? The ones who are training to fly the jets?"

"That's right," Elli said, as she handed the model to Knightly.

He took it from her and studied it. The plane had been put together with loving care. There was not a drop of excess glue at the seams and the painting had been done meticulously. Two tiny model pilots sat in the cockpit, forward and aft. They seemed to be ready even at this moment to take their craft into the skies.

"I remember I was in Delphi once," Knightly said, "and I heard a tremendous roar. I looked up, and there was a pair of jets, just like this one. They were flying through the valley, winding in and out of every turn of the hills, hugging the land. It was terrifying but it was thrilling, too. I've seen it on the islands as well—over on Lemnos or Samos. Did Giannakis ever experience that? Did he ever see them fly over?"

"There's a big base in Tripoli. They train there. Giannakis saw them fly over here many times. He absolutely loved that."

Elli smiled at Knightly, as she remembered.

"That's all he wanted to do, Will. That's what he wanted to be, when he was a young boy. He wanted to join the Icari. He told me he wanted to learn how to fly the jets. He wanted to be one of them. Boyish dreams!"

Knightly was about to say something but he looked at Elli and saw that once again her eyes were glistening. He put the model back on the desk and slowly wrapped his arms around her and squeezed her.

"We all dream like that. It's a beautiful thing. He took a lot of trouble making this, Elli. He must have dreamed about this a lot."

"It's all he would talk about, for years!" She laughed. "I wanted to show you, Will. It's another side of Giannakis, you know?"

Knightly nodded. "I understand."

"Let's go sit on the verandah," she said, taking his hand.

Elli closed the door behind them as they left the room. They walked down the hall and into the living room and went out through a sliding-glass door that led to the verandah. They sat down on a small wicker couch. Elli put her feet up on the thin iron railing and leaned back on a plump cushion and they sat there together and looked out into the coming night.

"I just can't believe what you had to deal with, Elli," Knightly said. "And all that time, I was clueless. I had no idea what you were going through."

"How could you have known? I didn't tell you anything."

"So that's why the letters never got answered?" he asked.

"I couldn't bring myself to tell you, Will. I was afraid of what you would think. And I didn't even know what to say. It was a horrible time—it's hard to imagine now."

"So my letters came just a little too late?"

"I'm not sure it would have made any difference. It's just the way it had to happen, I suppose. But maybe if I had been smart enough to steer clear of him—"

"Don't take any of the blame on yourself, sweet girl, no way!" Knightly said. "It belongs exclusively and solely to that bastard, believe me."

Elli flashed a smile at him and fell silent. Knightly stared into the distance.

"There's just one other thing, Elli," Knightly said. "It's been a long time. You've had to take care of Giannakis all on your own. Okay, Chrysa's been a huge help, but still wouldn't it have been easier with somebody else to help you? I mean, didn't you ever meet anybody you liked? You're a beautiful woman, Elli. You're intelligent, kind—you've got it all. So how is it that somebody didn't just come along and beg you to marry him? Honestly, I don't understand it."

"I never met anyone I wanted to marry, Will. That's all it was. I don't mean to say there hasn't been anyone at all. I mean, I would meet people and I went out on dates. I don't want you to think that I've had nothing but misery—I haven't been cloistered or anything like that. But look around here and look at Kremni. These are small towns and there aren't a lot of men to choose from. It doesn't help when you interrupt the natural order of things, either. If I had been in Tripoli or even gone to Athens, maybe I would have had a better chance of meeting someone. Or if I had stayed and gone through the courtship rituals around here, maybe things would have been different. But when I came back I already had a child. A lot of the girls and boys I went to school with had grown up and gotten married and their lives were on track. Even my old friends found it hard to deal with my situation, unfortunately. I found out that a lot of my former friends weren't all that open-minded or generous about what had happened to me."

"You've got to be kidding!" Knightly said.

"I wish I were. Like I told you, Chrysa is my best friend. My one true friend, really."

"I understand, Elli, but that still hurts a little," Knightly said wryly.

"Oh, Will, I was just counting my Greek friends, of course."

Elli winked at him and looked away. Knightly smiled at her and then looked away as well. It was a warm night and the cicadas were up late, chattering and sawing away at their summer-long recitativo. There was no breeze but even in the still air they would catch a breath that the yard exhaled and the porch would fill with heady draughts of jasmine and lemon blossom. The day had finally grown exhausted and the night was ready to claim its place. The curtained windows behind them were lit dimly and their weak glow began to yield as the dark gathered beyond the street and then inside the yard itself, spilling at last on to the verandah, painting the walls purplish-gray, then black, cooling the tile under their feet. The cicada-song faded to a distant murmuring. The sounds of the house itself, the faint ticking and humming one heard all day, reduced to nothing. Knightly took Elli's hand. He looked at her and he believed he could feel the heat of her eyes. The verandah sighed. Its last whispers surrendered to the silence. The vestiges of day dissolved, the lights trimmed, all giving in to embrace the overwhelming darkness, immortal and unbegotten night.

4.

"We arrived three and a half minutes too late. If we had gotten the word sooner, we might have saved the situation. If only. But we got there after the shooting started. There was already no chance of saving him by then. As it was, it was a bloody fight, even though we were just going in to recover the body. Three and a half minutes too late. Two hundred and some seconds. If only when Andreas had made the decision to call us in he had made it one tick earlier. If only, if only. But he didn't.

Joshua had come up with a plan, namely, to use a friend of Irini's to get at Skorpios. This friend of Irini's had gotten close to a guy who was one of Skorpios's drivers. Skorpios had more than one driver and he rotated them as a security measure. Even so, he saw this as a vulnerability. But give the devil his due. Skorpios realized he could turn the vulnerability into a strategic asset. The guy who drove for Skorpios who was supposedly getting set up by the friend of Irini's—he was in fact swinging the other way. He was a plant, a fake. Skorpios told him exactly what to say to this girl who was so inquisitive.

So what she ended up telling Andreas was exactly what Skorpios wanted-ed Andreas to tell whomever he was reporting to. The crazy man. *The crazy fucking asshole who shot up my club,* Skorpios must have said, *because I was supposed to be there that night.* An assassin with no conceivable motive. Until it dawned on Skorpios that what he was facing, perhaps the deadliest challenge he had yet faced, was in fact nothing more, or less, than a crusade. A campaign of liberation based on that trouble-making slut from—wherever she was from—Romania? Albania? Moldova. Right. The pair of them. Well, one was dead. The other had better go packing, back to her miserable country. So not liberation, after all. What was the assassin, the mad man after? Revenge. Revenge for the dead whore, the one that didn't get away. Pests, all of them, stupid pests. Got a problem with rats, lay a trap.

So he laid a trap.

Andreas got hold of us because he had finally freaked out. The girl was fine, Irini's friend, she could be trusted. But this guy, the driver—he had not been properly vetted. There was no time for that, Joshua said. *We're not going to let this slip away. We've got his location for tomorrow night. The man has told us where Skorpios is going to be and when he is going to be there. We're going to move. And this time we won't miss.*

For the first time, Andreas started to doubt Joshua's judgment. The assault was also planned too quickly, the plan itself rash, to the extent there even was a battle-plan. Andreas was to go through the front door, like a customer, while Joshua and Taz came in by the back door. But what if I get patted down? What if they stop me at the door or, worse, they see I've got a piece and something breaks out right there? The shit hits the fan and you guys are walking into a hornets' nest. Joshua was too impatient to listen. He just bullshitted him. Wear it around your ankle if you're worried about it. They're not going to do a careful frisk. You're a Greek, for god's sake! If they're on the look-out at all, they'll be looking for someone like me. *The crazy American.* Just put on your game-face and walk right in, like you want nothing more than to get laid. *Andreas, my man—don't stress yourself, for chrissake!*

They split up before the assault took place and Andreas thought about it and got cold feet. So he buzzed us and told us what was going down. It wasn't any fear on his part. He just saw at last the desperation that had taken hold of Joshua. The insanity that was now masquerading as what we all once acknowledged as the most extraordinary sort of bravery we'd ever seen, even among that population marked by the kind of courage we saw exhibited almost routinely.

We reacted immediately. Doc and Mac were in the best position. They were in the south already. The rogues were launching their attack on Skorpios at a club in Korídalos, a neighborhood just northwest of Piraeus, the port of Athens—in other words, in the southwestern sector of the greater metro area. So Doc and Mac jumped on bikes and they were on the spot relatively quickly. We were closer to the center and so we had to be a little more creative. Chrysostomos came up huge here. We were in the vicinity of a big hospital and I got Tommy to arrange for us to "borrow" a medi-vac chopper and its pilot. I went aboard along with Tex and Ricky, leaving Tommy to sort out the red tape—and to shoot anyone who tried to keep the chopper from getting off.

With the supernatural assistance of the chopper, we got there shortly after Doc and Mac, arriving like *dei ex machina.* Gods of the zip-line. We picked a roof-top that was just over four blocks from the club and I told Tex to deploy there with his TAC-50. A fifty-caliber sniper rifle, with armor-piercing rounds. The building the club was in was only two stories, while we had dropped from the bird onto a four-story building. So Tex was looking *down* on the roof of *their* building and from a distance of only about four or five hundred yards. The bastards who were set up on that roof were sitting ducks, once Tex opened up on them.

The bastards on the roof were the main problem. The attack started before Andreas had even reached the door. It was no attack, though—it was an ambush. Joshua had hardly gotten half-way down the alley before the guys on the roof opened up on him with Kalashnikovs. Weapon of choice for a lot of criminals in Greece nowadays. Joshua was hit and yet he managed to take cover. But he was pinned down and Taz was also pinned at the head of the alley. He couldn't get to Joshua.

That's when we got into the play. Doc and Mac came in on opposite ends of the alley and directed their fire at the men on the roof. That gave them something to think about up there, so that they weren't even looking when Tex opened up with the TAC-50.

He had a suppressor on the gun. What did it sound like when he fired a round? Imagine a pitching-machine, firing a wet baseball with a loose stitch or two at a brick wall at 120 miles per hour, that would give you some idea. The guys on the roof didn't even know they were getting picked off until at least two guys had gone down. They almost certainly figured it out because the guys weren't just getting shot. Their heads were getting blown off. Literally. So the other guys hunkered down below the lip of the wall that ran around the roof of the building. Only Tex's rounds went right through that wall like nothing at all. And their heads kept exploding.

It was a surreal scene. Doc and Mac had suppressors on their assault rifles, too, so their rounds were going off with muzzle flashes, but no sharp report, just a steady *thak-a, thak-a, thak-a*, while the Kalashnikovs answered in full voice, and the rounds that Tex was laying down on that roof were bringing up great puffs of plaster mixed with clouds of blood and brain and bone and hair. It was all the more surreal because I took it all in at a run. That is, I was seeing the whole thing peripherally. I got to the top of the alley where Doc was firing at the roof and Taz, too, with a handgun. 'Cover me,' I yelled and I sprinted for Joshua. When I got to him, I heard something coming up behind me. It was Taz. He had followed me down the alley. He barely looked at Joshua. One glance was enough. Joshua had taken numerous rounds and was bleeding badly. That one glance that Taz gave him was enough.

I saw anguish and hurt on the face of Taz, but also a frightening look, a furious anger and a hatred such as I have never seen, even having entered combat many times, on the face of any other human being, friend or foe. Taz bolted from where I was crouching down beside Joshua and burst into the building through the back door. The last thing I saw as he went in was how he jammed the pistol into his waistband and pulled out a knife, one that had a long curved blade, like the weapon of some aboriginal warrior. I knew what he was after. He was going to take the battle to the roof. He was going to fight his way up and murder any of the shooters unlucky enough to have survived only to face his rage or anybody else unlucky enough to get in his way. He was after scalps. What we discovered later was that Taz had moved through the club like sudden lightning and up to the roof, not only scalping enemies with that wicked curved blade of his but nearly decapitating several men with blows he dealt out with a savagery that was beyond human. That was how the battle ended. And that was how our man went down. Our brother."

"I was holding Joshua when he died," Daniel said.

5.

Knightly opened his eyes and saw that Elli was already awake and looking at him.

"Are you awake?" she asked.

"I am now—were you poking me?"

She looked at him sheepishly. "I was—I'm sorry."

"Don't be sorry—I'm glad you did!" He smiled as he put his arms around her. She nestled there with her head on his arm. Then she stretched and looked at him.

"I don't have anything for breakfast. Not even coffee. I'll go get some things in the village. Can you hold on until I get back?"

"I don't think so. But I'll try."

She hit him with her pillow as she climbed over him. She dressed quickly. Too quickly, Knightly thought—*quelle vision!* She came over and sat on the edge of the bed.

"You stay here and relax. I'll stop by the taverna and drop off my friend's pan, too. But I'll be right back, I promise!"

"I'll be fine," he said.

She smiled at him as she left the room.

Knightly heard the front door closing and the light scuffing sound of Elli's sandals on the stone walkway in the courtyard. He closed his eyes for a while, then opened them again, staring at the ceiling. He got up and went into the bathroom, splashed some water on his face and gargled with cold water. There was a fresh towel neatly folded on a wicker-table next to the bath-tub. "Why not?" he said to himself. He took a quick shower and dried himself off with the towel. After he dressed, he went down the hall. It was early but the sun was already warming up the windows of the living-room.

He sat down on the couch and looked around the room. Everything that he'd seen the day before was still there, occupying the same place, all the material relics of the family's history. The objects conjured for Knightly Elli's childhood and growing up, but these thoughts faded the more he reflected on the previous night's conversation. What Knightly kept thinking of—what he could not yet fully grasp—was not simply the enormity of the crime that had been committed against the young girl he had known twenty-five years ago. It was the calm of Elli's present attitude. It staggered him. Her peace. Not stoicism, he thought, just *peace*. What had happened to her, and then the painful turn that Giannakis's life took, the sinister addiction—it might have driven another person to despair or bitterness, if not madness. It wasn't that she was blasé about it, either. She was serene.

Thinking how Elli seemed to defeat the past, how their experiences were so different, Knightly saw a fearful asymmetry. How could he relate to what she went through, let alone help her? As if she needed his help! It finally occurred to him that the exact reverse might be the case. His suffering seemed trivial compared to hers. But it was fresh. A failed marriage. Miserably failed. He could barely think about the divorce without feeling the queasiness, the sickening sourness of it, deep in his gut. The asymmetry was real. But what needed to be brought level in fact was his incapacity for letting go of *his* pain and all of the toxic treasures he had buried deep inside himself. The asymmetry was in the gap between her way of handling things and his way of avoiding them.

As he contemplated the irony of this, he looked down the hall. "Why not?" he thought. He got up and walked toward Giannakis's room, where Elli had taken him the night before. It had seemed to do her good. Maybe it *was* a two-way street, after all.

There wasn't much to see, except for the fighter-jet, sitting on the edge of the desk, still pointing at the wide window and poised to take off. Knightly looked at it again and then looked out the window. In the daylight he saw that the courtyard below was farther down than he had realized. The ground sloped off somewhat on that side of the house. Where the stone pavement of the courtyard ended, there was some land, a few trees with an array of bright flowers planted between them, the garden wall and, just beyond it, the street.

Beautiful day, Knightly thought, as he turned to leave the room. On his way out, he passed the closet. Something made him hesitate—maybe something about an unopened door? So he opened it. What he saw was no surprise. A young boy's clothing. There was a shelf above the rod where the clothes were hanging, with just a few small boxes on it, nothing else. Down below there were some shoes arranged neatly in line and a couple of larger boxes. When Knightly lifted the lid of one he saw some of Giannakis's old toys. Next to this one, squirrelled away in the corner of the closet, there was a smaller box and it was open, its top thrown away long ago. The box was stuffed with papers. A layer of dust covered them and the other boxes that were sitting on the closet-floor. "Elli wasn't kidding when she said she doesn't come in here often," Knightly thought.

Knightly bent down and saw an old brown envelope standing up straight in the box. He took the envelope and looked inside it. More old papers. Knightly asked himself what in blazes he was doing. Is this the scholarly instinct in me, he wondered, or a natural inquisitiveness, or—hell, why beat around the bush or gussy it up—was it just a curiosity, rank and raw, that he couldn't control?

He pulled out a paper and shivered slightly when he saw that it was the original copy of the marriage license that Kazantzakis had referred to. *Holy smoke.* Knightly gave a low whistle. There were the two names of the wife and husband, Eleftheria Parthenis and Angelos Mavroudís, who were being joined, so far as the church was concerned, in an official and sanctified union, like that of any other couple. Knightly saw that Giannakis's birth certificate was also there, as well as another church document, a certificate of baptism. Knightly also saw diplomas Giannakis must have gotten during his schooling.

There was an old photograph in the envelope, tucked behind the school diplomas. Knightly took it out and looked at it. It was a picture of some young men—six of them, in fact. They appeared to be a group of some sort. A dining club or fraternity? Army buddies after their service was done? Part of a soccer team? They didn't look like athletes. The group was relaxed, no formal portrait. They were standing, leaning on each others' shoulders, some of them linking arms. Most of the young men were smiling. Except for those two. The one standing next to last, on the left, had a pinched expression on his face. It wasn't a scowl, but at the same time it was a pained and unpleasant expression. He was also slightly older than the others, if only by a year or two. The man standing next to him, on the end of the line, was also not smiling. It wasn't exactly a hostile expression either but it was a dull and vacant look that projected a vague menace. Knightly looked closer at the face of that one, the one who stood on the end of the line. Something about that face bothered him. The jutting brow, the bulbous nose. The jaw that made the whole head look too big and like it ought to be hanging from a lamp-post. Then all at once it hit him. He realized that he was looking at the face of Mitsos, the cop he had just met in Tripoli. A portrait of the unforgettably unlovely Mitsos as a young man.

Knightly looked at the back of the photo. There was a date, written in faded ink, but still easy to read: 1973. Someone had also put initials there that seemed to correspond with the figures on the front. The next to last figure must have had the initials A M. *Angelos Mavroudís?* Knightly looked at the pinched and unpleasant features of the man who stood next to Mitsos. Could it be Skorpios? Knightly tried hard to recall what Kazantzakis and Daniel had said about Skorpios. And as he studied the photograph, that face slowly took possession of its name. *Skorpios.* The initials that corresponded to the figure of the young Mitsos were M P. What was Mitsos's last name? He didn't remember if he had ever heard it. But what *was* it?

Knightly looked at the photo again. What did it matter *what* the M or the P stood for? The face of the young man in the picture was the same as the face he had just seen on the man sitting at one of those desks outside Kazantzakis's office.

Knightly put the box back in the closet and took the photo with him as he left the room. He walked down the hall and when he reached the living room he took out his phone and dialed the number Kazantzakis had given him.

It was Athena who picked up.

"*Nai?*" she said. "Yes?"

"Hello, Athena, this is Will Knightly."

"Hello, Professor," she said, "This is a surprise. What can I do for you?"

"Athena, I have an odd question," Knightly said. "Your colleague, Mitsos—what is his last name?"

"Pappas. It's Pappas. Why?" she sounded puzzled. "Why on earth are you asking?"

Knightly felt the floor sway beneath him.

"Athena," he said, "is Kazantzakis still in his office?"

"Yes, he is—"

"Do me a favor, Athena. Please, tell the Inspector not to go anywhere. I'm coming right over. I've got to talk with him right away—it's important."

Athena sounded grave. "Is there something wrong, Professor? Can you just give me an idea what you want to talk about with the Inspector?"

"I'm fine, Athena. There's nothing to worry about. Please trust me. But there is something I have to talk to Inspector Kazantzakis about. I've got something to show him."

He had almost finished, then he added, "Oh—please don't tell anyone else about this, okay? Don't tell anyone that I'm coming over. Not *anyone!*"

He closed the phone and wondered what Athena might make of that conversation. *Bizarre-o!* But he trusted her to deliver the message to Kazantzakis.

Knightly looked at the photo again. At the face of Angelos Mavroudís—Skorpios—and the face of Mitsos Pappas. The faces of two men, grim faces, barely young anymore, even then. Knightly now felt he could see in these faces a potential for evil, one evincing evil that was perhaps banal but the other an evil already beyond the ordinary.

Knightly's face felt hot and his throat constricted. He shuddered with anger. Then he heard steps outside and the front door opened. Elli stepped inside the house. She was holding a couple of plastic bags.

"Will, what's wrong?" Elli asked. "You look like you want to kill someone!"

"Elli, sorry," he said, startled. "I had a bit of a shock just now, that's all."

He walked over to her and handed her the photograph and as she looked at it he saw her face go white with astonishment.

"What is this—?!" Elli gasped. Then she looked at Knightly.

"This seems like a cruel joke, Will. What's going on? What is this? Where did you find it?"

"It's yours, Elli. It belongs to you. I found it tucked away in a box in the closet in Giannakis's room." He stopped, suddenly feeling embarrassed.

"I'm sorry, Elli! I guess I was feeling restless or something. I went back into Giannakis's room and I was just looking around. I apologize—I should have asked you if it was okay to go in there—"

"No, no—" she said emphatically. "It doesn't bother me at all. There's nothing sacred about it—I mean, I just don't go in there much. I'm not even here all that often, in Aetoráchi, that is."

She looked at Knightly and he could see she was puzzled. It was clear to him that she was trying to think back to that time that was now long past.

"He must have given this to me," she said.

"So it is Angelos Mavroudís?"

"Yes, it is," she said, somewhat distantly. "He must have given it to me when we went on one of our 'dates.' Or did I steal it from him? I really don't remember. I just can't believe I didn't throw it out. Maybe I kept it because I wanted something to show to people, in case he decided to renege on his agreement to support Giannakis."

"I'm glad you kept it," Knightly said.

Elli laughed and gave him a curious look.

"I don't go in that room very much because it's full of things I have a hard time dealing with. It's easier to ignore them or keep them at a certain distance. I don't think much about the past at all. Or at least I hadn't until you came back here."

Knightly didn't know how to take this. But Elli came close to him. She put her arms around him and looked into his eyes.

"What I meant is that I am grateful to you, Will. I'm very grateful. I just never had the opportunity to talk about these things with anyone. Even with Chrysa—we stopped talking about the past long ago. But I've realized I needed to talk about it, especially with someone who cares."

She was holding him tightly now as she spoke, her voice trembling.

"I'm very glad we talked. It helped."

Knightly folded her in his arms and held her close to him, kissing her hair.

"It helped me, too. Thank you for trusting me."

They stood there for a moment, holding each other tightly, neither of them saying a word, swaying gently. Finally Knightly broke the silence.

"I'm glad you kept the photo, Elli."

She gave a short laugh.

"Why are you *glad*?"

Knightly held up the photo and pointed to the figure on the end, the one next to Skorpios.

"That fellow is Mitsos Pappas. You know what he became when he grew up? A policeman. That's right, he became a cop and he joined the force in the city of Tripoli. He has been assisting the investigations of Chief Inspector Kazantzakis, on loan from Athens. And I'm quite sure he's been a huge help—he's been of inestimable value, I suspect—but not to Kazantzakis."

"Skorpios?" Elli whispered. "You think he's been helping this Skorpios?"

"Kazantzakis told me that the investigation keeps getting derailed. Every time he gets a lead on Mr. Skorpios, it fizzles. I'm no detective, but I think I get it. This guy Mitsos is feeding information to Skorpios and that's how the bastard keeps a step ahead of the inspector all the time."

"What are you going to do?" she asked.

"I'm going to Tripoli, Elli," he said, "and I'm going to give this picture to Kazantzakis. I think he'll know where to take things from there."

Elli smiled helplessly.

"My god, Will, are we ever going to get any peace and quiet?!"

"I know, Elli," Knightly laughed, "I know. But I think we're finally getting to the end of the tunnel. When I give this photo to Kazantzakis, that ought to be my final contribution to the case. I don't know what more I can do. Although—"

"What?" she asked.

"I hate to say this, Elli, but I will probably need to go to Athens one more time. That old student of mine, Daniel. I told you how he's involved in this business. But, well—it's complicated. He's not in direct contact with Inspector Kazantzakis. I think that Daniel needs to know about this, I mean, that the police probably now have a lead on Skorpios, something that may well take them all the way to Skorpios's front door. I think I'd better go to Athens and tell him what's going down. But I swear to you, on my dear mother's head and on my very first student copy of Homer, that I will come back to you immediately upon the completion of my mission! And I don't think I'll be going back to Athens any time soon, unless of course you want to spend a little time in the city with Giannakis and me."

She wrapped her arms around him again and kissed him on the lips.

"You go do what you have to do. I'll go back to Kremni and pick up Giannakis. Don't worry about me. I'll have good company! We'll be waiting for you."

"Amen," Knightly said.

He left the house and got into his car. Putting the photo into the glove compartment, he started up the car, rolled the windows down, and took off for Tripoli and his meeting with Kazantzakis.

After he had explained his business at the two checkpoints, Knightly entered the building. He took the elevator and got off where Athena had taken him. As he walked toward Kazantzakis's office, he saw that Mitsos was sitting at his desk and to all appearances checking over some files. Athena was there, too. Knightly saw her give him a sly wink.

"Hello, Professor. You've come to see the Inspector?"

"Yes, Athena, I have. He's in his office, I assume?"

"Yes, he is. Go right ahead."

Knightly went to the door and stopped, turning toward Mitsos.

"Oh, please forgive me, sir," he said with an emphatic politeness, bowing slightly toward Mitsos at the same time, "and allow me to wish you good day!"

"Και εσείς," Mitsos grunted, looking at him curtly. "You, too."

Knightly walked into Kazantzakis's office and while the inspector gazed at him with a mixture of mirth and curiosity Knightly asked if he might shut the door. Kazantzakis waved at the door as if to say, "of course." Knightly shut it and sat down. Without another word, he took out the photograph and put it on the desk in front of Kazantzakis.

Kazantzakis raised his eyebrows at Knightly and then looked down at the photo. Knightly was counting in his head. He had barely reached three when the inspector gave out a sharp gasp. It was as if he'd been hit with an electric prod. Kazantzakis flipped the picture over and looked at the initials and the date on the back, then turned it over again to inspect it more closely. At last he put the photo down on his desk. Knightly looked at him, but the policeman had fixed his eyes on a point somewhere on the opposite wall. What was at first a look of astonishment changed quickly to a puzzled expression that in turn yielded to a clouded expression from which Kazantzakis's features finally tightened into a grim mask of rage and disgust.

"Thank you very much for this photograph, Professor Knightly," Kazantzakis said. "I don't know quite how to express my gratitude. This will be very useful to us. Very useful, indeed."

"I'm happy to hear you say that, Chief Inspector. I thought you would know what to do with it."

"Where on earth did you find this, by the way?" Kazantzakis asked.

"I found it among Elli's things," he said.

Kazantzakis smiled.

"I'm not apprenticing myself to you, I hasten to add," Knightly said. "Elli—I mean, Mrs. Parthenis—had shown me some things that belonged to her son and I poked around a little more in there. It's a room she doesn't go into very much, you understand. Anyway, that's where I found the picture. I was shocked, as you can imagine. But when I saw what it was, I wanted you to have it."

"So I was right, after all, Professor," Kazantzakis said. "You are on the side of the angels. You did the right thing. I thank you again."

"It's going to help you in the investigation? You'll be talking to Detective Mitsos?"

"All in good time, Professor," he said. "Just between you and me, after I've turned Athena loose on a full and thorough investigation of everything remotely connected to our beloved colleague, Mitsos Pappas, he and I will be having a long talk. At that point, I am confident he will find himself thinking about the day of his birth and with a satisfactory measure of regret."

Knightly nodded, grinning. He was about to get up when Kazantzakis spoke again.

"This is truly remarkable, Professor. Yesterday I had very little idea what Skorpios looked like, never mind how I might track down the elusive beast. Now I am sure that fairly soon we'll be crawling into bed with him, before he even knows what's hit him."

"Please pinch him once for me!" Knightly said.

"I really am grateful to you for this," Kazantzakis said. "I would like to return the favor. I have some information—something I just became aware of myself—that I ought to share with you. It has to do with the two Americans we were speaking of the other day. One of them, you recall, had gone rogue and was involved in some very troubling activity. Well, I'm sorry to inform you that this man is now dead. He was killed in the same sort of incident he had been creating throughout the city."

Knightly was subdued as he listened to Kazantzakis.

"That leaves one other American. But my sources tell me that this other American could be described more as a solution than a problem. At least, that is how it will be expressed in the 'official version.' I trust this information will not be meaningless to you, Professor Knightly. Perhaps it may even be helpful to you. Again, I want to thank you sincerely for coming to me so promptly with your discovery."

Kazantzakis got up from his chair and extended his hand to Knightly.

"If you'll excuse me, Professor, I now have some things to attend to."

"I don't want to stand in your way, Chief Inspector," Knightly said. "Good day."

"Good day, Professor."

Knightly saw Athena on his way out. He turned and winked at her surreptitiously.

"Good day," he said. He tried to preserve a wan smile as he turned toward Mitsos.

"Good day, sir," he said politely.

"Fine," Mitsos grumbled, not even looking up.

And I sincerely hope that I've given the Inspector something he can use to deep-fry your sorry old ass, you miserable sonuvabitch! Knightly thought to himself as he walked away.

He left the building. When he got as far as the edge of the parking lot, he stopped there and took a deep breath. *That's done.* It felt good. He looked at the sky. The usual blue, stretched wide and high above the line of pines and a few cypresses that ringed the parking lot. Then he thought, *Damn it all. Joshua is dead.* And he began to worry about Daniel all over again. What would this mean for him? Well, he had to go to Athens. That was clear. So be it. He'd find Daniel once more, hopefully, and then he'd hear from him what it meant.

It occurred to him, as he got in his car, that when he left Kazantzakis he had forgotten to ask the policeman for a *mantinadha*. Come to think of it, Kazantzakis had offered none himself. Then Knightly recalled the look on Kazantzakis's face, after he saw the photo. A look of harsh fury and bitter loathing. The face of Justice, perhaps. Or of one deeply offended and seriously determined cop.

So be it, Knightly thought.

He started the car and took off, heading toward the road to Athens.

6.

NOT LONG AFTER HE LEFT POLICE HEADQUARTERS, KNIGHTLY HAD left the city limits, too, and in a space of minutes found himself on the national road and passing through the plain of Tripoli once more. As he looked around, he recalled his old edition of the Blue Guide and how the plain had been described so harshly there. He even remembered a few choice phrases, "*a monotonous plateau enclosed by an amphitheatre of barren mountains*." What's up with that, Knightly thought—"monotonous plateau," "barren mountains"? As compared to what? The lovely, languid landscape of the Lac de Genève? Or maybe the Scottish Bloody Highlands! Compared to nothing but itself, the plain of Tripoli, well-watered, fertile, ringed by mountains standing off in the middle-distance, was fair enough. Anyway, one was through the plain and out the other side so quickly, it was hard to see how monotony had much of a chance to set in.

He also recalled how the writer had named Tripoli the center of communications in the Peloponnese but then concluded by saying that it lay "*in a bleak situation*" among the peaks of the Mainalon range. "Sweet Jesus," Knightly groaned. *Bleak situation*? In light of what was coming down the road at the Corinth Canal, or Megara or Eleusis? The guide books could be as blinkered as history. And Knightly was moving once again in the very direction that history had gone. The city of Tripolis, or Tripolitsa, formed from the three ancient cities of Tegea, Mantinea, and Pallantion, received prime attention from Byzantines and Franks, was made an administrative center by the Turks and was fought over in the War of Independence, witnessing its full share of significant slaughters. But, fickle as ever, History decided, after Nafplio had served briefly as capital, that the city of Athens would be the seat of government and the permanent capital for young King Otto and the new country.

Nothing against Athens, Knightly thought, but once I'm done there, I'll be more than ready for the monotony of the plain of Tripoli again.

Knightly didn't relish driving in Athens, but once he arrived he brought the car into the city to save time. Luckily, he found a place to park not far from the Pelopidas. He walked to the hotel and checked in—more good luck, they had a room—and then headed at a brisk pace toward the *Scholar's Pub*.

When he got there he went straight to the bar and ordered a pint. Sharon was working and she glanced at him as he sat down. Her smile was cordial, but her face looked drawn. Knightly understood. He smiled palely in return. After he drained his glass, he waved for the check. "Thank you," he said, as Sharon put it on the bar in front of him. This time, she looked warmly at him. "Goodbye, Professor," she said. Knightly nodded and smiled at her. He left enough for the beer and a decent tip. Then he flipped the check over and wrote on the back, *Must talk!* He turned the check back over on the bar and left the pub.

He wandered down Ermou. The street was quiet, nearly empty. It left him feeling desolate. He was upset for leaving Elli so abruptly, especially after what they had talked about, everything that had come out—just the night before! But he was also thinking about Daniel. How would he be taking the death of his troubled friend? So much suffering and loss. He had been plunged into it without any warning. But what could have prepared him, after all, to share all of the sorrows of these people he cared for? It almost felt as if he'd brought the plagues on them himself, by coming here. That he was like the Ancient Mariner's bird of dread omen. Stupid fancy! The troubles he was sharing were all of them long in the making, that was painfully clear. It was just life, only offered up more abundantly. He thought of something he'd heard on the radio, before he'd left for Greece. An academic or social worker—what was her name—Brown? She talked about a link between vulnerability and courage. How vulnerability is always manifest in those who, as she put it, lead *whole-hearted lives*. She had a way of looking at loss, Knightly recalled, that cut it loose from a person's feeling of value or self-worth. It was coming back to him, what had really struck him. It was what she'd said about hope. That hope was not an emotion, it was a process. A cognitive process one undergoes while experiencing adversity. Through relationships—that was key—through the faith people place in you, to be able to help them get through a jam. Hope is something we learn, that we only obtain through struggle.

In that case, Knightly thought, we are all ripe candidates for this whole-hearted and authentic way of being! Every one of us—Elli, Daniel, myself, our much maligned Tripoli, with its "bleak situation"—for god's sake, even this country itself, with its economic and social crises and all. The corruption and exploitation, self-serving and recriminations, poverty and suffering, racism and crime, might all be for something after all, if the whole country could look itself and the world in the face after it's done and say, "thank you, but now we have found where our true hope lies."

He had reached Monastiraki. It was around five-thirty, too early for there to be a crowd in the *plateia*. But there were people here and there. He strolled slowly across the square. There was a small group of boys playing soccer. They were kicking a ball, passing it back and forth. When he walked by them, one spun out of control and ran right into him. Maybe it was his whimsical, melancholy mood, but Knightly didn't say anything. The boy looked up at him, startled, and apologized to Knightly as he backed away and rejoined his friends. Knightly just laughed. The kid had hit him right in the gut. Good thing he didn't have a *stiletto*, Knightly thought. He looked down and saw the kid had jammed a balled-up piece of paper into his hands. Knightly unfolded the wad of paper and saw there was writing on it. All it said was

SAD DANL

Knightly smiled ruefully. "We all are, Daniel," he said to himself. "We all are." He thought about the two words for a moment. Then he had it. SAD DANL...DAS LAND.

Das Land der Griechen mit der Seele suchend....

"Seeking the land of the Greeks with the soul...." It was a line from Goethe's *Iphigenie auf Tauris*—how many times had he belaboured that famous apothegm in front of his classes? Daniel must have remembered at least one such performance. The meeting place was obvious. Daniel had to mean the Goethe Institut. It was a venerable institution. Good choice for a rendezvous—it was close by. On Omirou, just off Panepistimiou. Knightly headed for the Institut as fast as he could go without looking too obvious about it.

He spotted Daniel loitering not far from the school, leaning against the wall of a building on the same block. He was dressed in jeans and a loose cotton shirt with long sleeves. He wore a light knit cap and—this made Knightly chuckle—reddish-brown dread-locks spilling out from under the cap and over his shoulders.

Daniel was looking straight at him and so Knightly walked right up to Daniel.

"Where are we going, Daniel?" Knightly asked. "And where are my dreads?"

"That's something you've got to learn, Professor. Everybody brings their own costume. Now just mind your manners and follow me."

They walked a few blocks until Daniel had led them to a café that was off the street, inside an arcade.

"Are we okay here?" Knightly asked.

"It's safe," Daniel said, "no one will bother us. This is the eye of the storm, so to speak. Besides, if it makes you feel any better, we're not alone. We're inside a secure perimeter."

"I'll leave all of that to you, Daniel. But, yes, it does make me feel better, thanks."

"So what's going on, Will?" Daniel asked. "Sharon passed your message on. It sounds like you've got something you want to tell me."

"I do," he said, taking a deep breath. "Boy, do I. Here's the thing, Danny. I happened to find a picture. It's of Skorpios, when he was young. It shows him standing next to a good friend of his. Long story short, this old buddy is now a cop. A cop in Tripoli who was privy to sensitive details of the investigation that the police are conducting into Skorpios's operation—emphasis on '*was* privy'! I gave the photograph to a policeman I've gotten to know. His name's Aris Kazantzakis. He's in charge of the investigation, in fact. He's solid. Anyway, he's going to screw that dirty cop to the wall and make the bastard sing *Tosca* to him. It's only a matter of time before the cops get Skorpios, that's my point."

Daniel looked at Knightly without expression.

"Where did you find this picture?"

"I found it in Elli's stuff. She—" Knightly hesitated. "She had a kind of relationship—a strange one, actually—with Skorpios, a long time ago."

Daniel was wearing shades but even so Knightly could see his eyes widen.

"As I said, it was a long time ago. Skorpios was someone else at the time. I mean, his name back then was Angelos Mavroudís. Anyhow, Daniel, the point is that Skorpios is cooked. His defenses are for nothing now. The cops finally have their hooks in someone on the inside. And this guy is going to give them what they need to nail Skorpios. I wanted you to know this because I think it means that now you can stand down."

Daniel said nothing. He looked at Knightly with affection, but at the same time Knightly could see that Daniel wasn't buying it. At least, not easily. Knightly also could see that Daniel was tired. For the first time, Knightly thought, he looks tired.

"I'm sorry about Joshua, Daniel. I heard about what happened. I'm very sorry."

"It's awful, Will. It's unbelievable. I just can't take it in. I think I'm still fighting it, trying not to believe it. But I was there. I was with him. I was with him the whole way, when we took him to the embassy."

Daniel breathed in sharply. A waiter approached their table slowly. The place was empty. It was early, barely six in the evening.

He asked Daniel what he would like and Daniel asked for Greek coffee. The man looked at Knightly.

"The same. Thanks."

"No problem." Then he left.

Daniel opened a leather bag he had with him and pulled out a small lap-top. He flipped it open and handed it to Knightly.

"Check this out," he said.

"What is it?" Knightly asked.

"It's Joshua's. He left a kind of notebook behind. It's a commentary on the world's ills, at least those that bugged him the most, along with a plan of action and proposed remedies."

"Like the papers of Lysander that Plutarch says the Spartans found in his house after he died?"

"Apocryphal or not. These are real, unfortunately."

Knightly looked at the computer's desktop and saw a single icon. It was titled JERRY CO. He groaned and looked at Daniel, who just shrugged. Then Knightly clicked on it. He saw a long list of files, each bearing a name of an organization or group of people that, Knightly assumed, had drawn Joshua's attention. Some of the names were familiar, others sounded ad hoc:

The NRA

Climate-change deniers

Radio evangelists

Radio shock jocks

Union-busters

Unionizers

Quick-buck frackers

Waste-spewing inhumane industrial farmers

Creationists

Anti-abortion taliban

Sex traffickers

Drug traffickers

Dope-smoking shareholders of the cartels

The "stars" of Pranked

Partisan media pundits

Partisan lobbyists

Car salesmen

Pulp fiction writers

Gangs

Gang-employers

Homophobes

Holocaust-deniers

Anti-Zionists

Ultra-Zionists

Neo-Fascists

Skinheads

Entrenched pseudo-Lefties

Neo-Stalinists

Tea Partyists

The ISI

And on and on. Knightly stopped scrolling down. Reading through the list fascinated and repelled him. It also made his eyes tired. He began clicking on some of the files. Each one contained a tirade against the group whose name was in the title of the file. The NRA, according to Joshua, was "*a sad collection of anti-patriotic pussies who claim to bear arms in defense of OUR FREEDOM as if me & my boys who are out here getting shot at aren't doing shit to keep America free!*" Knightly started to read through Joshua's ideas for dealing with this organization but quickly shut the file in disgust. He clicked on the file *Partisan lobbyists* and read Joshua's views about who exactly these people were and who in particular posed the greatest threat: "*... esp. the supra-type who have the gall to dictate to elected representatives of the People.*" There was reference to a *No-Man-Is-An-Island-But-We-Own-An-Island Pledge*, followed by a passage describing in lurid detail the measures Joshua proposed "*to deal with self-appointed legislators like Gruber Sunkist, or whatever the fuck his name is.*" Curious as he was, Knightly couldn't endure reading past the words, "*...with a light ball-peen hammer.*"

Every file that Knightly opened sounded depressingly the same. There was a file at the bottom of the list labeled A DECLARATION. There Knightly found a manifesto of sorts, in which Joshua pronounced on what he saw as the chief evils of the day. There was a preamble whose salient phrase seemed to be: *"the eternal non-contest of American society (& elsewhere): pusillanimous left vs. pugilist right."* The declaration insisted that what it advocated was *"NOT Anarchy, NOT Terror, but ANTI-TERROR."*

THE PUNISHMENT OF EVIL—NO, THE ANNIHILATION OF EVIL! THAT IS THE MISSION. WHAT IS EVIL? THE STRONG WHO PREY ON THE WEAK. COMPETING INTERESTS, LONGSTANDING GRIEVANCES, FLASH-POINTS OF CONFLICT, CLASHES OF FAITH (NOT TO MENTION POVERTY, CRIME, SLOW PACE OF DEVELOPMENT, BLOATED PUBLIC SECTOR, POLITICAL GRIDLOCK, ETC)—WHAT ARE THESE BUT PROPS AND SCENERY? SAME OLD LAME ASS DUMBSHOW. NAME ANY INTRACTABLE CONFLICT AND WE'LL NAME YOU ANY NUMBER OF SELF-SERVING FUCKS WHO ARE MAKING A JUICY PROFIT OUT OF IT. FEEDING THE EXTREMES FUELS CONFLICT AND KEEPS THE EVIL ONES CLOSE TO POWER AND IN THE $$$MONEY$$$.

Elsewhere there was an odd digression on the soullessness of the times. How the present age made a person yearn for the time of the nameless bureaucrat. *Automated answering systems and the like have made even the old bureaucratic encounter seem like a lost paradise. PLEASE SELECT FROM ONE OF THE FOLLOWING OPTIONS—*"self-service" *my ass! Shameless insufferable doublespeak!* Robotic technologies had added a thick, impenetrable layer to the lattice-work hive, so it went, *hiding the honey and maddening the sick and needy beast in us.* Then the manifesto returned to its political themes. It ended with a reference to what it called *"the need for ULTRA CENTRISM,"* which it never defined, except indirectly in pithy phrases, such as *"the need for extreme violence on behalf of moderation and justice."*

Knightly hardly knew what to make of it. He closed the Notebook, handed it back to Daniel, and sighed.

"Wow. There's a lot of hurt there."

"In all directions."

"It's such a farrago of ideas. I mean, what's the connection between drug lords and legitimate companies who install automated answering systems, for example?"

"Right, it is bizarre. But I think he explains that one somewhere as 'an identical callous indifference to the quality of life of those you oppress, delude, and profit from.'"

"Hm. I guess that did bother me—I found myself agreeing with some of what he said."

Daniel grimaced. "No kidding. He was upset with the way he saw things were going back home, that's putting it mildly. Back home and around the world. When we were on an assignment, wherever we were, if it was half-civilized, I started hiding the newspapers and unplugging the TV. But I couldn't shut down the Internet."

"Seems he saw himself as a Robin Hood," Knightly said.

"Robin Hood *manqué*," said Daniel.

"A very wrathful Robin."

"A real fucking Robin Fucking Hood!" Daniel tried to laugh as he said this, but his voice caught. He stopped and fell silent. He wiped his eyes.

Neither of them spoke.

Daniel sat for a long while, staring at the small laptop. Then he reached out and put his hand on top of the device, as if he were laying it upon the chest of his fallen comrade.

"Joshua needed help, and what did I do about it? Nothing. He needed a lot of help. I wish I could do this over again. At least try—"

Knightly was about to speak, but Daniel held up his hand, as if he knew what Knightly was going to say.

At last, Daniel put Joshua's computer back in the bag and looked at Knightly.

"So you think I should just give it up?"

"Yes, I do. Come on, Daniel. Let the police handle it—this Skorpios character. That's the way it should go, isn't it? And it sounds like you are going to get out of this without too many repercussions. You're lucky, you know, as far as that goes."

Daniel made a face. "Yes, as far as that goes."

"What about Ariani? How is she? Take care of her, Danny, just worry about her. Weren't you going to take her back home? I think that would be the best thing now, for all concerned."

"She's doing okay, Will, thanks. Or I should say she's doing okay where I'm concerned. But I don't know what's going on in her head. Not every-thing, anyway. The problem is that she still wants us to get Skorpios. I know that for a fact. She's still grieving for Irini. She always will be—that's never going away. But right now it's still raw. She tries to hide it from me but she can't. She wants revenge, Will. That's it. She wants us to kill him."

"But the police—"

"She doesn't have time for the police. She doesn't have any faith in them. She's seen too much. I really don't know how I'm going to convince her that we should go—"

"So you agree that you're done here?"

The waiter came over with the coffees and two glasses of water and asked if they would like anything else.

"No, thanks," Knightly said.

Daniel picked up his cup and took a sip.

"I've got no orders at present. Just that I'm supposed to be in Frankfurt in five days."

"That would give you enough time to get Ariani back home, wouldn't it? Take her back to her family, help her start to settle back in?"

"If she's willing, sure."

"You've got to convince her, Daniel."

"Or I could fire up the *dictyo* one more time."

"Oh, Christ, Daniel—I've got to be honest, I don't think that's a good idea."

"Never mind what I'm going to say to Ariani. What do I tell *them*? They're pretty motivated right now, as I'm sure you can imagine. We're close, Will. Why not go for it? Get the son of a bitch. Why not do it? Then we can all go home."

"That's asking for trouble, Danny. I can't believe you didn't get into trouble already."

"Well, as a matter of fact, it's kind of surprising, but I didn't. According to the official version, I did an outstanding job. A member of the team suddenly went AWOL, inexplicably, and went on the war-path. I responded to the situation with prompt and judicious action and limited the damage done by the individual in question during the aberrant period. I'm walking away from this with a commendation, in fact. So, yes, the sensible and reasonable thing would be to get my men out of here, to signal the 'network' to stand down, pack our bags and take Ariani back home."

"You could get elements of your *dictyo* to work with the police, couldn't you?"

"Some of them *are* the police. And the very fact that these guys have preferred to work with me, in the way we've been doing it—well, what does that tell you?"

"There are a lot of good cops, Daniel. I know one of them personally."

"Of course you're right, Will. But what about it? Can you tell me it will all work out just as we want it? That the cops will get Skorpios and that they will take him to trial and that they'll get a conviction? Can you sit there and tell me with a certainty that that dirty motherfucker will pay? That he will serve one day—even one stinking day? Or that he won't 'escape' or just sit in prison, wherever they put him, and go on running the business, just from a new and slightly less convenient location?"

Daniel took a sip of water, looking at Knightly. Knightly stared at his cup of coffee.

"Jesus, Daniel," he finally said, "you know how cynical I am. But it's what you've got to do. You can't go after revenge. You've got to leave Skorpios to the police. You have your orders—"

"Orders are to be in Frankfurt in five days. That creates space."

"You can't do it, Daniel. Maybe he deserves to die, no argument there. But it's not your role to decide on punishment or to execute it. Not now. That job belongs to the police. Or the law. That's what you and the men who serve with you are all about, right?"

"I and the men who serve with me are also all about killing the bad guys, Professor."

"You are the Guardians," Knightly continued, ignoring him. "Think of it that way. Your job—what you're sworn to do, I dare say—is to protect and defend the constitution. Okay, of the United States. But by extension it's about the Law. You are the guardians of the Law. *Don't look at me like that!* Exploited, adulterated, abused, underused—it's the best we've got. Depressing as that may be. It's vulnerable, from within and without. You help to keep it safe for the rest of us. Talk about creating space. The Law operates within a certain space and you patrol its perimeter, so that in effect you define that space. You are an *akrítis*, Daniel, do you see? You are a warrior on the margins, the boundaries of what's civilized. You are facing both ways, son. Toward the light and toward the dark. But here you are standing in the light. Right now, Daniel, you've got to stay in the light. It's over. You did your job. And you lost your friend. But to seek revenge will not be to honor him. To seek revenge, now, would be to perpetuate his error. Enough, Daniel, enough. Send your friend back home. And take Ariani and bring *her* back home. I am proud of you, Daniel. You saved this girl. You have done what you were called on to do. Now take her back home."

Daniel said nothing. Knightly could see he was listening, thinking.

"God damn it, Will. You're reminding me of all those times I'd come to class and I thought I had you but you'd come up with something and win the argument—"

"Thanks for telling me now—I never thought I won a single one!"

"If you ask me to read between the lines, where my orders are concerned, I am to get to Frankfurt in five days, which gives me just enough time to put the rest of this business in order and *don't fuck it up anymore*! If I'm honest with myself—"

Knightly laughed softly. Daniel gave a vague smile.

"If I'm honest with myself. So that's what I'll do."

"I meant what I said, Daniel. I am proud of you. I'm not taking any credit, mind you. Not one whit. I'm just incredibly proud."

Daniel smiled more broadly.

"I wish Elli could meet you," Knightly said.

"I do, too, Will. I'm sorry we had so little time. It won't be like this forever, though. Next time, hopefully it won't be quite so crazy."

"I hope so."

They got up. The waiter saw them and came over. Knightly scowled when Daniel beat him to the check. As they left the café Daniel turned to Knightly and said,

"I can't wait to take off these fuckin' dreads—"

Knightly laughed.

"Take care of yourself. And take care of that sweet girl. She needs you."

"I will. Take care of yourself, too. And give my best to Elli."

"I shall, Daniel. Goodbye."

"Goodbye, Will."

And they parted there on the avenue of Eleftherios Venizelos.

—◊—

Daniel got back to the apartment and Ariani was waiting for him. She kissed him. Daniel put some music on and they sat down and ate supper. They were just finishing when a song came on. Lucinda Williams. One that Ariani loved. She took Daniel by the hand and as he got up she drew him gently into her arms and they slow-danced there. When the song was over, they went to bed. They lay there and talked together for another hour.

In the wilderness, at night. You have shared supper. You build up the fire, circle its light and warmth. Talk rises, soft as smoke. Crackling, an occasional spark. An hour or two, who would know. No one cares. The fire dies. But when you poke the ashes there are embers underneath, breathing, a low red pulse, glowing with heat. Pushing at them, you heap the coals together and set one last log on top and it catches and as you see the fire coming to life again and as you feel it come to life your face burns but it is pleasurable.

After they made love, they held each other in silence and finally fell asleep.

—◊—

And Daniel had a dream. And heard a voice as well. Or it was his own voice in the dream.

Thrones, Princedoms, Powers, Dominions. Our brother is dead. Why do you weep? Whether it is nobler to die in this way or some other, let it be. He raised his hand against the enemy, our brother showed no mercy, let mercy and goodness be. Give him peace. He cried out before his enemies, THEY HAVE REWARDED ME EVIL FOR GOOD, AND HATRED FOR MY LOVE. LET THERE BE NONE TO EXTEND MERCY UNTO THEM. *Let it be.*

He knew no fear, except a holy terror for the weak that the strong prey upon, all the helpless whom he loved not wisely, but too well. He pursued justice, to extremes. Greater passion had no one. In the hour of his anger, he delighted too much. His wrath dripping like honey, filling his nostrils, his mind and eye. Hatred and sweet gall, richer than all his tribe.

Brother, why did you leave us? Where have you gone? Will I go that way, too? As we remember you, remember us. Earth does not contain you. You are a spirit. And have vanished. Leaving us without a question. Give us peace. Brother. Peace.

7.

It's an up and down life. Every morning a new day, but from one day to the next no one knows. No one really knows. Knightly had left the city in the morning. He was already on the coast road when he got the call from Chrysanthi. Where one begins to get the views that are breathtaking. When Knightly heard the phone and answered it and listened to what Chrysa said it took his breath away.

"Are you driving?"

"Yes."

"Will, we need to talk. I'm afraid it's bad news. I'll call you back in five minutes. Can you stop somewhere? I don't think you should be driving. Pull off the road, if you can. I'll call you back."

Knightly closed the phone and found a place to pull over. It was overlooking the sea. He sat in the car, wondering what Chrysa was talking about. Something was wrong. He felt sick. *What the hell is wrong?* He got out of the car, leaned up against it. He suddenly felt enervated, anxious. He stared out over the sea. Its brilliance. Intense.

His phone rang.

"Hello, Chrysa? No, I'm not driving—yes, I stopped, it's ok. Chrysa, what's going on?"

There was silence on the other end, though Knightly could hear Chrysa was trying to say something. She was having difficulty speaking.

"Will, I'm sorry—I have some terrible news."

"Chrysa, what happened? I don't understand—"

"It's Giannakis, Will—Giannakis."

"Chrysa," Knightly said, "please, tell me—what's going on?"

She was trying to speak, but her voice was choking with sobs.

At last she burst out, "Giannakis is dead."

Knightly fell back against the car. He couldn't speak. Chrysa herself was sobbing now. Finally, Knightly managed to ask, *Where are you?*

"Aetoráchi!" Chrysa moaned.

I'm coming.

Knightly didn't remember closing the phone, saying goodbye. He didn't recall anything later about the end of the conversation. He slid down and sat in the dirt, leaning against the car on the side of the road. The sea lay before him. Shining. Expansive. And he sat there and looked over the sea and tried to understand what he had just heard. Giannakis is dead? How did it happen? What had Chrysa said? He couldn't remember. She had been sobbing and she had not told him what had happened.

Elli! Where was *she*? Why did *Chrysa* call him? Was Elli hurt? What was going on?

His head spun. His eyes were fixed on the sea, its shimmering brilliance, rolling in endless low waves toward the rocks below him. He watched it scintillate, searing his eyes. He couldn't bear to look at it anymore, and yet he could not look away. It was too lovely. He felt as though just beneath the radiant sheet that covered the bay there was a vortex, ready to suck him in. He felt the glare blinding him, felt its fiery joy. He felt he might be lifted from the earth, suddenly, without resisting, and plunge into the sea, the great sea, and be lost forever.

Later he would barely remember getting back in the car. Had anyone with sense been present, they wouldn't have let him drive. But he had gotten back in and made it to Aetoráchi. He did recall later how, when he had reached the village and walked up to the door of Elli and Chrysa's house, Chrysa had come out to meet him. She seemed to recognize that he was still in shock. It made her burst into tears.

She embraced him. They clung to each other.

"What happened, Chrysa?" Knightly said. "Where's Elli? What happened? Giannakis—" he had a hard time saying the words. "Giannakis is dead?"

Chrysa looked at Knightly imploringly, as if she did not want to have to say it.

"It's impossible!" Knightly shouted. "What happened, Chrysa? What happened, for god's sake?"

She took his arm and sat him down on the front steps of the house as she sat down next to him. She looked exhausted. Knightly realized that Elli was in the house, even as they sat there. But in what state? Elli must be beside herself. Knightly felt the urge to rush in and be with her. But his legs were numb, his whole body. He waited, listening.

"It was an accident. He fell—" It looked as if Chrysa was going to cry again.

She took a deep breath and looked straight at Knightly.

"He fell, Will," she said, "He fell off the roof of the house!"

Knightly looked at her in horror.

"What?! How could that happen?"

"We don't know!" Chrysa cried. "He had never done anything like this! We don't know why he went up on the roof."

Now the sobbing started again. Knightly put his arms around Chrysanthi, trying to comfort her. Her body heaved with the sobs, so much that it made Knightly himself feel exhausted. Then she sat up and, wiping her eyes, forced herself to speak.

"I don't know why he was up on the roof. He's never done it, ever. Elli went into the village—she had left him in the house, just like she'd done a thousand times—everything was fine, Giannakis was fine. Only this time—this time he climbed up on the roof."

She shuddered.

"The doctor said that he fell badly. He said that Giannakis went off the roof but must have realized something was wrong. He was twisting himself, he must have tried to reach backward—there were scrapes on his arms and chest—he must have been trying to grab on to the roof—"

Knightly remembered how the ground slopes away on one side of the yard. He also recalled seeing an iron ladder attached to the side of the house. It was common for houses in the area to have some way up to the roof—spiral staircase or ladder—for maintenance of chimneys, antennas, solar panels. He was starting to understand how the accident might have happened. But what he could not even begin to understand—what he thought he'd never understand—was *why*. Had Giannakis known what he was doing? Had he wanted to hurt himself, then become afraid when he felt himself falling? Or could it have been something else entirely? Had he simply wanted to *fly*?

"The fall broke his neck," she said. "He died instantly, the doctor said."

Chrysa said this with conviction in her voice, but her eyes held a question. Knightly said nothing.

"Where is Elli?" he asked, finally.

"She's inside. She's sleeping. The doctor gave us something for her."

Knightly just shook his head.

"She was not in a good way, Will," Chrysa said.

Knightly nodded. "She must be devastated," he said, grimly. "I can't even begin to imagine—"

They looked at one another.

"Can I see her?" he asked.

"She's asleep—"

"I know," Knightly said, "I won't disturb her. I just want to see her."

Chrysa looked at him as if to say she understood. They went into the house. Knightly walked into Elli's room. She was in her bed. She was sleeping peacefully, Knightly noticed, but when he came closer and looked at her, it startled him. Her eyes were red, and though her features were composed now, it was as if a cry had been caught on her lips. Her face was still contracted with pain even though she was now under the influence of the sedatives. Knightly looked at her with a helpless grief. He wanted to touch her, stroke her hair, but the thought of waking her scared him.

He left the room and sat down next to Chrysa in the living room.

"What are we going to do, Chrysa?"

Chrysa looked at him. Her face was streaked with tears and she looked drained. Yet the way that Knightly had put the question seemed to please her.

"There's nothing much we can do, Will," she said, "except to make sure that Elli rests as much as possible."

She held up a small bottle of pills and put it down on the coffee table in front of them.

"If you don't mind, I think I'll get some rest, too," she said to him. "I haven't slept much since it all started last night."

"Go get some sleep, Chrysa," Knightly said. "I'll stay right here."

She looked at him, trying again to smile. As she got up, she leaned over and kissed him on the cheek.

"I guess we'll deal with this as best we can," she said, and walked down the hall to her parents' old bedroom.

Knightly sighed. He stretched out on the couch. His head hurt. He forced himself to close his eyes. And before he knew what had happened he had fallen asleep himself.

He had a dream. It was the same dream—or another version of it—that he had when he slept that first night in Elli's house in Kremni. He dreamed he was on the slope of a hill. He was a young boy again. He recognized the place. It was a hill just below the house of a childhood friend, where they often played. It felt like winter. The air was cold but the sun was high overhead and hot, and the combined heat and the cold had made the snow on the slope of the hill crusty and slick. Knightly found himself struggling to get up the hill. He was wrapped in heavy clothes and he was laboring as his feet kept slipping on the icy sheet of snow. He looked up in the dream and saw that his mother had come for him. She was waiting at the top of the hill. She was waiting to take him home. But he kept slipping and every time he fell he slid further down the hill, increasing the distance he had to climb. He was overheating, he couldn't get any traction, couldn't break through the surface of the snow or find his footing at all. His lungs were bursting as he tried to scream for help, tried to call out to his mother. She was looking down at him, waiting for him to climb up the hill. She waited there in silence, never making a move to help him. He was suffocating under the cruel glare of the sun reflected blindingly off the crusty slope of the hill.

He woke up with a start, drenched in sweat. When he came to his senses, he got up and walked down the hall to Elli's room. He pushed the door open carefully and looked in. She was still asleep. Knightly watched her from the doorway. He could scarcely tell if she was breathing. He came into the room. Walking up to her bed as softly as he could, he looked at her as she lay there. Her chest and shoulders barely rose and fell, her mouth was slightly parted. She still was sleeping deeply, thanks to the merciful balm of whatever the doctor had prescribed. And, though Knightly doubted his eyes at first, he swore to himself that the tortured look he had seen on Elli's face only an hour or so before was beginning to appear less desperate, less wild. The grief was there, but now her look seemed to be changing slowly into an expression of some sort of acceptance.

8.

No one was out at this hour. It was too early. No one on the streets. A bakery showed signs of life—the grille was up, some lights on inside. Otherwise, the street was peaceful. Or dead.

Everything was where it was supposed to be. The neighborhood was unfamiliar, but everything matched what the source had described. There was the alley. This was where you had to be careful. Scan the roofs across from the back door. That's how Joshua got it. There was no lip or rim on the roof of the building opposite the one where Skorpios was supposed to be. No place to hide up there. All clear. One hazard out of the way. The alley itself was clear as well. All the way to the back door.

The idea was to go in with the nine millimeter in hand. That gave a measure of comfort. The gun had its specific weight, a certain heft to it. It felt strangely good. Plenty of power in a small package. Knock on the door and step back. When it opens, see what you're dealing with. Any messing around, you start shooting. Any surprises, just keep shooting till you're sure they're the ones who buy it. Not you. You're not going to be taken down by any foolish surprises. Like poor Joshua.

The door opens. Just like he said. You knocked and he opened right away. He's ready. I guess he's a pal, after all. Or he really needed the money. It ought to be enough. Good luck with it. He only looked at it quickly. He's trying not to look too nervous, but he must be scared. He's fucking with Skorpios, if he thinks about it. But the idea is that Skorpios will be dead in just a few minutes. He's banking on that better happen. Still, he didn't stay around too long. Just opened the door, took the money and got out of there. *Now it's up to me.*

The hall is dark. There's the door that goes downstairs. There must be people further down the hall but you can barely hear them. Skorpios is downstairs all by himself, with any luck. Having breakfast all by himself. But not for long.

There was a corridor that turned left at the bottom of the stairs. The first door on the corridor was closed but a dim light was filtering through from underneath it, just an inch or two into the hallway. *That's it.* The bastard is in there, sitting at a desk. Having breakfast and whatever else he does to get ready for his ungodly days. Counting his dirty money, reading the newspaper, reading porn. Who the hell cares? His morning is going to be different today.

Ariani opened the door—it wasn't locked—holding the gun at waist level. The look on Skorpios's face, when he saw her walk into the room, was nearly too wondrous for words. Utter surprise and shock turning into anger, especially when he saw the gun. Contempt played on his features for only a second, but just as quickly a flush of terror chased away the contempt. It was the gun and the look on Ariani's face. Black hatred sitting on a twisted smile. Ariani raised the barrel several centimeters and smiled more broadly. *Good morning, Mr. Skorpios.*

Skorpios raised himself slowly from the chair, almost without thinking, sneering at Ariani, instinctively but also from shock. Then a thought must have flashed through his mind, she saw, because his eyes suddenly darted toward the desk in front of him. *He's got a gun in the desk. But it's been so long, he doesn't remember which drawer it's in.* She laughed to herself. *He doesn't know what the fuck he's doing! Getting other men to do your dirty work for too long, Mr. Skorpios.*

As he reached for one of the top drawers, she fired a round that hit the top of the desk, glancing off and striking the wall to the side of where Skorpios was standing. She fired again, hitting Skorpios a little above his right knee. That one was right where she wanted it. He squealed in pain and fell back down, hitting the chair heavily. The look on his face was confused, rage mixed with a growing fear, the redness and the pallor of each in turn making his face break out in peculiar blotches. He hissed at Ariani as she walked calmly toward the desk.

She fired another round. It hit Skorpios in the left shoulder. He screamed aloud, then moaned softly as he touched the hole in his jacket where the bullet had entered, now welling with blood. He looked up at Ariani.

"What do you want?" he shrieked at her.

"I can't have what I want," she said.

If Skorpios had known any pity himself, his eyes might have filled with some sort of sign for mercy. As it was, Ariani saw nothing there to move her in the least. No human emotion. Just a desperate, self-involved will to escape the situation. An abject terror mixed with an urge to fight. But Skorpios knew he was helpless. He would have reached for the weapon in his desk. But he seemed robbed of the power to act. He looked up at Ariani with hatred, unable to stop her, and incapable of thinking what he might say that could possibly sway or appease her. *That smile of hers!*

She had him in her power.

Except for the fact that the first three shots had gotten someone's attention. She could hear noises through the door, which she had locked when she came in. There were sounds of a commotion, coming from down the hall. Skorpios had some of his men in the building, but they must have been having their breakfast upstairs. They had been alerted by the shots. They were running downstairs and had just gotten to the landing. Not much time left to do what she needed to do.

She raised the gun and pointed it straight at Skorpios's chest. Pulled the trigger. A dark young rose blossomed in the middle of Skorpios's shirt. His spitting and hissing turned raspy, the look on his face passed from anger and fear to a growing despair. He was dying, and he knew it.

The sound of footsteps in the hall got louder, until Ariani heard them right outside. She saw shadows flitting along the bottom of the door itself. *Let's not take chances.* She lifted the pistol one final time and squeezed. The round tore into Skorpios's forehead and painted the wall behind him in a shock of crimson.

Skorpios's men kicked the door open. Ariani had already turned, crouching low. She fired off two quick rounds. No fooling around this time. One man stood in the doorway and the two rounds hit him in the chest, knocking him back. He cried out and began to sink slowly toward the floor. But the man behind him had crouched as well and got off one shot and another right after it from underneath the arm of his comrade, before he went down. Ariani fired at almost the same time. She thought she had hit the second man but she wasn't sure. The rounds he'd fired hit her squarely in the chest and knocked her down. She hardly knew what had happened. She had fallen and rolled on her side, trying to get up. She didn't have enough strength to push herself off the floor and she just lay there, a few feet from the first man who had come through the door. She couldn't hear anything. She tried to look up. Nothing moving. She could barely make out the form of the second man, lying on the floor, just behind his comrade. She had hit him too.

It was hard to say how she felt at that moment. Very weak. She felt very weak, mostly. But she had done what she came to do. *Victory*. She lay there, letting her head roll back. No need to look now. Skorpios was dead. She tried to recall the expression on his face when she first came into the room, then how he hissed at her as she strode up to the desk and shot him, taking away his power, over herself, others. She tried hard to concentrate, so that she could relive those moments, fleeting as they were, of her revenge. Of Skorpios's punishment. But it was too hard. She was tired. She fought to keep her eyes open, but she knew she was failing. She knew the room was flooded by the fluorescent lights that were burning underneath plastic panes in the ceiling above, and yet she could not focus on anything, near or far, even as she felt her body floating away into a gathering darkness.

—✳—

When Daniel woke up, it surprised him how light it was. What time was it? *Shit!* What time *was* it? His head was filled with a cloying sensation, more than just a good rest. Was that the wine? They only had a couple of glasses last night. Was he really that tired, that he slept like a stone, all night and right into the morning?

That's when he realized he was alone in the bed. *Ariani—?*

Ariani wasn't there.

He jumped out of bed and went to the dresser. He looked in the bottom drawer, on her side. Shit. Her gun was gone. A snug, pretty little nine millimeter he had given her, to protect herself in case anyone came to the apartment. And he had given her a crash course in how to use it. She had been an avid pupil. Too much so. He rooted around in the drawer. The money was gone, too. They had kept a stash there—the money they were going to use to take Ariani back home and set her up in her town. In her father's café, or in another business. They had saved a decent amount from "taxes" collected from the hoods who were Skorpios's couriers and bag-men. Anyway, the money was gone. Daniel had gotten the picture.

He threw his clothes on, grabbed his phone, and went into the living room. There were the glasses from last night. He dipped a finger in the dregs of his glass. A faintly bitter taste. *She slipped me a mickey,* he thought. *Clever girl!* Not enough to knock me out for good—thanks for that much. Just enough for golden slumbers.

"Radio," he barked into the phone. "We have a problem—a *major* problem. Ariani is gone! She's after Skorpios. Light up the goddamned *dictyo—light that fucking thing up, now!*" he roared. "I want to know where she is. Tell everybody we've got to find her—*and I mean now!* Call me the minute anybody calls in with anything."

He pulled on his shoulder holster and a loose cotton shirt over it and left the apartment, taking the steps three at a time until he was out the front door of the building and on the street.

—◦◦◦—

Daniel.

That song. The words—what were they?—"*You were born to be loved.*" *Thank you, Daniel. Love. You gave me hope, so I could do this. Hold me. Dancing—? No, I can't—I'm sorry! Too tired, can't move. Help me, Daniel. Please. Daniel—I'm sorry.*

Where was he?

She felt he was near. Up ahead—she felt as if he must be ahead of her. Call to him. She wanted to speak but her voice—she couldn't make it work. She couldn't move. Tired. Her arms, too heavy. The walls of the room—hard to see. Were they close or far away? They seemed wet. Like a cave. Where was she? Where was he? Was he coming back for her? She tried to think what his name was. It didn't matter. She could not think of her own name. And the more she thought about it, the less any of it was coming back to her. She didn't care. It really didn't seem to matter.

She thought of nothing now, for the nothing had her.

9.

"Nothing?" he asked the inspector, who was sitting across the table from him. "You wouldn't like anything with it?"

"No, thank you," Kazantzakis replied, "just the coffee will be fine."

Knightly asked the waitress for two coffees. She smiled, nodding slightly, and went back inside the café.

"So you were saying what happened after Skorpios was killed—"

"Well, our good colleague Mitsos tried to hold out, but he crumbled quickly. Athena made short work of it. She found an apartment he was keeping in Loutraki. It seems our man liked to gamble. He was well known at the casino. Not the face of a matinee idol, but memorable in its own way."

Knightly smiled.

"The concierge at the casino recognized him right away when Athena showed him a picture. He said that Mitsos came nearly every other weekend and—you'll like this—with a different woman each time!"

"Sly bastard!" Knightly said. "Who said money can't buy you happiness?"

"It seemed to have afforded Mitsos a certain amount of comfort. It turned out, though, that he was not particularly good at saving money.

When Skorpios was killed, it pretty much sank his chances of getting a fancy lawyer."

"What a pity—rotten luck!" Knightly said.

"Indeed, he's been cleaned out."

"What will you do now, Inspector?" Knightly asked.

"I have to take care of some loose ends, before I go back to Athens. Athena will take over the investigation of Skorpios's organization here in Tripoli. She's been promoted, you know."

"That's excellent. She strikes me as a very capable young woman."

"She's wonderful, I agree," Kazantzakis said. "I'll miss her when I go. It won't be long now. I'll be back at headquarters in just a couple days."

"Won't you get any time off?"

"Not for now, no," Kazantzakis said. "Maybe at the end of August or early September. I'd like to go back to Crete for a week or so."

The coffees came. Knightly sipped his, looking around the plateia, and sighed.

"This is where it all started."

It was Kazantzakis's turn to smile.

"Is this where you were sitting when you saw your student?" he asked.

"Yes, it was. You see, Inspector, apparently I can't take a hint. I jumped up and went barrelling after him, as soon as I saw him."

"You had no way of knowing what was going on."

"I suppose that's true," Knightly said. "It's funny. It's occurred to me— what would have happened if I hadn't been sitting here at that precise moment? What if I had been inside the hotel, just unpacking my suitcase, or taking a nap? What if I'd gone straight to Elli's place, or to Vasses? Or if I simply hadn't noticed Daniel, or god knows what else? What if none of it had happened? It's a bit bizarre to think of that."

"It's true, it is odd. We probably would not have met, Professor," said Kazantzakis.

"That would have been a shame!" Knightly said. "It's just strange. I might have found that picture of Skorpios and Mitsos and not seen anything significant about it at all."

"In that case, I might very well be working on the Skorpios case still, without making any real progress, and still feathering that damnable Mitsos's love-nest in Loutraki!"

The two men fell silent for a moment, sipping their coffee.

"Are you married, Inspector?"

"I was. My wife passed away."

"I'm so sorry! When did it happen?"

"She passed away three years ago this last Spring."

"In the Spring—"

"One week before Easter."

They fell silent again.

"Do you have any children?"

"Two. A son and a daughter."

"Same here. My daughter's in India on a Fulbright and my son's doing an internship in California. They're great kids. They grow up so fast. What are yours doing now?"

"My son is in the navy and my daughter is in America. She's also in California, in fact. You would approve, Professor—she studied classical philology. She's a teacher now."

"Good for her! So she's picking up the cudgels for her old man—"

"I could not be prouder, it's true. I suppose you could say she's fulfilling a dream of mine, one I had long ago."

"That's another funny thing. You became a policeman, and yet I believe that you are a philologist at heart, Inspector—I'll never forget those *mantinadhes*!"

Kazantzakis laughed, "While you, my dear Professor, are a philologist who became, somewhat unexpectedly, a policeman this summer!"

"I may have to work on a few more cases to come up to your pay-grade, Chief Inspector."

"You never know, Professor. You never know what the future holds—"

"Sounds ominous. You'll notice I'm studiously ignoring the crowd in the *plateia*."

"Trying not to let any more trouble find you!"

"I'm planning to let the rest of the summer be utterly boring."

"Somehow, I find that hard to believe. Will you be staying with Mrs. Parthenis?"

"Yes."

"How is she doing, by the way?"

"You heard about Giannakis?"

The inspector nodded.

"She's doing better, thanks. It's still difficult."

"I feel for her. It must be very hard," Kazantzakis said.

"You said your wife's been gone three years now, Inspector?" Knightly said. "That must be hard as well."

"I still forget she's gone sometimes," he answered, "when I come home, I'll think she's in the house. Sometimes, I almost call out to here, then I remember—"

Knightly looked at Kazantzakis, considering his words carefully.

"I don't want to offend you or say anything inappropriate, Inspector. But Athens is a big place—do you ever think you might meet someone?"

Kazantzakis shrugged, as if to say no. "I don't have much inclination, to be honest. My work keeps me busy enough. I suppose I allow it to absorb me. How could I replace her, after all, my Aphrodite—that was her name, Professor! I have a hard time imagining myself with anyone except her, especially now.

The old dog, grown dull, sees the rabbit, and he hardly cares.
What use then has the hound anymore to sniff the weary air?

"Ah, nicely turned. But that's our calling, my good man, to show that these old dogs can learn new tricks!"

"I'll meditate on that bit of encouragement, my friend, I promise," Kazantzakis said.

He looked at his watch.

"Speaking of my calling, I'd better get back to work. Thank you very much for the invitation, Professor, and for the coffee. I hope you will visit me in Athens, some time this summer, before you return to America. Do you still have my card?"

"Please, call me Will. I do have it, Inspector—"

"It's Aris, Will. Call me Aris."

"I'm sure I'll be back in Athens before the end of the summer, Aris. I'll give you a call when I do."

Summer goes and the days grow short, as they flee the strength'ning cold.
Then set a place beside the fire—I'll be coming down the road.

"My dear Professor—I mean, Will! Don't tell me I've succeeded in turning you into a singer, just like a native son of Kríti?"

"That would be even more presumptuous than hoping to turn detective, my dear Aris. But I tried to tell you—you are a gifted philologist and a damn good teacher. I think some of your Cretan song-making may have rubbed off on me!"

Kazantzakis chuckled. "Goodbye, Will. My very best to you and Eleftheria."

"Thank you, Aris. Till I see you again, take good care of yourself."

And the two men parted in the shadows of Agios Vasilios and its sturdy towers.

⎯ⵯⵯ⎯

Knightly had just arrived in Aetoráchi when he spotted the taverna sitting at the head of the village's small square. It reminded him of how Daniel had surprised him at that very spot just a couple weeks ago. He had been out for a walk and had stopped at the taverna to say hello to the owner, who was sweeping in front of the shop, when a car pulled up. Knightly had only glanced at it, but then saw a familiar figure get out and wave at him. It was Daniel.

He had decided to visit Knightly before he left the country. He was leaving the next day, to bring Ariani back home. He had wanted to say goodbye to his old teacher. Knightly was moved and told him how much he appreciated the gesture.

Daniel had looked good, especially considering all that he had been through. He seemed rested and composed, though subdued, it was true, even grave. That was only to be expected. Knightly had heard about Ariani's death. Sharon had called him—Daniel had asked her to do it, and she had found Elli's number somehow—and told him everything that had happened.

He had asked Daniel how he was doing. Daniel had answered, "Okay, I guess," and shrugged. Knightly told him how sad he had been when he heard about what happened to Ariani. "I don't know what to say, Daniel, I feel so bad." And Daniel had thanked him.

"She made the wrong choice, Will. But I know she felt she had to do it. I wish she had been able to walk away from it. She couldn't. Was it just in the cards that she would have to go that road? The moment she and her sister were betrayed in that way? Was it all determined right then? Or even before—?"

"She was dealt some awful cards, Daniel," Knightly agreed. "Did she leave anything behind for you—a note or anything like that?"

"She left me a note. Basically, she just said she was sorry. She couldn't live with the thought of her sister being the one who had to die. It made her feel that she hadn't done enough to save Irini. She couldn't be the only one to survive. Especially if she did nothing to avenge what they did to her sister. She hoped she would see me again. But she said that if she didn't make it, after she did what she had to do, then she begged me to forgive her. She said she loved me—"

Knightly could still recall the look on Daniel's face when he said those words, one of a painful joy wedded with helplessness.

Daniel had continued, explaining that Ariani had ended her note by saying that she hoped Daniel loved her, too. "She wrote, '*Don't forget me, if you can help it,*'" he said. "'*I will wait until the time when I see you again. That may not sound like much comfort to you, my sweet boy. But where I may be going, I don't think it will seem like much time at all, until I can be with you again. I have no words to thank you for all that you did for me. My love is yours forever.*' And she had signed her name."

Daniel said that she had left some money with the note and a postscript: *This will pay for my trip back home.* He said that she must have bargained hard with the guy who gave Skorpios up—there was a decent amount left. He was going to give the money to an organization in Moldova. It had been Ariani's wish. A group that worked to educate women about the sex trade and help those who had already been trafficked. A different kind of network. Daniel said that he and Ariani had wanted to help them do their work.

Daniel asked if he could meet Elli. Knightly had to explain what had happened to Elli and her son. Daniel looked shocked. After all *he* had been through! Knightly had to explain that Elli still wasn't up to seeing people—it had only been a day or two at that point. Daniel had understood.

Knightly thanked Daniel again for taking the trouble to come all this way to say goodbye. He said he hoped they would see each other again, sooner rather than later. Daniel had said he hoped so too. Then he pulled out his wallet and took out a business card. It had Daniel's name and rank and the rest, including an e-mail address. Knightly couldn't help but laugh when he saw it. "You mean to tell me I could have used this all along?" "Come on, Will, I never check this thing, not when I'm working." "Okay—" Knightly had said, puzzled. Daniel had smiled and promised that he did check it fairly often when he wasn't too heavily engaged. "So give it a try from time to time, okay?" Daniel had said. "I want us to stay in touch."

Knightly had done a good job of keeping his composure until Daniel drove away. Then he walked over to a bench in the little *plateia* at the center of the village, just a handful of paces away from the taverna. He sat down, and he wept, for the second time in only a few days.

He wept as he thought of all the damage that had been done. He wept to think both of those who were lost and those who were left behind, bereft. He could not help thinking of Daniel, who had lost two of his best friends, one of them a lover. He thought of Ariani, but he also thought of her father. How would he take the news—*both* of his daughters? He thought about his own children. How much he loved them, how much he missed them. How grateful he was that they were safe and flourishing. He thought of poor Giannakis, who never knew his father. And then he thought of Elli. That is when he had gotten up, after sitting for a moment, and made his way back to Elli's house.

—⁓—

He pulled up beside the garden wall of the house across the narrow street from Elli's house and left the car there. He walked up to the front gate. All was quiet, not a sound to be heard, until the heavy gate swung open with a creaking moan and announced his arrival.

There was Elli, kneeling in the garden. She was putting in tomato plants. She wore a straw hat and as she looked up when he came in a strand of her hair fell across her face. She wanted to brush it away, but her hands were caked with soil.

"Let me help," Knightly said. And he brushed it out of her face and behind her ear.

"Thank you," she said, looking up at him, wiping off her hands.

"Are you ready for lunch?" he asked.

"I don't know—okay, maybe I've done enough for now," she said.

Knightly knew they would be going to the cemetery later that afternoon. The visits from neighbors and people in the village had begun to taper off, growing less frequent now, though food was still delivered almost daily by one or another lady, friends of Elli's parents from long ago. Maybe they could get some food from the taverna tonight, just for a change. He could walk into the village and pick it up. Elli wouldn't have to go out.

"Will we get any visits today?" Knightly asked.

"Maybe," Elli said, "no more than one or two."

"What should we have for lunch?" he asked.

"I picked some lettuce and cucumbers this morning. And we still have peppers. Do we have any bread?" she asked.

"I got some on the way back from Tripoli—I stopped in Kato Doliana."

"Oh, how's the inspector, by the way?"

"He's fine. He told me to say hello."

Suddenly some clouds rolled overhead and blocked the sun for a moment.

Elli shivered.

"Don't tell me it's going to rain," Knightly said.

"Probably. But only for ten minutes or so," said Elli.

And the rain started. They felt a few light drops at first but then some big drops hit them and ran down their noses so that they could taste them on their lips. Knightly took Elli's hand and helped her get up. The rain falling in thin streams already puddled the yard. The earth exuded a heady smell, of freshly pressed linen mixed with gently decomposing jasmine petals. Knightly looked at Elli with a crooked smile, and she looked back at him, almost laughing, the rain trickling down their faces.

"I guess we should get out of the rain," he said.

So they took their steps, wandering slowly, hand in hand, by the garden path, back to the solitary house.